Plain Christmas

The Amish Classic Series

For a complete listing of books, please visit the author's website at www.sarahpriceauthor.com.

Plain Christmas

A Plain Fame Novel

Sarah Price

Waterfall
PRESS

Published by Waterfall Press, Grand Haven, MI

www.brilliancepublishing.com

Amazon, the Amazon logo, and Waterfall Press are trademarks of Amazon.com, Inc., or its affiliates.

ISBN-13: 9781503934832

ISBN-10: 1503934837

Cover design by Eileen Carey

Printed in the United States of America

About the Vocabulary

The Amish speak Pennsylvania Dutch (also called Amish German or Amish Dutch). This is a verbal language with variations in spelling among communities throughout the United States. For example, in some regions, a grandfather is *grossdaadi*, while in other regions he is known as *grossdawdi*. Some dialects refer to the mother as *mamm* or *maem*, and others simply as *mother* or *mammi*.

In addition, there are words and expressions, such as *mayhaps*, or the use of the word *then* at the end of sentences, and, my favorite, *for sure and certain*, that are not necessarily from the Pennsylvania Dutch language/dialect but are unique to the Amish.

The use of these words comes from my own experience living among the Amish in Lancaster County, Pennsylvania.

Chapter One

"Careful with the garland, now!"

Amanda stood in the center of the living room, overseeing the workers decorating the house for Christmas. She tried to hide her impatience. It was taking them far too long, and she had other things to do. They had arrived three hours earlier, and while the rest of the rooms were coming along nicely, the two men in the living room appeared to be struggling. Now, as they stood on metal ladders bookending the fireplace, she could see disaster ready to unfold. The marble wall was presenting them with a problem: they couldn't figure out how to drape the eighteen-foot garland over the mirror.

Amanda was on the verge of offering her assistance when it happened. The young man wearing clothes too large for his small frame almost dropped his side of the garland, scattering hundreds of needles onto the white floor in front of the fireplace. Then, as the ladder began to wobble, he lost his footing. Amanda caught her breath, knowing exactly what was going to happen but unable to do anything to stop it. The man held on to the garland like a monkey swinging from a vine, his dark eyes large and anxious, before stumbling from the ladder and falling to the ground.

Pine needles went everywhere as ornaments shattered into small shards and spread in every direction.

"Oh help!" Amanda muttered as she rushed forward and knelt beside him. "Are you all right?"

From the way the color drained from his face, she doubted that he was. But it was probably from embarrassment, not from physical injury.

She held his arm as she helped him back to his feet. She peered into his face. To her surprise, she realized that he was just a teenager, perhaps a few years older than her fourteen-year-old adopted step-daughter, Isadora. And from the looks of his clothing, he was certainly not a regular employee. It appeared that his loose-fitting pants and shirt had been borrowed from a much larger man. Most likely, he was the younger brother of the other worker and had come along to see the inside of the Diaz mansion.

She didn't need to wonder why; she knew the answer: curiosity.

Amanda wasn't surprised. After nine years, people were *still* curious about her.

When she had first met Alejandro, quite by accident in New York City, she hadn't known who he was or how closely the media—and the public—followed him. As it turned out, he was the man known as Viper, an international music sensation with a reputation for loving and leaving a trail of beautiful women in his wake. But because he always did it with style, his fans adored him for it.

Then the paparazzi discovered his unexpected relationship with Amanda Beiler. Their brief courtship was very much in the public eye, and it led to a quick engagement and tumultuous first year of marriage. She wasn't prepared for his lifestyle, nor was he for balancing his professional success with married life. And, of course, neither of them had been prepared for the surprise that awaited them in Brazil: Isadora.

Over the years, curiosity about their married life had not dissipated, meaning that security had to be vigilant at vetting workers and checking credentials and identification before letting anyone into the gated community and onto their property. Occasionally, someone slipped in, like the young man standing before her. It wasn't the first time someone snuck through protocol—and certainly would not be the last, she thought.

"Lo siento," he said, apologizing with a trembling voice.

"Tranquilo," Amanda said in response, hoping to reassure him that there was no need to be afraid. Of course, that was easy for her to say. Since he hadn't responded to her in English, he was most likely not a native-born Miamian. His accent sounded Latin American, but she couldn't quite place the exact country of origin, despite how often she traveled to Central and South America with Alejandro.

She heard the sharp sound of footsteps approaching from the foyer.

"Whatever is going on here?" The shrill voice of Amanda's housekeeper echoed from the open doorway.

For a moment, Amanda thought the boy might run. A look of panic crossed his face, and his dark eyes quickly turned toward the other worker, who still stood by the other side of the fireplace. Amanda gave him a reassuring smile, pausing to gently pat his arm. Like most fans, he was harmless. Alejandro had made sure to teach her that when she first met him, though he also made sure to travel with proper security, just in case.

Taking a deep breath, Amanda turned and walked toward the foyer where Teresa stood, hands on her hips and a scowl on her face, leaving the two workers scrambling to gather the garland and hang it properly while another quickly swept up the mess on the floor.

"Everything is fine, Teresa," Amanda said, placing her hand under the housekeeper's arm and guiding her in the other direction. "How are they coming along with the dining room? I want everything just *perfecto* for when Alejandro gets home tonight."

They walked through the grand foyer, passing beneath the large crystal chandelier and the staircase that curved along the wall to the second floor. From the moment the real estate agent had opened the double doors and stepped back for Amanda and Alejandro to enter the house, Amanda knew that her husband had fallen in love with it.

Sophisticated in its simplicity, it had satisfied Alejandro's need for impressing guests who met with him at their home. It was also open and airy, which reminded Amanda of the large open spaces typical of the Amish barns from her youth. In fact, there were parts of the house that were similar to her childhood home: a large family kitchen with an area for the family to gather after meals, and the master bedroom on the first floor. That, however, was where the similarities ended. Other rooms were constant reminders that she was most certainly *not* living in Lancaster County, such as the large formal dining room reserved for when all of Alejandro's friends and family came for meals and the soundproof recording studio on the far side of the house.

While she had fallen for the simple and open floor plan, Alejandro loved the ornate grandeur of marble walls, massive windows, and rich woodwork. The majestic columns that adorned the entrances into several of the more formal rooms were awe-inspiring. While it was much more ostentatious than their penthouse, Amanda knew that Alejandro wanted something to show for his hard work and sacrifices over the years. So despite feeling uncomfortable with the extravagance of the house, she had supported the move, especially since the children would have more privacy and a real backyard.

As far as decorating, Amanda had insisted on not crowding the space with too much furniture, so as not to overwhelm the senses. She wanted to create an aura of simplicity. Luxurious simplicity. Alejandro let her deal with all of those decisions, and whenever he returned home from his frequent trips to Los Angeles or New York City, he always appeared interested and pleased with any changes to the house.

For the most part, every room remained a neutral color: cream. The three exceptions were the children's rooms. Otherwise, the only time Amanda added color to the cream décor was during the holiday season. And that was another reason why she insisted on personally overseeing the hired service that put up the tree and the wreaths, garlands, lights, and bows. After all, she wanted to be a part of the festivities. She couldn't imagine someone else doing it completely. It simply wasn't Christmas if she couldn't decorate her own home, filling it with personal touches and creating a warm, inviting place to celebrate with family and friends.

One of her most cherished childhood memories was of helping her mother with decorating the large kitchen gathering room. Their decorations, however, consisted of only a piece of yarn hanging between two walls. Every day during the holiday season when Anna and Amanda came home from school, they would run to the old gray mailbox to see if any Christmas cards had arrived. There was nothing the two girls enjoyed more than hanging all of the Christmas cards from that yarn.

The Amish simply hadn't bought into the commercialism of Christmas, preferring to keep the holiday focused on what was truly important: the Christ-child, who was born to take away the sin of the world. It had taken Amanda quite a few years to really get into what the Englische called the spirit of Christmas—and she had learned that the Englische version of Christmas spirit usually meant little battery-operated lights on the windowsills and lots of greenery with bows and fragile figures or ornaments. That was when she started hiring professional decorators for the holidays.

After inspecting the dining room, Amanda and Teresa headed toward the grand salon. It was the main gathering room at the rear of the house. The back wall consisted of floor-to-ceiling windows. Whenever she and Alejandro entertained, they could slide back the windows opening the room completely to the outside patio that surrounded the pool. Usually, the room contained just a few pieces of furniture—several chairs, two sofas, and a coffee table—set up to present casual sitting areas where Alejandro and Amanda sometimes sat after dinner so that they could catch up with each other. The simplicity of the décor made the room feel rich and sophisticated.

Today, however, it had been transformed into a magnificent winter wonderland.

Amanda gasped, her eyes taking in the large sixteen-foot Christmas tree, decorated with thick white ribbons and an assortment of gold ornaments. Strands of lights had been hidden within its branches, and it seemed as though thousands of them were twinkling among the greenery. And all along the top of the back wall, there were beautiful boughs of evergreens festooned with ornaments and lights. The elegance of the tree and the simplicity of the room were simply breathtaking.

"Alejandro will love this," she said, more to herself than to anyone else. But she heard Teresa make a noise in the back of her throat that indicated she was in agreement.

He had been traveling for almost ten days, having left for the first of his annual Christmas concerts the day after Thanksgiving. His first stop had been Los Angeles because the tour was starting on the West Coast this year. Even though the Jingle Ball concerts continued for another two weeks, it was fortunate that there were small breaks in his busy concert schedule, including the next few days. Alejandro would fly home from Texas tonight. His manager, Geoffrey, had arranged for a private jet to fly him back to Miami as soon as his set was finished. Amanda suspected it would be the early hours of Sunday morning by the time he walked through those double doors, and she wanted him to feel the peace and joy of the upcoming Christmas holiday.

Christmas was the one holiday that he insisted on spending at home and with family, and she couldn't agree more. For the past few years, his mother would arrive several days early, her arms laden with bags of food as she marched directly into the kitchen and plopped everything onto the counters. Behind her would trail two of the house staff, toting her suitcases and packages while waiting for instruction on what to do next. No sooner would Alecia have greeted Amanda and the children than she would begin working in the kitchen, directing the staff to fetch her pots and pans, chop vegetables, or do any other task that she felt they were sufficiently qualified to accomplish, with one exception: the actual cooking. She never once delegated that duty to anyone else.

With Alecia in the house, there was constant energy in the kitchen. Alejandro's mother was always a whirlwind of energy, but she went into overdrive during the month of December. Amanda never complained, though. It was one of the many things she loved about Alecia.

Alejandro's aunts, uncles, cousins, and friends would begin arriving in the early afternoon on Christmas Eve, long after the caterers got busy roasting the pig, a tradition in Alejandro's family. It had taken Amanda a few years to get used to the unique foods served by his family over the holidays: rice and beans, pork and chicken, fresh *chicharrones*, fried plantains, and other Cuban dishes. Rich in flavor and varied in spices, each dish was part of her husband's heritage—and a far cry from what she, as a youth, had eaten on Christmas Eve dinner back on the farm in Lancaster County.

An hour after the decorators left, thankfully with no further incidents of runaway garlands or dropping pinecones, Amanda slipped outside through the sliding glass doors in her office. Isadora's orange cat, Katie Cat, that she had adopted almost nine years ago when staying with Amanda's family in Lancaster County, slept on a chair at the table. Amanda shooed the cat off the chair and, after brushing aside some cat hairs, sat down to relax. She needed to steal a few moments just to sit in the shade on the patio and enjoy the fresh afternoon breeze. Within an hour, she would have to meet Jeremy at his studio, her favorite stylist, who had won her heart and friendship when she began touring with Alejandro so many years ago.

Jeremy always told her that truly glamorous women wore stunning gowns or classy dresses with perfectly matched shoes and accessories. And, of course, every outfit needed to be adorned with complementary jewelry that accentuated her beauty and declared how much her husband loved her.

Knowing that Amanda never spent money on herself, Jeremy frequently provided Alejandro with a long list of what Amanda "absolutely, positively" needed to have. Amanda knew there was no point in trying to argue with Jeremy. He wouldn't hear it, waving her off in his typical overdramatic way. Despite their occasional pseudo bickering, Amanda had to admit that her fashion stylist (and, secretly, one of her few trusted friends) had impeccable taste. As did her husband. Every year, Alejandro would find a way to bestow upon her pieces of jewelry that took her breath away, especially when he helped her put them on and stood back to admire her, a loving look of approval in his blue eyes.

She shut her eyes and let her head fall back. There was no denying that she was dreading the evening she was about to face. Charlie, her assistant, would arrive shortly and begin to talk nonstop, directing his team to take notes, make calls, or send e-mails, all the while telling Amanda what she needed to do. Her head would no doubt be swimming with endless details and a headache would be forthcoming, and they'd soon be at Jeremy's studio, where her stylist would make his grand entrance. Jeremy never entered a room quietly. And then the fireworks would begin. Jeremy had been with Amanda for almost eight years, and it was no secret to anyone that he was not fond of Charlie.

The feeling, apparently, was more than mutual.

When working with them, Amanda often felt as though she were mothering two children instead of working with two adults. Quite often, she compared them to oil and water: necessary for the recipe but difficult to mix together.

"Ma'am?"

At the interruption, Amanda opened her eyes and looked toward the house. A timid woman in a maid's outfit approached her, holding a small white envelope in her hand.

"Yes, Renata?"

"Teresa asked me to give this to you," she said and held it out for Amanda to take.

She sat up and removed her sunglasses, tipping them up so that they rested atop her head. It must be important, Amanda thought. Otherwise, Teresa would instruct the staff to put it on her desk in her office. "Thank you, dear," she said as she reached for it.

Immediately, Renata disappeared.

The handwriting was instantly familiar, and even though there was no return address, Amanda knew who had written to her: her mother.

She felt a moment of remorse. She hadn't been home to see her family in a while. Years, actually. Life had been too busy, first with the children and then with the move to their new house. Now that the children were in school, Amanda's schedule had become a succession of dinners and banquets, meetings and fund-raisers. And she often traveled with Alejandro for interviews, award ceremonies, and other events where her presence was requested.

The envelope felt light in her hand but heavy in her heart. She tried to think when, exactly, they had been back to Lancaster County, Pennsylvania. Certainly after Sofia was born, she thought, trying to remember. But had Sofia just been a baby? And during one of her quick trips north, Amanda had taken Isadora back for a brief visit with her grandmother, aunt, and cousins. But that had been when Isadora had turned ten years old. Was it possible that Amanda hadn't visited her family in four years? She questioned herself. Could that be true?

More guilt.

Life certainly had a way of taking over, she thought. A tightness formed around her heart.

With a sigh, she slid her finger under the flap of the envelope and extracted a card that contained a single piece of paper. Reluctantly, for she knew that the letter would certainly include not-so-good news, she began to read.

Dear Amanda,

It was so good to read your letter. I'm glad things are going well for you.

I had a busy autumn, which is why I have not responded in a timelier manner. Now that Thanksgiving has passed, I finally have a moment to sit down and catch up with my correspondence.

Anna and Jonas are doing well. The days are shorter and there isn't as much to do beyond our regular chores. Hannah and Rachel are busy at school preparing their pageant for the parents. Sylvia and Elizabeth are still home yet, and Samuel had his first birthday last month.

Went to Walmart last week. I ride the bus for free now, you know. Can you imagine that? I'm a senior citizen now! Reckon that's not something to brag about. You couldn't believe how full the bus and the stores were! Then I realized they were all shopping for Christmas.

On the bus ride back to Lititz, I looked at all of the other people with their packages and bags. There were only a few Amish women on the bus. We stood out, not just because of our dresses but our lack of packages, too!

While we have never been ones for exchanging gifts, I realized that we have not celebrated Christmas together since you married Alejandro.

Which is why I am writing to you.

Would you consider coming to Lititz for Christmas? I want to see you and the kinner. *Such a gift cannot be purchased in a store or carried in a bag, but it would be the best present that I could ever receive.*

With prayers and blessings,
Your loving mother,
Lizzie

Amanda tapped a well-manicured finger against the arm of the chair as she tried to figure out what, exactly, bothered her about her mother's letter. Perhaps it was the fact that it had not been solicited by one of Amanda's letters or postcards. She'd sent the last one over two months ago. Nor was her letter in response to one of the voice messages she sometimes left on the phone that Jonas had installed in the dairy barn behind the farmhouse. No, her mother had simply written to her out of the blue.

Oh, Amanda remembered far too well how hectic autumn was in the Amish community, between final hay cuttings and baling on the farm and the commitments within the church district in October before the rush of November weddings. But her mother always found time to write her a letter or call whenever Amanda had reached out to her.

Not this time.

And then there was the content of the letter. Just a brief update and one short, simple question: *Would you consider coming to Lititz for Christmas?* Amanda shut her eyes and leaned her head back against the chair's cushion. Something must be wrong, something that her mother didn't want to put in writing. After all, Lizzie's letter said nothing that could insinuate anything was amiss. Rather, Amanda suspected the problem was with what had not been stated at all: just as Amanda had two daughters, so did her mother, and clearly, she wanted to enjoy the holiday with *both* of them.

It was an impossible request and that made Amanda feel even worse. There was no way she could change the Christmas Eve tradition of the Diaz family, and not just because of Alejandro's commitment to his extended family or even their commitment to their own children. She simply didn't have the heart to disappoint Alejandro's mother. Alecia was a strong woman who had struggled most of her life as a single mother raising her only child, an equally strong-willed son.

Amanda didn't question the fact that Alecia ruled the extended family when it came to certain things, and tradition was definitely one of them. Amanda had accepted that from the very beginning and had actually come to enjoy her mandated holiday each Christmas.

Until now.

Amanda couldn't help but ask herself *when* she had become so Englische that she had forgotten about her own family and traditions.

Would you consider coming to Lititz for Christmas?

Traveling to Pennsylvania for Christmas was *simply not possible*. She knew that without even asking. If she did ask, Amanda knew Alejandro would move heaven and earth to try to make her happy, but with Alejandro's schedule—and hers—it just couldn't happen. Even their free time was scripted. And even though Alejandro had nothing on the itinerary during the week before Christmas, Amanda knew how much he was looking forward to a few weeks at home with only a handful of meetings in Miami. There was also the five-day yacht trip to the islands that they had planned long ago with three of Alejandro's cousins and their wives. And, of course, he was scheduled to perform in Atlanta *and* New Orleans on New Year's Eve.

No, this was an *impossible* request.

And yet . . .

A small noise broke her concentration. Amanda glanced over her shoulder, not surprised to see their aging housekeeper, Señora Perez, leaving the house. She shuffled toward Amanda, a light tray in her hands. Amanda started to get up to help, but, as usual, Señora Perez ignored her efforts as she set the tray onto the round table on the patio.

"*Gracias,* señora," Amanda said as the housekeeper set down a pitcher of cool water and an empty glass.

The older woman started to turn away, but then her tired eyes noticed the neat handwriting on the letter. She looked at Amanda. "*¿Hay un problema, Señora Diaz?*"

Amanda tried to smile. She certainly did not want to burden her housekeeper with any concerns regarding Lancaster County and her mother's request.

"It's a letter from home." As soon as she said those words, she quickly corrected herself. "I mean Pennsylvania. Where I grew up."

"Ah *sí.*"

Señora Perez knew better than to ask too many questions. Even after so many years of working with them, first just for Alejandro and then, after Amanda arrived in his life, with her and their children, the housekeeper had never once interfered in their personal lives.

"*Si usted necesita algo . . .*"

"*Danke*, señora. It'll be fine, I'm sure," she answered in a reassuring voice. Amanda didn't want her to worry.

As Señora Perez quietly slipped back through the open sliding doors and disappeared into the kitchen, Amanda stared after her. She was getting older, Amanda reckoned. At seventy-four, how much longer could she continue watching over the household? Alejandro and Amanda had discussed the situation several years prior and decided that the woman who had treated them so well over the years was just as much a part of their family as Alecia. She had a home with them until the day she wanted to leave. But even though her health was strong, Señora Perez needed help managing the increasingly busy household. The previous year, Amanda had hired Teresa to manage the rest of the staff, instructing the younger woman to always defer to Señora Perez.

So far, it was working out well, especially since Teresa had the energy and stamina to keep up with the children. But it was another problem for Amanda to worry about. Not only was she concerned about her own aging mother, she was also worried about Señora Perez.

Her thoughts were interrupted by the chiming of the clock in the foyer. It was almost three o'clock. She sighed, her cheeks puffing out just a little. Soon the sun would begin its descent, and Señora

Perez would oversee the preparations for the evening meal, a meal that Amanda would miss. Again.

It was Saturday night, which meant that she had an evening obligation. As usual. Tonight she had two charity events—one in Miami and one in Palm Beach. Even though she would much prefer to stay home and spend the evening with her children, her presence at both events had been contracted through Alejandro's people almost a full year in advance.

The only good news was that she had only a few more commitments before the holiday season was over. Amanda had insisted that her publicity staff not overschedule her. She wanted to focus on her family, not the public. She knew, however, that the time to help with fund-raisers was when people were feeling charitable—and that meant participating in these events during the holiday season.

Once New Year's Day arrived, both Alejandro's and Amanda's schedules would open up for a few weeks, and they could concentrate on spending more time with each other and their children.

With a heavy sigh, she stood up, pausing to retrieve the letter, and walked into the house. The children would arrive home by four o'clock, and hopefully, Charlie would be early enough that they could leave for Jeremy's studio before that time. She knew far too well that avoiding the children, especially Nicolas, was a must. They'd delay her departure, and the last thing she wanted was to irritate Jeremy.

An hour later, Amanda was ushered through the doors to Jeremy's studio, security not even stopping her at the entrance. They knew who she was even before she stepped out of the car.

"On time?" Jeremy stood at the back of the massive room, his hands on his hips and his eyes wide open as if surprised. "Let me guess. Grace has your"—he hesitated and pursed his lips—"*children.*"

Amanda set down her wrap and handbag on an upholstered bench. "You say it with such love, Jeremy."

He rolled his eyes. "Hmmph. I don't have time for love, darling. We are on a very tight schedule."

She tried to hide her smile. As much as Jeremy complained about how her attention to her children often made her run late, she knew that deep down he cared about her *kinner*. In fact, when Amanda had taken Isadora to a movie premiere earlier in the autumn, he had commented on how beautiful she was becoming.

With a look of impatience, Jeremy clapped his hands to get the attention of his staff. "Let's go, people! We have a lot to do, and *we* don't want to be late." He paused before adding, "For a change!" Amanda noticed him glance in her direction, and she knew he was referring to her. Amanda didn't take it personally. She knew Jeremy well enough by now to not take any of his jibes to heart.

Familiar with the routine, Amanda walked over to the dressing room. For the next two hours, Jeremy would fuss over her, directing the hair stylist and makeup artists. Everyone would quietly accept his criticism and, ultimately, obey his direction. He was particular about perfection, especially when it came to Princesa. Jeremy was not about to produce anything but what both Alejandro and the public expected. After all, he had a reputation to uphold as one of the most sought-after stylists in the country. Nothing short of spectacular would do.

Amanda didn't complain as she let Jeremy's staff work their magic on her. Long ago, she had stopped feeling uncomfortable with so many people working on her hair and makeup, talking about her as if she weren't even there. Quietly, Amanda followed Jeremy's instructions as he snapped commands to his staff of three men and one woman.

"No, no, no!" His voice carried throughout the otherwise empty studio. "What are you doing, Marcus? She's a princess, not a harlot! Redo that eye makeup!"

Amanda peeked in the mirror and caught Jeremy's gaze. She shook her head once, just a slight gesture, indicating her disapproval of his comparison. But she remained silent, holding on to advice that her mother had taught Amanda when she was a child: Silence was the best recourse to sinful words. It did give her comfort to see Jeremy guiltily cast his eyes down. After years of working with her, Jeremy understood her limits well.

"Cell phone!" someone called out from the other side of the room, causing Amanda to jump. "You want it, Amanda?" But she didn't need to respond. Someone ran across the room and thrust her phone into her hands. Despite the many years of practice, people doing things for her was one thing Amanda hadn't become accustomed to.

She thanked him and lifted the phone to her ear, although she already knew who was calling. "Hello?"

"¡Ay, Princesa!" Despite his grueling travel schedule, Alejandro always sounded so cheerful and energetic. She had no idea how he managed to do that. "You are getting ready for tonight, sí?"

Without realizing it, she smiled and lowered her eyes as if creating a barrier between herself and the other people in the room. They seemed to shuffle away, disappearing from her side so that she could have privacy while she spoke to her husband. "How is it that you are so busy yet still keep track of my schedule?" she marveled.

She heard him chuckle. "Ah, that's a secret, mi amor," he said, his voice low and teasing. "Shall I whisper it into your ear when I arrive home tonight?"

Even though he couldn't see her, she knew that he'd sense her cheeks had grown pink from his suggestive tone. "I miss you, Alejandro," she said softly into the receiver.

"I'll be with you very soon, and we will pick up where we last left off. Do you remember?" he murmured into the phone.

Remember? How could she forget? Even after hanging up and when the hair stylist had resumed fussing with her long brown hair, she quietly sat, thinking about the romantic evening she'd spent with her husband just before he left for this last grueling tour. They'd shared an intimate candlelit dinner alone by the pool. It was a rare treat to have the house to themselves. The children had been invited to spend the night at their grandmother's house, so they made the most of their quiet time together. There was no one interrupting, no last-minute calls to make, no one seeking their attention. She had even given the staff the night off and convinced Alejandro to silence his cell phone, which was a monumental task! But that night, he didn't protest and let her set the phone down on the table without a single word.

What a wonderful night, she thought as she blushed yet again, remembering the way Alejandro had insisted that they take a midnight swim in the pool.

"Amanda," he had crooned into her ear when she shyly swam up to him and let him take her into his strong arms, "you are so beautiful, *mi amor*. Such a vision under the moonlit sky." When he kissed her, she felt so perfectly content. It was as if they had the whole world to themselves.

She sighed, realizing how impossible it would be to have a night alone with Alejandro anytime soon.

The sounds of the studio brought Amanda back from her thoughts. She heard the clucking of Jeremy's approval from behind her as the hair stylist swung her chair around to face him. Her friend immediately beamed with pride.

"Now *that* is much better!" he exclaimed. "Finally! I knew you were hiding in there somewhere, deep down." He pointed his finger accusingly in her direction.

She returned his smile, practically glowing. Jeremy turned to bark more orders to his staff, convinced that Amanda was happy because of the results of his hard work in transforming her. Little did he know that Amanda's happiness had nothing to do with her hair or dress or the fact that she had a limo waiting to take her wherever she wanted to go. No, tonight had nothing to do with her public role as the wife of the most famous singer in the world. Instead, it had everything to do with her husband, Alejandro, the loving man behind the wild persona, and all of the possibilities that lay in front of them tonight. In a short few hours, they would once again be reunited, and he would hold her in his strong arms.

And for Amanda, nothing mattered more than that.

Chapter Two

In the early-morning hours, the heat woke her long before the sunlight did.

With a soft sigh, Amanda opened her eyes and blinked, her mind slowing catching up with her body. Overhead, the blades of a white ceiling fan slowly rotated, making a soft clicking noise. She glanced at the windows, squinting as she waited for her eyes to adjust from sleep to morning.

The white plantation shutters were open just enough so that she could see the changing colors of the sky. What had been a dark, chalky blue began to change as the sun rose, slowly changing to lighter shades of indigo before shifting to warmer colors: red, orange, yellow. Behind the palette of God's brush was a new morning that, from the looks of it, was going to be another picture-perfect Miami day.

Picture-perfect, she thought, but muggy.

In the first week of December, the Miami air had been unusually thick with an oppressive humidity. Throughout the day, it would increase, and by ten o'clock, Señora Perez would turn on the central air-conditioning to cool down the many rooms of the house while directing one of the other house staff to shut any windows that Amanda had opened the previous night.

It was like that every morning. There was nothing Amanda preferred more than fresh air, even on mornings when there wasn't a soothing breeze. She hadn't grown up with all of the luxuries that now surrounded her: air-conditioning, housekeepers, personal assistants, private jets. And, while other people might take advantage of the comforts of fame and fortune, Amanda frowned on excessive opulence, even in the form of unnecessary air-conditioning at night.

Humid days like this one in December sometimes made her long for the snow-covered fields of Lancaster County. She often called to mind the stillness of the Pennsylvania mornings and the feel of the frigid air against her skin as she slipped out of her warm bed. She would make her way to the bedroom window and take a minute to savor the beautiful sight of snowflakes falling outside before getting ready to tackle the day's endless chores.

A soft noise next to her jarred her out of her thoughts and made her smile. She had sensed his presence long before she had felt him begin to stir.

Pulling the white sheet over her shoulder, she pressed her back against his side. The warmth of his skin seemed to burn through her sheer white lace nightgown, but she didn't mind. She could hear his gentle breathing and lightly feel his breath on the nape of her neck.

He was finally home, and she was utterly content.

She instinctively blushed, calling to mind the night before. She had found Alejandro sitting in a lounge chair on their outdoor patio, nursing a drink. He was patiently waiting for her to return from her charity event. Apparently, he had remembered their midnight swim as vividly as she had and wished to recreate the evening. When she walked slowly toward him, his eyes drank her in from head to toe. Her spine tingled with the intensity of his stare as he stood up and extended his arms toward her. She nestled into his chest and breathed in his scent. At that moment, nothing mattered but having her husband home.

Now they were together, in their bed, enjoying the warmth of each other, as they had done so many mornings since they were married.

Just a few weeks ago, they had celebrated their ninth wedding anniversary and, shortly after that, Sofia's eighth birthday and then Nicolas's seventh. Time seemed to know no mercy when it came to how fast it passed by.

Sometimes when Alejandro was touring and traveling, Amanda would wander through the beautifully landscaped gardens in the rear yard, reflecting on how much her life had changed in such a short time. It seemed like just yesterday that she was a young Amish girl, living a plain life on her family's farm in Lancaster County, Pennsylvania. Now, she was famous in her own right, as not only the wife of Viper, an international superstar-rap-singer-turned-music-producer, but a woman adored by millions of people in countries that she had had no idea even existed when she was a child.

In fact, she had never heard of Viper or rap music or the multitude of tiny Latin American and European countries she now visited frequently with Alejandro. Knowing what she knew today, she better understood why the public was so fascinated with their relationship. What were the odds of the biggest rap star in the world falling for a sheltered Amish girl? The story had been in the tabloids for months on end, with daily headlines that claimed all sorts of details about their whirlwind courtship. She remembered one article in particular that made her blush with embarrassment. "The Odd Couple" read the headline. "Plain Amish Girl and Latino Lover, Viper—One of Rap's Sexiest Stars—Find Love!" it continued, while inside it featured a multitude of photographs that showed Amanda in her simple clothes and white prayer *kapp*, doing her daily chores on the farm. Next to those pictures was a series of photos of Alejandro dancing on the stage as hundreds of his young female fans screamed his name and held up signs professing their undying love for him.

It wasn't often that plain fame happened.

Fate, Amanda thought as she slowly opened her eyes and stared up at the ceiling, the blades of the fan moving so fast that she couldn't pick an individual one unless she concentrated intently while trying to follow them. Like the fan blades, fate was a moving target. She understood that few moments in time could be pinpointed as the single moment that could change the the trajectory of one's life. That Manhattan day when they had collided on the busy city street was one, a moment in time that instantaneously changed the course of both her and Alejandro's lives.

For the better.

Amanda took a few moments to lie in her bed, snuggled into the warmth of Alejandro, and thought about quietly getting out of the bed to close the slats to the plantation shutters, which were now allowing a stream of sunshine into the room. She decided against it. Along with her habit of constantly opening windows, she also hated to close the plantation shutters. The large backyard and tall fence that surrounded the property, along with the tall bushes and trees that protected them from prying eyes, not to mention the room-cooling film on all of the windows, made her feel safe enough.

Alejandro, however, preferred the shutters closed when the sun set, for security reasons as well as for privacy. When he was away, she left them open. Last night she'd forgotten to close them.

Just as she started to move about, hoping that she wouldn't disturb him, he slid his arm over her shoulder, gently pulling her toward him. She shut her eyes and smiled, enjoying the moment: the two of them alone, the warmth of his skin through her nightgown, the pressure of his arm against her chest.

"Morning," he mumbled into her hair.

"Good morning," she whispered back. "You didn't come to bed last night."

After their unforgettable reunion, Alejandro had gently carried her into their bed like a bride on her wedding night and softly kissed her forehead as Amanda quickly drifted into a dreamless sleep. But several times throughout the night, she awoke to find the pillow beside her untouched and the bed beside her empty.

He exhaled softly. "I couldn't sleep, and I didn't want to wake you, Princesa." He paused. "By the way, the house looks *magnifica!*"

She smiled to herself. He noticed. He always noticed. Even the small things. When she put out fresh-cut flowers, he always commented on the arrangement. If she wore a new dress, he would compliment her on how it flattered her figure. His attention to detail, especially when it came to his wife, was just one of the many things that she adored about him.

"What time did you finally come to bed?" she asked as she placed her hand on his wrist, gently stroking his skin with her fingers.

He gave a soft groan. "Late. Three o'clock, I think." He paused. "Maybe four."

"Oh, Alejandro!" Abruptly, she twisted herself around so that she faced him. That was one thing that had not changed over the years— his propensity for pushing himself. "It's too much!"

While he had cut back, just as he had promised her on that cold day when he found her standing alone beside her father's grave, his idea of cutting back was not typical of most people. The way that he pushed himself always worried her. "You should go back to sleep! It's not even six thirty!"

He responded by pulling her even closer and resting his chin atop her head. "Umm, no, Princesa." She nestled against him, his arms encircling her tightly so that she had no option but to stay where she was. As if she would have made any other decision. "This is what I want. You. Here. Just like this in my arms."

23

She relaxed a little, her fingers tracing the fading blue tattoo on his bicep. "Isadora," it read. He had tattooed Sofia's name on his other arm shortly after her birth. His girls, he always called the three of them, even though Amanda wasn't so thrilled about his tendency to mark up his body. *Ink,* he called it. She felt *personal graffiti* was a much more fitting name for it. Yet, it was his way of expressing his love for them, a permanent mark on his body as well as in his heart.

For a few minutes they remained like that, their bodies nestled together as morning became a reality. She could hear his breathing slow once again, and while he fell into another light sleep, she lay there and listened to him. Each breath matched the beating of her heart. They were connected in more ways than just marriage, a bond that extended beyond the physical.

He had never been much of a sleeper, and she knew that soon he would awake for the day. He often slept just a few hours, going to bed long after she retired and rising with her in the early hours of the morning. While she was eager to ask him about Los Angeles and the recording sessions, as well as the concerts, she knew that his sleep was much more important. She also craved just a few moments without any mention of contracts or music or recording stars and tours. If he wasn't traveling for concerts, he was in meetings. Since their first year together, not much had changed in that regard. Everyone was still seeking a piece of Alejandro. The only difference now was that he had scaled back his travel schedule and tour dates. He wanted to spend more time with his family while Amanda wanted time alone as a family *without* the all-too-familiar entourage that seemed to accompany Alejandro whenever they traveled or the inner circle of people who frequently hung around their house whenever he was home. Even worse, of course, were the constant prying eyes of strangers whenever they went out in public.

He had, in fact, settled down quite a bit—as much as a world-renowned celebrity could without retiring completely from the constant scrutiny of the public eye. Retiring was something she knew he'd never do. Performing was as much a part of him as breathing.

From another room, the sound of the coffee grinder broke the silence. Probably Señora Perez starting breakfast, she thought. Since long before Amanda had married Alejandro, the housekeeper rose with the sun so she could prepare for her day in the silence of early morning. It wasn't unusual, though, for Amanda to join her, the two women working quietly, side by side. Despite the fact that Señora Perez worked for Alejandro and Amanda, she had given up resisting Amanda's efforts to help her. She knew how much Amanda enjoyed doing things for her family. But not today.

Today, Amanda didn't want to rush into her regular morning routine. Instead, she wanted to enjoy the warmth of her husband's body beside her as the sun filtered through the open slats of the plantation shutters that covered the windows that looked out onto their lush backyard.

After a few minutes, the whir of a lawnmower caused Alejandro to stir. There seemed to be quite a few landscapers rushing about to get the grounds in perfect order for their upcoming Christmas Eve celebration. After all, hosting a winter extravaganza wasn't easy. He tightened his hold on her and sighed. "The calm before the storm, eh?"

She gave a soft laugh. "You don't know the half of it," she muttered, remembering the poor worker hanging by a garland in the living room. He chuckled as his lips nuzzled into her neck.

When Alejandro was home, there was always a different energy level in the house.

"The trip was good?" she asked with interest.

She felt him nod as he answered her with a drawn-out "*Sí, claro.* Just long." His thumb caressed her bare shoulder as he held her. "And the children?"

"Fine," she answered unconvincingly.

"Just fine?"

"Well, you know how they are . . ."

"Ah *sí.*" He chuckled softly. "I should have known the answer before I asked the question." He kissed her shoulder. "You need a break, Princesa. You and me. Alone."

"Hmm," she replied noncommittally, thinking of her mother's letter. She had decided that she would speak to him, perhaps even ask him for his thoughts about returning home for Christmas. But she knew this was not the right moment. He had just returned from a grueling trip and was clearly tired. No doubt, he had a million decisions to make, and she didn't want to add one more. At least not today.

When she felt the intensity of his touch increase, she shut her eyes and smiled. His absence had seemed especially long. Even with their three children in school, Amanda found juggling schedules, after-school activities, and her own appointments stressful, despite all of the household staff that she had come to depend on.

It felt good to have him home.

It felt even better to know that she had nothing scheduled for the day but to spend time with her own family.

"Perhaps after a few days," she answered at last. "The children have missed you, Alejandro."

"And I have missed *you.*"

Her skin heated from his touch and the soft purr in his voice, but the sound of running feet down the hallway suddenly interrupted them. The door to the master bedroom suite flew open and, within seconds, their privacy was invaded.

"Papi!"

The little voice that cried out his name didn't startle Amanda. Alejandro, however, hadn't been prepared for the soft body that scaled the bed like a monkey and, with a delighted shout, jumped on top of him. "You're home!" Sofia excitedly shouted with her sleepyhead curls flying in different directions.

Amanda held back a smile as Alejandro made an *oomph* sound from the sudden weight of Sofia landing atop him.

"Who's this?" he said sleepily but good-naturedly. He removed his arm from around Amanda and reached out for Sofia. "A Sofia? I don't recall ordering a Sofia for breakfast!" She giggled as he wrapped his arms around her and planted soft kisses on her cheeks and neck. "Umm . . . Sofia kisses for breakfast, *sí?* What a treat!"

More giggles followed as Sofia tickled him.

Alejandro glanced at Amanda over Sofia's dark curls and mouthed the words, "Door locks?"

Amanda shrugged, still smiling as she watched her husband with their daughter in his arms.

"Papi! Papi!"

Alejandro looked up in time to see seven-year-old Nicolas charging across the room. With his thick, wavy hair and vibrant blue eyes, he was a miniature version of his father. And his intense energy was often too much for Amanda. He loved wrestling and climbing, often scaling the wall that surrounded their property. On more than one occasion, a security guard had knocked at the front door, a sheepish-looking Nicolas standing beside him, his eyes on the ground.

As Nicolas took a leap, Amanda moved away from Alejandro in time to escape the small tank of a boy who landed on the bed next to his father. When the boy sat up, he tried to shove his sister away, but, as usual, Sofia fought back, claiming the spot right by her father's side. Alejandro laughed, putting his arms around the both of them and giving them a big hug.

"Looks like it's time to get up," Amanda said as she slid out from beneath the covers while Alejandro dealt with the two overly energetic children, both of them fighting for his undivided attention. She took advantage of their focus being diverted on to Alejandro—usually they were clamoring for her attention—and hurried into her walk-in closet and dressing room.

Let's hope he can keep them occupied for a few minutes more, she thought as she hastily got dressed before her two children started wrestling at her feet, which was the general course of her mornings.

In Florida, although early December days tended to be a little cooler in the mornings and evenings, the midday sun still felt like August. Amanda quickly selected a pale-blue sundress and pair of matching leather thong sandals, making certain to grab a light white cotton knit cardigan just in case she was chilly later in the day when the sun went down. As she finished getting ready, she could hear the giggles and laughter of Sofia and Nicolas coming from the bed. While it wasn't a conventional family, Amanda convinced herself that she wouldn't have changed one thing about their lifestyle. After all, this was her life, and she thanked God for it every day. She knew that she had to take the good with the not-so-good. To lament otherwise would be to question God's plan for her, and that was something Amanda wasn't willing to do.

She glanced in the mirror and smoothed her hair back before twisting it into a bun.

Well, *one* thing she might change, she thought as she remembered her mother's unexpected request. Some time over the next few days, she would need to broach the subject of the holidays with Alejandro. Her mother would need a response one way or another.

"Mami!"

At the sound of Nicolas's voice and the patter of his bare feet running across the bedroom floor, Amanda braced herself for what she knew was heading her way: a very happy—and physical!—good morning greeting.

He wrapped his arms around her legs and squeezed as tight as he could. Amanda held on to the dressing table to avoid stumbling backward.

"Oh help!" she said in a teasing tone. "Such a greeting!"

"Papi's home! Papi's home!" he squealed in excitement.

"I know!" She laughed. "Isn't that wonderful?"

Nicolas tilted his head and grinned up at her. "He said we don't have to go to school today."

"It's Sunday," Sofia's voice called from the doorway. "We don't have school on Sunday, silly goose!"

Amanda gave her daughter a look of reproach. Despite her young age, Sofia was the bossiest of the children and lately had taken to name-calling. Amanda was more than certain that she'd picked it up from watching videos on YouTube.

"Alright, both of you." Alejandro stood behind Sofia and clapped his hands twice. "Give your mother some space, *sí*? Go get changed and ready for breakfast. And no electronics at the table, eh?"

Without questioning him outright but with a slight groan, both Sofia and Nicolas scampered out of the bedroom. Amanda couldn't help but smile.

"If only I could bottle up their energy . . . ," Alejandro said wistfully with a grin.

Amanda laughed. "Oh, please! You have just as much energy on your own. I'd hate to think of what would happen if you had more!"

"Simple, *mi princesa*. We'd have many more nights like the one we had last night," he teased in a low voice, arching his eyebrow in mischief.

Amanda blushed on cue and shook her head. "You must have been incorrigible as a child," she observed.

"Of course I was. Why do you think I give my mother the world? She's a saint to have put up with all of my antics."

"Well, I believe the apple hasn't fallen too far from the tree. Your children are a bundle of energy. They certainly keep me on my toes."

"And what lovely toes you have," he playfully observed.

As Amanda finished pinning her hair, she looked in the reflection of the mirror as Alejandro leaned against the doorframe. He wore black gym pants and no shirt. With his arms crossed over his chest, he looked especially muscular, something that had not changed over the years, although he complained he had to spend more and more time at the gym in order to maintain his physique.

"What are you thinking?" she asked, still gazing at his reflection.

His eyes stared back at her with such intensity that it made her blush. "I was thinking how you haven't changed at all. Still so very beautiful."

"Of course I've changed. I've gotten older."

He shook his head in denial. "That's not possible. You are still the young girl I fell in love with."

He took a step toward her and stood behind her, their eyes meeting in the mirror. He raised his hand and ran his finger down the back of her neck. Shivers ran up her spine, and she caught her breath. How was it possible that, after all these years, he could still have such an impact on her?

"I think we've *both* changed." She reached up and covered his hand with hers.

"Oh? How so?" he asked with interest.

"You have calmed down a bit, don't you think?"

He laughed at her question. "Just a minute ago, I was a hurricane of energy. Now I've calmed down."

She smiled at him. "You know what I mean."

"*Sí, sí*, I know what you mean, and you are right, I have calmed down . . . maybe a little. And you? How have you changed?"

Amanda thought carefully about the question before answering. "Well, I've adapted to being more worldly, I reckon."

He laughed again, raising an eyebrow as he repeated her words. "You reckon? I haven't heard you say that word in years!"

"Mayhaps I haven't become so worldly after all," she said, teasing him by deliberately responding with another word from her past.

But she wasn't certain if that was true. She was just as surprised as Alejandro that she had used that phrase, so reminiscent of the simple vocabulary from her upbringing on an Amish farm. Had she said it subconsciously because of her mother's letter? This might have been a reasonable segue into mentioning the correspondence, but she didn't want to have this conversation with him. Not now, anyway. So she merely smiled and turned around so that she could kiss him on his lips.

"Mayhaps you need to give me another kiss like that," he requested with mischief in his voice. "*Gracias a* Dios! Your lips haven't changed at all."

"Alejandro!" But she smiled at his playfulness. It felt good to have him home. "Let's get some coffee and plan the day before the children are finished getting ready. I have the feeling that once they get hold of you, I won't see you again until tonight."

"Umm," he sighed, his voice deep and husky. "Until tonight then, Princesa." Leaning down, he placed a tender kiss on her neck, his one hand dropping from her shoulder to her slender waist. The heat from his embrace and the passion of his kiss caused her to flush and look away from the mirror. He could still make her feel as if each kiss was the first one, and she found herself vividly reliving the memory of that long-ago day.

When he separated from her, his hand lingered for just a moment on her hip, the corner of his lips lifting in an all-too-familiar way, when the color flooded to her cheeks.

The rest of the day was spent preparing for the holiday. There were so many things still left to do and so very little time.

"After breakfast, I want you and Nicolas to help me wrap some gifts," Amanda told Sofia as she sipped her coffee and made a long mental list of the tasks that needed to be done.

"Can I wrap Papi's gift?" Nicolas begged. "Pretty please!" he added, his big blue eyes open wide.

"Of course you can!" Amanda replied at once, enjoying Nicolas's excitement at the prospect of wrapping his father's gift. But no sooner had she uttered the words than she found herself wondering about the special meaning this simple deed represented for her son.

Despite all these years spent with Alejandro and their family, she still had a difficult time comprehending why people would shower each other with so many often useless and extravagant gifts around Christmastime. Back home in Lancaster County, Christmas among the Amish was not about giving gifts. It was about celebrating the birth of the Savior. About spending time with one's extended family and rejoicing for the bounty of God's gifts to his children. For humbly thanking him for the abundance of blessings bestowed upon their community. For the more conservative members of the *g'may*, it was also a time of peaceful reflection and atonement. It was not about sharing material gifts with one another.

Sure, some Amish people, perhaps influenced by the Englische tradition, had started to give their children little gifts around that time of the year—a sewn handkerchief, a new pair of shoes, a new Sunday shirt—but these were always practical items and certainly did not come with all of the commercialism and fanfare associated with the Englische Christmas.

While the glimmer in Nicolas's eyes made her happy, she felt a certain anguish building up in her heart. Indeed, it was nice to see the love and adoration for his father that was brought about by the simple act of wrapping a present. But at the same time, it made Amanda ponder the gifts that Alejandro was planning to give his friends and family—especially his mother.

After all, this gathering of family and friends had become a strong tradition with her husband and his entourage. He loved to shower them all with presents and throw a lavish party with exquisite food, fancy wines and liquors, a band, and gifts for everyone—gifts that often included fancy cars and expensive jewelry. He loved to have his mother cook the special Christmas dishes for him, and he loved making her feel special. Alejandro was generous to a fault, and that generosity also gave him great pleasure. Could she possibly ask him to give that up in order to spend their Christmas with her own family in Lancaster County?

Yes, she thought. By asking him to celebrate with her own family, she would be denying him the one gift he enjoyed above all others: celebrating with his friends and family.

And while that thought left her sad, she knew that she had no choice but to try to give her mother the only gift she had ever asked for.

Chapter Three

"The holidays are coming soon," Amanda said as she stood at the granite counter and rearranged some freshly cut flowers in a Lalique crystal vase.

It was her morning ritual: waking before everyone else so that she could enjoy a few quiet moments by herself. Some days, as the sun barely crested the horizon, she would escape to the gardens and weed, plucking the uninvited growths and then cutting some fresh flowers for the staff to put out in various areas of the house: the entrance room, the family's kitchen table, the different hallways, and, of course, their master bedroom. It was one of her favorite things about living in Florida: everyday access to fresh flowers.

When Alejandro was traveling, early mornings were Amanda's favorite time of the day. She could ease into her schedule without too many interruptions from the children and staff. For once, her cell phone remained silent and she could simply . . . be. It reminded her so much of her life before Alejandro.

Today, however, Alejandro had been home from his tour for several days and was back to his own early-morning routine. He joined her in the quiet of the kitchen.

Despite having been away for so long, he was already leaving again the following afternoon, right after the photographers were finished with the family photo shoot. It was for the cover of a magazine to be published in June, the main reason why the company wanted to conduct the shoot under the sunny Florida sky, right in their own backyard.

Alejandro's day was full of meetings with different people: his manager, his promotions team, other artists, and even several business professionals who wanted Viper's endorsement on their products. Amanda knew the only time she would be able to speak to him about her mother's letter was now, before the daylong interruptions began.

"The holidays? *Sí*, Princesa, I am well aware. In fact, my mother is already busy planning—or so she reminds me whenever she can." He gave her a wink as he leaned against the counter, dressed simply in pressed black dungarees and a light-cream polo shirt. There was a steaming mug of coffee by his side, and he leafed through several newspapers and weekly tabloids, which a staff member set out for him each morning. He looked relaxed, but Amanda wasn't certain that he was paying attention to her. He glanced at his watch distractedly. "I need to leave in an hour. Meeting with Geoffrey and Rudy before having lunch with that new recording artist I told you about last week."

Her concentration broke. "You haven't even had breakfast yet!" It was an ongoing battle between the two of them. She always complained about his horrible tendency to skip meals, especially when he was bouncing between a tour schedule and being at home. He would merely laugh while flexing his muscles, telling her that he was just fine and in top shape.

"I have a little time, Amanda," he said. "But I'd be happy to take it with me if it's not ready." It was his way of compromising with her.

Señora Perez was already at the stove, cooking the breakfast. From the familiar smell, Amanda could tell that she was cooking Alejandro's favorite: *tostada*, eggs, and sausage, with freshly sliced papaya on the side. And, of course, fresh-squeezed Florida orange juice, which he insisted on having each morning.

Amanda poked her head around the corner and caught Señora Perez's eyes. "When Alejandro's breakfast is ready . . ."

She didn't have to finish her sentence. After so many years working in the family, Señora Perez was very familiar with Alejandro's routine, which was unpredictable, at best. "*Sí*, Amanda. I'll pack it for him to take."

Amanda smiled her appreciation and, before returning to the counter where Alejandro stood, picked up the coffeepot to refill her husband's cup.

"We should discuss our plans before you leave," Amanda said casually as she set the piping-hot mug before him.

"Ah *sí*," he replied while he flipped the page of the newspaper, his eyes scanning the headlines. "I'll be back on Sunday morning, but don't forget that next week we are traveling to Michigan before the New York and Miami concerts."

She sighed. That wasn't what she meant. Her mind had been so preoccupied by the letter from her mother that she had almost forgotten about their travel plans for the following week. It had completely slipped her mind. There was so much to remember, dates were a blur to her.

"What's in Michigan, again?" she asked. It wasn't a state that they often visited.

"The children's book," he said. "The one to raise money for your cancer center."

"Oh help! I had forgotten about that!"

He glanced up from the paper and gave her a mischievous smile. "Well, you will be thirty next year, no? They say that the memory is the first to go," he teased, while tapping the side of his head with his index finger.

Playfully, she tossed a hand towel at him as he laughed.

How could she have forgotten about the book recording to benefit the Princesa Cancer Center? After all, it had been her idea to raise money for the children's center she had set up to help families.

When her assistant, Charley, had mentioned that a publishing company had contacted him, asking if she would be willing to provide audio recording for a children's book, Amanda had immediately said yes, provided that all the proceeds from the sale of the books were donated to the children's cancer center that bore her name in Miami. It had been a cause she'd supported since Alejandro had introduced her to a little boy with cancer in a Chicago hospital. When Alejandro had volunteered, too, Brilliance Audio had excitedly given the project a go-ahead. Making a difference in people's lives was one of the things she felt the most proud of. If her status as the wife of a megastar gave her the ability to help those in need, maybe it was worth the traveling and endless events.

The reading had fit in their schedule, too. They would fly out of Miami at six o'clock in the morning on Tuesday, and the following day, they would travel to New York City. She knew that Thursday was fully booked with Alejandro's scheduled performance on *The Today Show* and a meeting with several aspiring artists in the early afternoon. All of this before the Jingle Ball concert at Madison Square Garden, Amanda thought wearily. It would surely be well past midnight before they boarded the private jet that would fly them home to Miami in time for the Friday night concert at the American Airlines Arena.

"Alejandro, I was thinking . . . ," Amanda said in a long-drawn-out manner before she paused, giving him time to realize that she wanted to discuss something of importance with him and sought his undivided attention.

He tilted his head as he watched her, his mouth pursing just a little. *"¿Sí?"*

"I'm sure it's not possible . . ." Again, another pause. She picked up a crystal vase and walked around the counter to place it in the center of the large family dining table.

"*¿Qué, mi amor?* Ask and I will make it happen," he answered earnestly.

She took a deep breath. "You shouldn't say that, Alejandro. You have no idea what I am about to say."

For a long moment, he studied her, and she could see that he was thinking. She rarely asked him for anything, mostly because she didn't want for anything. Whenever she did, it was always a reasonable request and always within his schedule. Even though they hadn't dated for a lengthy amount of time, just a few months really, she had married him knowing that his profession called for unusually high demands on his time. But she had never made a request like this. And while the last thing she wanted was for him to feel guilty, she also knew that her mother had never requested anything. In the days since receiving the letter, Amanda had concluded that it was important to her that sharing the holiday become part of the family tradition.

"Fair enough," he said. "Let me rephrase that. I will certainly try to accommodate you."

"I received a letter from my mother yesterday," she hesitantly said.

"She is well?" he asked, his forehead creasing with concern.

Amanda wavered before answering. Her mother hadn't actually mentioned anything about her health or well-being. "I believe so," Amanda answered. "She didn't necessarily say. But back home, people rarely say much about themselves."

Alejandro stood up and crossed his arms over his chest, clearly curious now. "So what was the real purpose of the letter, Amanda?"

She swallowed before she spoke, preparing herself for his reaction. "She asked if we could come to Pennsylvania for Christmas." Her tone had a tinge of guilt in it for asking but also held a tremor of longing for him to acquiesce. It was important to her. With her mother getting older and Alejandro's schedule, Amanda wondered if this might be one of the last opportunities she would have to enjoy the holidays with her entire family in Lititz. A bucket-list wish of sorts from her mother. Would Alejandro understand this? Would he sense the anguish that was building up in her chest? She knew he was quite adept at reading people's emotions and inner thoughts—that was what had attracted him to her in the first place—but when she was a young girl, she had learned that the Amish community frowned upon displays of emotion and internal turmoil.

He groaned, his shoulders slumping forward as he rubbed his temples with one hand. "*Ay* Dios, Amanda! You know we can't do that! Everything's been settled, and to change it now, well, so many people would have to change their plans as well."

His schedule was busy, that was for sure and certain. But Amanda had looked at it the previous day, and she wasn't so convinced that he couldn't make this happen. She knew better than to say that to him, though. Besides, it was more than just his schedule. There was also his mother to consider. She would never let them break tradition without an earth-shattering fight. While Amanda had always gotten along with her mother-in-law, the relationship between Alecia and Alejandro was like a rubber band. If one pulled away, the other one did the same, creating tension between the two that often caused one of them to snap.

"She's never asked before," she replied, trying to hold back her emotions.

He looked miserable, standing there before her, still rubbing at his head.

"And the children don't even know their cousins," she added, feeling a tightness in her throat.

"Amanda," he said gently. "I would do anything for you, but I cannot make this one thing happen."

Slowly, she nodded her head. "I know, Alejandro. I just thought I would ask." She forced a faint smile and averted her eyes, knowing full well that she, not he, was in control of this. "It is, after all, such short notice."

"*Sí*, too short notice. If only your mother had asked a few months ago. Things might have been different. My mother has already started the preparations, and my cousins are expecting us to host everyone."

Amanda picked up a vase and started to walk out of the room toward the hallway, where she planned to put the flowers near the front entrance. "She just doesn't understand that your schedule is booked so far in advance," she added.

"*¡Exactamente!*"

As Amanda began to leave the room, she paused at the door, as if thinking of something important. Slowly, she pursed her lips and she said in a drawn-out way, "However, I don't think we've ever celebrated Christmas with my family, at least not since the children were born."

She didn't have to turn around to know that he had slapped his hand against his thigh. "That's not right, Amanda! It's not as if I don't want you to go."

As she continued walking, she knew that he was following her. She walked through the family entertainment room and paused in the hallway that led to the glass atrium. Setting the vase onto an otherwise empty reception table, she rearranged and fluffed the flowers as she listened to Alejandro pacing back and forth behind her.

"It's just not possible, *mi amor*," he said, trying to sound convincing. "I know it doesn't sound fair . . ."

Amanda stopped fussing over the flowers and turned around to face him. She gave him another smile. "You don't have to explain anything," she said as she took a step forward, leaning up toward his face to give him a soft kiss on the cheek. "As long as we are together with our family, everything is fine. My mother will have to understand."

She walked away, wondering whether he would drop the subject or continue mulling it over. After all, he had meetings in the afternoon and had promised to take Nicolas fishing after school. Given that he was leaving the following day, Alejandro certainly had other things on his mind and didn't need to be bothered with last-minute requests to change his demanding itinerary. He was always willing to squeeze in more appointments for the sake of his career and to accommodate others, but he never responded well to unplanned changes in his personal life.

Nevertheless, she hoped that a seed had been planted. Not a flower seed but more like . . . a weed. It had not been her intention to burden him with making this decision, however important it was to her. She just thought that there might be some way to compromise, some way to satisfy both sides of the family. She felt a lump building up in her throat as she realized that her husband did not need the additional stress; he had enough to deal with on his own.

It wasn't until later in the evening that the subject was brought up again. After spending the rest of the day away from home, Alejandro had returned with a pensive expression on his face. Amanda noticed it right away and kept her distance. She knew better than to interrupt Alejandro when he looked deep in thought. Those were the times when she kept to herself, knowing that he would come to her when, and if, he needed to talk about something.

By the time he finally approached her, it was well into the night. Amanda was already in bed reading a book when she heard the door to their bedroom open. She looked up and smiled as Alejandro walked in and yanked at his tie. Tossing it onto a nearby chair, he crossed the room and sat next to her on the edge of the bed.

"Everything go well?"

He nodded. "*Sí*, quite well. The new LP is going to set many new records on the charts."

Folding down the corner of the page she had been reading, Amanda shut the book and set it on her lap. He glanced at it before pushing it aside so that he could lean over and rest his arm across her thighs. He stared up at her. "I thought about what you asked today, Amanda."

"About?"

He raised an eyebrow, suspicious of the genuineness of her reply. "About Christmas, *sí*?"

"Oh?"

"You know my mother will have a—*¿cómo se dice?*—temper tantrum," he said. "But if you are willing to deal with her, then we can go to Lititz."

Amanda caught her breath. "Really?" she asked, her eyes wide and disbelieving. She hadn't expected him to be keen on spending the holidays with her family. Her mother had never really approved of their relationship, especially during the tumultuous beginning. Even the last time they had visited, Lizzie made a disapproving noise whenever Alejandro talked about the music industry with Anna's husband, Jonas.

"*Sí*, really." He reached out and tugged at the long brown hair that hung over her shoulder. "You are right about the cousins. And your mother is their grandmother, too. Besides, you never complained once, in all these years, about spending all these holidays with my friends and family. It's time for us to spend it with yours. But," he said abruptly, holding up his hand in an effort to stop her from saying anything, "we can only stay for a few days. Geoffrey has his people making the arrangements. And remember"—he lowered his voice and stared into her eyes—"you agreed to break the news to my mother, *sí*?"

Barely able to contain her emotions, Amanda threw her arms around his shoulders and hugged him. She couldn't believe that he had agreed so easily! She felt his arms wrap around her waist and pressed her cheek against his shoulder, beaming with joy, even though—or perhaps because—he couldn't see her.

"Oh, Alejandro! That is the most wonderful Christmas present ever!"

Chapter Four

"What do you mean we won't be home for Christmas?" Sofia cried out in alarm.

Just the way Sofia enunciated the word *Christmas*, her blue eyes bulging out of her head and her mouth hanging open in surprise—and not the good kind of surprise—made it sound as if Amanda had proclaimed that there would be no Christmas at all.

With the exception of Alejandro, the rest of the family gathered in the large kitchen at the back of the house. They were waiting for the photographer to call them to come out and take their places in the garden. A team of people had descended upon the house earlier in the morning, setting up equipment in the backyard for the photo shoot. While they were waiting, Amanda had mentioned the big news as casually as she could.

Sofia had been putting on her shoes and was standing the closest to her mother when the announcement was made. "We're *always* home for Christmas!"

Isadora looked up from her cell phone and asked, "What's this about Christmas?" She was sitting at the table with her textbooks spread out before her, but as far as Amanda could tell, she hadn't done anything more than check her social media.

Amanda gave Isadora a look. "How about some more homework and less texting, Izzie?" She glanced over her shoulder in time to see Grace struggling with Nicolas, trying to keep him from getting his clothes wrinkled or dirty before the photography team was ready. He was trying to run away from her, and her attempt to contain him in the large atrium was not going well. "Nicolas! Calm down and listen to Grace. Please!" Amanda called out, but he ignored her.

"What? We won't be here for Christmas?" Isadora's voice sounded as horrified as Sofia looked. "Please tell me not Tia Maria's house! It's so small for all of those people, and Papi's cousin Adolfo still pinches my cheeks!" She rolled her eyes and groaned. "Doesn't he realize I'm not a little kid anymore?"

"No, no, sweetheart. Not Tia Maria's house. We're going out of town instead," she exclaimed cheerfully.

Suddenly, a look of excitement crossed the fourteen-year-old's face. "Out of town?" Her blue eyes flashed as her mind clearly began to check through all of the possibilities. "Where to? Europe?" She gasped. "Paris?"

Amanda started to respond, but Isadora talked right over her.

"Wait, no. That's too far away, right?" Isadora pressed her lips together, thinking of her next guess. "Oh! I know! New York City? You know how much I love New York City." She practically squealed in delight at the thought. "Fifth Avenue! Here we come!"

"No, not quite like New York City," Amanda said as she knelt before Sofia and tried to buckle her daughter's shoes. Of course, Sofia didn't like the shoes that Jeremy's team had picked out for her to wear, whining that they were too babyish for an eight-year-old. She kept swinging her feet away from Amanda, no matter how hard her mother tried to hold each foot still. "Sofia, please," she said softly. The foot finally remained motionless long enough for her to fasten the buckle. "There! Next foot."

"Los Angeles?" After a brief hesitation, Isadora's expression changed, and she gasped. For a moment, she looked as alarmed as Sofia had just moments ago. "I'm not going to miss the Miami concert, am I? You know I told everyone I was meeting Banff! That would be an epic tragedy! Please tell me I won't miss it!"

This time, it was Amanda who fought the urge to roll her eyes. When had the holidays become about everyone else's needs? Didn't anyone think of other people at Christmas? She sighed. Apparently not in her family. Like sharing the holidays with her family, giving to others was another change that needed to happen to their family holiday tradition, and she didn't mean giving material gifts. "No, Izzie," she said at last. "You won't miss the concert."

Glancing over her shoulder, Amanda looked at Grace and Nicolas. They were standing in the hallway. Nicolas was still trying to run from her, but Grace had a firm grip on his arm. "Please, Nicolas," Amanda said in an exasperated tone. His energy was exhausting her patience. "You're going to knock something over."

No sooner had she said the words than the small boy swung his free arm and hit the flower vase on the table. The vase shattered, scattering broken crystal and water across the floor. Startled at the noise, which echoed against the cathedral ceilings, Grace released the little boy's arm, and the now-free Nicolas ran out of her reach. As he sprinted past Amanda, she just barely managed to grab him.

"Nicolas!" she snapped at last. He finally stopped squiggling and stared up at her, his big blue eyes searching her face. Immediately, Amanda took a deep breath and counted to ten. Twice. It wasn't even ten o'clock, and with the three children home from school for the photographer, Amanda could tell it was going to be a very long day. "Please, sweetheart," she said with forced calm. "I need you to calm down. Just for an hour or two."

"Mami!" Isadora interrupted, ignoring Teresa and Grace as they cleaned up the mess that her brother had made, even as Teresa swept up the shards under the table by her feet. "Could you please answer me? *Where* are we going for Christmas?"

"I want to be home for Christmas!" Sofia cried.

"We *will* be at home," Amanda said with as much patience as she could muster. "*My* family's home."

The color drained from Isadora's face. "Pennsylvania? They don't even have electricity! How will I charge my phone?" she said in a panicked voice.

Amanda counted to ten again and then tried to reassure her daughter. "You know they have solar electricity. We've been there before, Izzie." When she noticed the scowl on Isadora's face, Amanda reminded her, "You loved it there once. Remember? When you adopted Katie Cat?"

Isadora rolled her eyes. "That was *eons* ago, Mami!"

"I doubt much has changed since then," Amanda said softly. "It's the same place."

"Well, I sure hope they have good cell service," Isadora said, not directing her comment to anyone in particular. "It's out in the middle of nowhere."

At this last comment, Sofia made a face. "Middle of nowhere? How will Santa find us?"

Already Isadora was notifying her friends, first holding up the phone to snap a selfie and then tapping furiously on it.

"Izzie, please. Do not broadcast this information." All Amanda needed was for one of Isadora's friends to post their plans on social media, and the paparazzi would have a field day.

Dropping her phone on her open textbook, Isadora rolled her eyes and sighed. "How long will we have to be there?"

"Will we still get gifts?" Sofia asked. "You know I asked Santa for a laptop." She tilted her head and eyed her mother suspiciously. "The purple one with the special unicorn case, too. You told Santa, right?"

Amanda frowned. Her patience was wearing thin. "Santa?" She took a deep breath. Santa Claus. Every year it was the same thing, only now it was multiplied by three.

Each year, it started earlier and earlier. The list of things that they wanted for Christmas now began shortly after Labor Day. How could they help it, Amanda wondered, when the world of advertising kept finding new ways to brainwash the children to promote its products? The only problem was that they wanted everything. Whether it was the coolest electronic toy, newest connected gadget, or latest fashion style, they simply expected it to magically appear under the Christmas tree.

"You do remember that Christmas is much more than receiving gifts, right?" Amanda said, finally finishing with Sofia's other shoe. "It's about Jesus."

"The little baby?" Nicolas asked.

"Yes, baby Jesus."

Sofia looked at Nicolas. "Like him?" she asked and pointed at her brother. He responded by sticking his tongue out at her.

"Sofia. Please don't antagonize him." Amanda stood up and ran her hands down the front of her black skirt. The two younger children were like cats and dogs, constantly bickering. The one-year difference in their age had done nothing to make them close friends. Instead, they squabbled and argued nonstop.

Isadora stood up and with a mischievous smile said, "Yeah, Sofia. Otherwise *Santa* won't bring you any presents in *Pennsylvania!*"

"Will Jesus bring us presents, then?" Nicolas asked, his eyes wide as he stopped fussing.

"But what does baby Jesus have to do with Santa's presents?" Sofia demanded.

Inwardly, Amanda groaned. This conversation was heading in the wrong direction.

In their world of excess, it seemed increasingly hard for Amanda to keep her children grounded. Over the past few years, Amanda had tried unsuccessfully to take the children to church. But between the family's chaotic travel schedules and the invasion of both paparazzi and fans, she had finally abandoned the effort. Instead, she tried to read them stories from the Bible at night, even though Sofia cried for her *Dora the Explorer* books. Eventually, Isadora and Sofia began negotiating with their mother: one Bible story for each storybook.

To Amanda's shame, she had eventually given up arguing with the children and, instead, did what she could to instill values in the children, talking about God and Jesus as often as she could.

Clearly, that wasn't enough.

"Amanda, the photographers are ready."

Grateful for Alejandro's reemergence, Amanda turned to face him and gave him an exasperated look. If only he would support her in her efforts to provide a religious education to their children. "Honestly, Alejandro, we need to have a talk about Christmas."

He stood there, his black suit crisp and fresh, his sunglasses resting atop his head, and stared at her with a blank expression on his face. Behind him, Amanda could see the media team out back by the pool, fiddling with their lights and equipment as they waited for the Diaz family. The photographers were on the magazine's time clock, not Alejandro's, so Amanda didn't mind keeping them waiting. Besides, this was more important than any magazine cover.

"What about Christmas?" he asked at last. "We agreed we're going to Pennsylvania, no?"

Isadora and Sofia spoke up simultaneously.

"Why do we have to go away? I'll miss everything that's going on here!"

"What about Santa? He'll never find us! We won't get anything!"

At the mention of not receiving presents, Nicolas joined them. "I want to stay here for Santa!" He began to cry.

Amanda tilted her head and spread out her hands, as if presenting the very problem that vexed her.

"Ay, mi madre," Alejandro mumbled, rubbing his chin and glancing toward the ceiling. Then, he turned to Nicolas and pointed a finger at him. "No crying, Nicolas!" he said in a stern voice. "Big boys don't cry over such things!" To his daughters, he merely raised an eyebrow and gave them a warning look. Immediately, the complaining ceased, although based on her quick return to her phone, Amanda suspected Isadora was sharing her distress with her friends once again.

"We will discuss this later. For now, I want happy faces for the camera, and"—he directed another firm look at Nicolas—"our best behavior."

Outside by the pool, the media team was still fussing over their equipment: lights, reflectors, and cameras. There were wires everywhere. As Alejandro walked ahead of his family, one of his numerous assistants hurried to meet him to discuss something in Spanish. Amanda held Nicolas's hand, but it didn't make a difference. He was too busy staring at the cameras and, distracted, tripped over a wire and fell, cutting his knee.

"Nicolas!" Immediately, Amanda scooped him into her arms. He sobbed into her neck, blood from his cut staining her silky white blouse.

"Amanda! Let's go!"

Alejandro's voice carried through the open space between them. She turned to face him, their whimpering son in her arms, and his eyes quickly assessed the scene. The camera crew stopped what they were doing to watch. Quiet swept through the group. It was well known within the industry that when schedules were delayed, Alejandro became irritated. Yet, his ire was most often directed at others and very rarely at his wife and children.

"Ay, Nicolas!" His eyes narrowed as he crossed the distance between himself and Amanda. When he noticed the stain on her blouse, he reached up and ran his fingers through his hair, frustrated at yet one more delay. Amanda glanced over his shoulder and noticed the

magazine's stylist frown and roll his eyes, shaking his head in dismay while tossing a hairbrush over his shoulder.

Unmoved by his son's tears, Alejandro took the seven-year-old from Amanda and passed him over to an assistant. "Clean him up, *sí?*" As the assistant led the boy by the hand, Alejandro smiled at the young woman with gratitude. *"Gracias."*

Behind Amanda, Isadora sighed, but it was Sofia who spoke. "How long is this going to take?"

Alejandro turned his head in the direction of Sofia's voice, but his eyes fell upon Isadora, who, once again, was taking a photo of herself, her tongue sticking out of her mouth as she rolled her eyes for the picture. He frowned. *"Ay, hija,* can you put down your phone for the next hour?" It was not a question but a demand. He reached out and took the phone from her. "Give the world of social media a reason to miss you, no?"

A tall man approached them and extended his hand toward Alejandro, who responded by pulling him into a warm embrace.

"Geoffrey! What's the good word today?"

Amanda smiled at Geoffrey, Alejandro's manager. "Merry Christmas," she said when he leaned over and kissed her on both cheeks.

"Merry Christmas to you, too." He walked with them toward the photography equipment, where the team was waiting. "This should only take about an hour," he explained, glancing at his watch. "And then we'll have to leave for the airport, Alejandro. Oh, and the arrangements have been made for getting everyone to Pennsylvania after the Miami concert."

At his words, Amanda felt her heart flutter. She shouldn't have been surprised that Geoffrey had already made the arrangements. Whether by text, e-mail, or phone, the two men were always communicating.

"Miami concert?" Isadora perked up and ran forward, placing her hand on Geoffrey's shoulder as she walked behind him. "Did you find out if I can bring my friends, Uncle Geoff?"

Amanda had forgotten about Isadora's request to bring her friends with her to the Jingle Ball concert in Miami. With all of the top bands and singers that were performing at the event, everyone wanted a ticket. Isadora, however, wanted to be backstage so she could meet the performers.

"Izzie, you shouldn't ask for such favors," Amanda said. She was always wary of Isadora getting hurt by people trying to take advantage of her. At the same time, she knew their daughter needed a social life, too. Most of her friends attended the same private school and came from privileged backgrounds, but none of them came from a family that had so many ties to the entertainment industry.

"Unfortunately," Alejandro said, answering for Geoffrey, "that cannot happen, Isadora."

"Papi!" she whined. "Why not?"

Amanda frowned. Wasn't it enough that Alejandro had agreed to let Isadora attend? While he usually let her attend his Miami concerts, this one was different. The backstage scene would be more chaotic than usual, and Alejandro normally objected to Isadora attending a concert with so many performers and their entourages. It simply was too mature an environment for a young girl. But now that she was fourteen, he had agreed to let her come, especially since Banff, her favorite band, was performing.

While Alejandro often gave in to his firstborn's demands, this time he held firm. "Not this year, *hija*."

"Can we at least get some tickets for Jennifer and Cathy?" she pleaded. "You know I told them you would!" She stared at her father and then, when he didn't answer right away, she looked imploringly at her mother. "Mami! If I don't get those tickets for them . . ."

"We'll see," Alejandro finally answered but in a far too noncommittal way to sound convincing.

Amanda reached over and touched her daughter's shoulder. They both knew that a "we'll see" from Alejandro usually meant no.

Isadora groaned as she covered her face with her hands. "I'll be a social outcast if they don't get to go!"

"At least you won't have to see them afterward," Sofia said sarcastically as she walked past her sister, "since we're going to *Pennsylvania* for Christmas!"

Alejandro pointed his finger at her. "That's enough, young lady." He turned to look at Amanda, giving an irritated shake of his head. "Ay-yi-yi!"

"Can you manage while I go change, or should I send Grace or Renata to help?" she asked as she started to walk back toward the house.

He shook his head to indicate that he didn't need help, but by the time she reached the door, she knew that he was on his cell phone, and the two girls were already bickering.

She hurried to their bedroom, removing her blouse as she walked into her closet. Jeremy had probably spent weeks selecting the perfect outfit for her to wear for the photo shoot, and she knew she would hear about it from him. Nothing she chose for herself would rise to the level of perfection her stylist demanded. She sighed as she rummaged through her closet trying to find something that was at least similar.

"Amanda," she heard Alejandro call out to her, his voice carrying from the backyard through the open window. "*Con rapidez!* The photographer doesn't want to miss the morning light."

"I'll be right there."

Amanda sighed again as she buttoned up her new blouse. She wondered if there would ever be a time that they could enjoy a normal day without the constant demands that came with Alejandro's fame.

For the next hour, the family stood together, the photographer's crew directing their every movement. It wasn't the first family photo shoot, and although Amanda suspected that it would not be the last, she hoped it was a long time until the next one. The smiling and posing became painful after the first fifteen minutes, the children losing interest and Alejandro starting to glance at Geoffrey, who was pacing on the grass, his cell phone held to his ear. Clearly, something was amiss, and that made Alejandro fidgety.

"Nicolas, look this way," the photographer said. Amanda looked at her son and saw that he had turned around, his shoulders slumped from boredom. "Amanda," the photographer said to her, "can you please try to keep the children still?"

She placed her hand on Nicolas's shoulder and gently pulled him against her.

"When will this be over, Mami?" he whispered.

"Soon, sweetheart. Just try to smile and not look away. Think of something wonderful, and it will help."

"Like Christmas?"

She laughed. "*Ja*, like Christmas."

She followed her own advice and let her mind drift to the upcoming family sojourn. For just a few days, life would be simpler. There would be no demands made of their family, at least not from the outside world. A serene smile graced her face as she imagined the children with no cell phones or tablets as they played in the hayloft, and Alejandro with no one demanding his time, relaxing and just . . . being. There would be nothing to do but take in the fresh air and enjoy one another.

"That's perfect!" The photographer moved around as he took a final series of photos. "Beautiful, Amanda," yelled the photographer. "Whatever you're doing, keep doing it!"

Finally, the photographer lowered his camera. "That should do it." He called out to the rest of his crew, "It's a wrap!"

No sooner had he said those words than Alejandro hurried over to Geoffrey, and the children scattered in different directions. They were all clearly grateful to be finished with another mundane chore. Amanda stood there alone, watching as everyone in her family disappeared into their individual worlds, a world that centered strictly on them and no one else. She sighed, wondering how she had let this happen. She was finally realizing that instead of easing up, Alejandro's chaotic lifestyle had not only increased but now trickled into her children's lives.

Chapter Five

Amanda paced the floor in the sitting room. Her high heels left little marks in the white carpet, creating a trail of polka dots behind her. She didn't know why she felt so nervous; it was just one holiday. At least that's what she tried to convince herself. How bad of a reaction could Alecia have?

Yet, try as she might, there was nothing she could tell herself to quell her anxiety.

She paused at the window and stared blankly outside. A man wearing khaki pants and a white shirt stood by the pool, listening to music while he vacuumed it, and two landscapers tended to the rest of the backyard.

A typical day. At least on the surface. However, Amanda knew that it would be anything *but* typical.

The previous afternoon, Alejandro had left after the photo shoot. Just prior to walking through the front door, he reminded Amanda again of her promise. Then, after placing a soft kiss on her lips, he was gone. Standing in the doorway, she watched her husband as he got into the waiting car, pausing to give her a final wave before it drove away.

As she shut the front door, she had known that she couldn't make any more excuses. With a sense of growing anxiety, she headed to her office. She had to make the dreaded phone call to Alecia.

She had promised Alejandro that she would inform her mother-in-law about their decision to spend the Christmas holiday with her Amish family in Pennsylvania, not with Alecia's family in Miami. Avoiding the situation would only make matters worse. Amanda couldn't even imagine Alecia's reaction if she heard the news from another source. Regardless of how tight-lipped Alejandro's and Amanda's inner circles were, word traveled quickly once someone slipped up. Amanda learned *that* a long time ago.

Isadora and her cell phone didn't help.

Technology, she thought with a shake of her head. The way that their daughter depended on her cell phone and laptop to communicate with the world bothered Amanda. Whether they were out in public or relaxing at home, Isadora seemed to always be hunched over, her fingers tapping furiously. When had she grown so dependent on technology?

Amanda hated feeling as though she was always talking to the bent-over form of her daughter, but it was even worse that she had to filter everything she said in the presence of the children. Too many times the family had planned a private outing, only for Isadora to comment about it on social media or for Sofia to confide in her friends. The blunders were innocent lapses in juvenile judgment, but the result usually was the same: chaos. Especially in Miami, there was always a readily available mob of paparazzi eager to snap a photo of the Diaz family. They simply didn't care if they ruined what should have been a peaceful family affair. All they wanted was to sell a photo or video to the highest bidder.

It would be good to get away, Amanda thought, to a simpler environment without housekeepers and personal assistants. Best of all, there would be limited access to technology.

Still standing at the window, she looked toward the side yard, taking a moment to admire her flower garden. As much as she loved cutting the flowers in the mornings, she missed the planting and weeding of truly working in a garden—a real garden with vegetables that would feed her family. While Alejandro hired landscapers to tend to her flowers, Amanda knew she was too busy to care for the type of garden she would have preferred.

A wave of guilt washed over her. Despite her love for gardening, now her days were filled with interviews, photo shoots, and attending events on behalf of Alejandro. When had she lost that passion for connecting with nature instead of with cameras?

Her life, like an untended garden, seemed consumed with weeds. And while her actual flower gardens flourished from being cared for by many people, including herself, Amanda knew that her life-garden needed weeding in order to let the flowers grow.

She heard a noise from the hallway and turned toward the French doors. Glancing at the clock on the wall, Amanda realized that Alecia must be running late. It was almost time for Nicolas and Sofia to arrive home from school. She'd have to hurry to ensure that any emotional outbursts from Alecia were long over before then.

When she heard the telltale sound of Alecia's footsteps approaching, Amanda took a deep breath, said a quick prayer for strength, and braced herself for the storm that would, undoubtedly, descend upon her in just a matter of seconds.

Teresa appeared first, her expression unreadable as she opened the glass doors so that Alejandro's mother could enter the room. From the sound of Alecia's rapid-fire Spanish, Teresa was receiving a litany of either requests or complaints. Amanda couldn't quite determine which. Knowing her mother-in-law, it was probably both. Alecia's partiality to Señora Perez's authority over her son's household had been challenged when Teresa had been hired. In Alecia's view, a housekeeper needed to be quiet and in the background. Teresa's stern, confrontational manner rubbed her the wrong way.

Once she had finished with Teresa, Alecia swept into the room, her arms laden with shopping bags. Her blue eyes, so similar to Alejandro's and the children's, met Amanda's and lit up. "Amanda! *¡Querida!*"

When Alecia walked into a room, it was always with a great flourish. People stopped talking and turned their heads in her direction, her presence commanding respect from those who willingly gave it—and demanding it from anyone who didn't. Amanda fell in the former category, while Alejandro leaned toward the latter. Amanda couldn't count how many times she had been forced to run interference between the two over the years, usually calming Alejandro enough to make quick peace with his mother.

That was one of the reasons Amanda had always gotten along so well with her mother-in-law.

With great joy, Alecia crossed the room and embraced Amanda. "What a pleasant surprise! I was so thrilled that you called me." Kissing Amanda's cheeks, she added, "We need to do this more often, no? Not just when Alejandro is away." Then, she took a step back, her hands still on Amanda's shoulders, and gave her a quick study. "*Ay*, you look beautiful . . . as usual." She laughed.

"And you look—"

Alecia interrupted Amanda. "The decorators! Ay-yi-yi!" She shook her head approvingly and made a satisfied noise with her tongue. "Just beautiful." She paused for a long second. "Although I would have preferred more red. It's just a little bland without it, no?"

Amanda bit her tongue. "I don't think it—"

Ignoring her, Alecia gave a little laugh. "You won't mind if I add a few red bows here and there before Christmas Eve."

"Alecia—"

"Now, let me show you what I bought, *querida*. Two new dresses for Sofia! I know how fussy she can be, but she *is* still a little girl, *sí*? She can pick which one she prefers for our family gathering."

Amanda gave up trying to speak and stood there watching as Alecia hurried back to where she had dropped the bags.

"Neiman Marcus had some wonderful sales the other day," Alecia said in an excited tone. With great pride, she carried the bags to the sofa and sat down, gesturing for Amanda to sit next to her. "Not that it really matters."

Since Alejandro had started paying his mother's credit cards, Alecia had gone overboard more than once. While Alejandro grumbled about it from time to time, usually around April 15 when his accountants complained about her expenses, he'd never once questioned her spending habits. Amanda, however, knew far too well that Alejandro had become an enabler to his mother's addiction to lavishing gifts on her grandchildren.

"*¡Ven!*" With a big smile on her face, Alecia patted the seat beside her again. "I also picked up a pair of dress shoes for Nicolas. Perfect for the holidays, no?" She began rummaging through the bags, pulling out a few items to display for Amanda. "Sofia will wear this, no?" she asked and held up a very childish white sleeveless dress that was covered in polka dots. It had an abundance of ruffles around the collar, and a big gaudy sash circled the waist.

With one glance, Amanda knew that Sofia would never wear that dress. Not by choice, anyway. Besides, at school, her children wore uniforms, and Jeremy oversaw what they wore at public events. He always insisted that everyone be coordinated and in the most current styles. Simple elegance was his motto. Amanda agreed at least with the simple.

"I—"

Once again, Alecia reached into the bag for another box. This one was small, and she held it with both hands.

"This," she said proudly, "is something that I picked for you."

Taken aback, Amanda temporarily forgot about Christmas. "Me?"

Alecia nodded and handed the small box to her. "*Sí, querida.* For you."

The box felt light in her hand. Amanda frowned as she looked at Alecia. "Whatever for?" Her birthday wasn't until after New Year's, and everyone knew that Amanda was much more practical than her husband and children. While she didn't mind outfitting everyone else with the latest and greatest things, she tended to shy away from buying things for herself.

With an overly modest shrug of her shoulders, Alecia looked away. She was trying to look demure, but Amanda saw through it.

Carefully, she opened the box and saw a charm bracelet set against the blue velvet case. It was silver—which Amanda preferred to gold—and had a toggle clasp. And while it was beautiful on its own, it was the charms that gave Amanda reason to pause: six little people charms—two men and four women. For a moment, Amanda didn't get it.

"It's lovely, Alecia," she said, even though she did not usually wear bracelets. "Thank you very much. So thoughtful."

"There's one for each member of your family," Alecia said proudly as she leaned forward and pointed to each one. "Alejandro, you, Isadora, Sofia, and Nicolas."

But that left one unaccounted for. "And this one?" Amanda asked.

"Why, that's me!" She smiled. "It's our family."

Amanda set the box upon her lap and took a deep breath. "Alecia," she began, trying to pick her words carefully. "I have something to tell you."

The night before, she had practiced her speech for hours, sleep evading her until she finally turned on the light and began to write out what she wanted to say. In the morning, she had practiced it with Teresa and Grace. Neither one offered her any advice, although Teresa gave her a generous pat on the back and wished her good luck, barely able to hide a smile.

Now, with Alecia staring at her, a smile plastered expectantly on her face, Amanda forgot what she had planned to say. "I . . ."

"*¿Sí, querida?*"

Struggling to remember her prepared words, Amanda felt her heart begin to beat rapidly and she swallowed. "Well, I wanted to let you know—" She paused, and that was all the opportunity that Alecia needed to let her thoughts run wild.

"*¡Gracias a* Dios!" she exclaimed.

Amanda blinked, startled by Alecia's reaction, especially given the fact that she hadn't said anything yet.

Before Amanda could say another word, Alecia clapped her hands together in delight. "You're pregnant? *¡Yo sabía!* It's time for you to have another baby before you get too old for more children!"

Amanda's mouth opened. For a moment, she could not respond. Finally, she shook her head. "No, no! That's not it at all. We already told you last time that we decided no more children."

The previous winter, when Amanda had taken ill, Alecia had rejoiced and began telling the family that she was going to be a grandmother again. It was no secret that her own regret at having only one child drove Alecia's eagerness for Alejandro to have a large family. And while Amanda adored her children, she knew fulfilling her mother-in-law's wish was impractical.

When Alejandro had shared their decision with Alecia to not expand their family, she hadn't spoken to either one of them for two weeks.

Upon hearing that Amanda was, in fact, not expecting, the enthusiasm drained from Alecia's face. "I see," she said in a flat voice. For a moment, she stared silently at Amanda. Then, suddenly, she gasped and grabbed Amanda's wrist in panic. "A divorce? *¡Ay* Dios!" she cried out. Her lips tensed as she became steely-eyed. "What has he done now, that son of mine? Whatever it is—"

This time, Amanda interrupted her. "Alecia! No! Nothing like that, I promise."

"What is it, then?" she asked in confusion.

Amanda stood up and took a few steps. She hated feeling so nervous. It was silly, she told herself. After all, her mother-in-law didn't *own* the holidays, and surely she could understand that they hadn't been back to Lancaster County for years. Feeling a new measure of strength, she turned and said, "It's about Christmas."

Alecia leaned back into the sofa with her mouth agape. "Christmas?" Relief washed over her face, and she gave a short laugh. "All of this over Christmas? Oh, *querida*. You had me worried."

Amanda clasped her hands behind her back and tried to meet her mother-in-law's eye. But she couldn't. "We're going to Lititz for the holiday." She quickly blurted it out, feeling as shell-shocked as Alecia looked.

A moment of silence fell between the two of them. It felt like a long time to Amanda but in reality was only a few drawn-out seconds before Alecia rose to her feet and hesitantly moved so that she stood in front of her daughter-in-law. The color had drained from the older woman's face, and Amanda braced herself for hysterics.

Instead, she was shocked when she felt Alecia wrap her arms around her. "Oh, Amanda," Alecia said sympathetically. "It's going to be all right."

Pulling back, Amanda stared at her. "It is?"

She nodded solemnly. "I'm here for you, and I'll be happy to look after the children," Alecia continued, her voice calm and reassuring. "They'll have to attend my church, of course, on Christmas Eve, not that Lutheran one that you always insisted on taking them to. But with all of the cousins here, they will hardly notice that you're away for the holiday. And Alejandro . . ." She waved her hand dismissively. "He's gone so often that it won't be much different, no?"

"It's not what you think," Amanda managed to say.

"Now, tell me, *mi hija*, who has fallen ill? Is it your mother?"

"No, it's—"

Alecia gasped and covered her mouth with her hand. "Not your sister, bless her heart. Five children in eight years and all daughters!" Automatically, she reached for the gold cross that hung around her neck, made the sign of the cross, and kissed it reverently before dropping it back onto her chest.

"She does have one son," Amanda gently corrected her. "The baby."

But, as usual, Alecia simply wasn't listening. "Is she going to the doctor? Or is she risking it by trying natural remedies?" The way she said *natural remedies* clearly indicated her disapproval, as if it was akin to drinking spoiled milk. "Alejandro must arrange for her to go to the Columbia Presbyterian Center, *sí?* They are the best in the north, especially if it's cancer."

"Alecia—"

"Since I know she won't fly down here." Another disapproving noise.

Amanda closed her eyes and shook her head, raising her voice to be heard. "Anna is not sick, Alecia."

Silence filled the room, and when Amanda opened her eyes, her mother-in-law was staring at her with a confused expression on her face.

"We are going to Lititz for the holidays," Amanda said slowly, hoping the words would finally sink in. "All of us."

"The children?" she asked in disbelief.

"Yes, Alecia. The children, too."

The astonished look on her mother-in-law's face said it all. "I . . . I don't understand," she stammered. "What have I done to upset you?"

Alarmed, Amanda reached out to touch Alecia's arm. "Oh no, Alecia, it's nothing like that!"

But Alecia raised her hand to stop Amanda from trying to explain. "Two weeks before Christmas and you tell me this? That you are taking my grandchildren away from me? Leaving me all alone over the holidays?"

"That's not exactly true," Amanda said softly. She fought the urge to remain calm and patient, but she was beginning to feel flustered. Once again, Alecia turned the situation into a personal affront. While she loved her mother-in-law, Amanda wished that Alecia would be mindful that Alejandro had in-laws of his own. Clearly, Alecia had never learned to play fair in the sandbox. "Tia Carmen and Tio Juan and all of their children are still here, Alecia. I hardly doubt that you will be *alone*."

"To celebrate with the Amish?" The way she said the word *Amish* always sounded demeaning, as if the plain lifestyle was equivalent to living in a third-world country.

"I grew up in the Amish community," Amanda reminded her mother-in-law, her patience truly being tested.

"And you left them," Alecia said, the sharp tone of her voice cutting through Amanda. "Now you want to go back to celebrate a religious holiday with them? Don't they *shun* those who leave?"

Amanda took a deep breath and counted to ten. She didn't want to explain, again, that she had never become a baptized member of the church. The stereotypes the media promoted were common among the public, and that included Alecia. "They can't shun people who never took the kneeling vow, Alecia," she said with a calm she did not feel.

There was no more time for the conversation to continue. The sound of running feet and happy voices burst through the doors, causing both Amanda and Alecia to look up as Sofia ran into the room. Nicolas trailed behind her.

"Abuela!" Sofia reached her grandmother first and gave her a warm hug, even as Nicolas tried to wedge his way between them. "Are you staying until Papi comes home?"

Pushing his sister away, Nicolas managed to work his way into Alecia's arms. "Stay until Christmas!" he cried out.

Sofia gave him a little shove. "We're going to Pennsylvania for Christmas, goose. Remember?"

Amanda was too tired to reprimand her for calling Nicolas names. She shifted her weight and leaned into her hip, one arm wrapped around her waist as she rubbed at her temples with her other hand.

"We aren't seeing Abuela for Christmas?" Nicolas asked, a hint of sadness in his voice.

Amanda heard Sofia whisper in a too-loud voice, "We're seeing our *other* grandmother."

Inwardly, Amanda groaned, knowing that this was not exactly helping her.

Despite Amanda's family's own simple life on the farm, Alecia never hesitated to remind anyone willing to listen how she had been a single mother when she emigrated from Cuba with Alejandro. Raising a child alone in a new country, with a different language, had not been easy for her, especially as Alejandro had been unruly, even then. Her survival and his success had translated into a victory against adversity, giving her a feeling of personal superiority that she did not hesitate to lord over others.

And that especially included any occasion when she felt her grandmother status threatened.

Over the years, she had grown increasingly vocal about her opinion that there was only one good thing that had emerged from Lititz, Pennsylvania: Amanda. And at the mention of anything related to her daughter-in-law's family, the tension in the room became palpable.

Now was no exception.

"Why are we going there without Abuela?" Nicolas cried out, turning to look at his mother.

"Nicolas, please!" Amanda said quickly, her tone much sharper than she intended it to sound.

But he ignored her plea. "Why can't Abuela go with us?"

With a forced smile on her face, Alecia reached out for Nicolas's hand. He took it and let her embrace him, not seeing the look that passed from his grandmother to his mother over the top of his head. "Such a fuss, no?" Alecia said. "And for such a big boy. No tears."

He sniffled and used the back of his hand to wipe his eyes.

"Besides," Alecia said, "who said you won't be with me on Christmas?"

Sofia jumped up and down. "Are we coming back to Miami, then?"

"No," Alecia said as she straightened her shoulders. With a look of victory on her face, she pivoted her gaze toward Amanda. "But *I'll* be going with you to Pennsylvania."

Chapter Six

"It will be good for them to spend time with my family," Amanda said as she stood in the center of her large walk-in closet. She wasn't certain if she was trying to convince Alejandro or herself.

The children had slowly stopped grumbling about leaving Miami for the Christmas holiday, especially when Amanda told them about how they would make cookies, milk cows, and even ride in a horse and buggy. While Sofia made a face at the prospect of milking cows, Nicolas had perked up at the idea and started to get a little excited. Isadora, however, seemed pensive and did not comment about the upcoming trip. She often seemed to withdraw into her own thoughts at the mention of Pennsylvania and the Amish.

It was something Amanda had asked Grace to keep an eye on while she was traveling with Alejandro that week.

She riffled through some dresses. There were so many outfits in her closet, she never could decide and usually stuck with the same ones: a simple black skirt and white blouse or a plain black dress. "They can learn a lot from my family," she continued. "How to make do with less." Frustrated with the clothes clogging her closet, she gestured with her hand toward the racks. "Look at this, Alejandro. This is outrageous.

Where does all of this . . . this . . ."—she struggled to find the right word—"extravagance come from anyway?"

Alejandro looked up from where he was leaning against the doorframe, having alternated between looking at his cell phone and watching Amanda as she assessed the different outfits. He didn't appear concerned as he lightly commented, "That's Jeremy for you. Always wanted the best for you, sí?"

"The best for *me*?" She dropped her hand to her hip and stared at him. Hadn't he seen the price tags still hanging on some of the clothes? "Who pays for all of this? Not Jeremy!" she said. "And I certainly don't need so much. It's obscene."

She paused, waiting for him to look up from his cell phone. When he did, he gave her a sheepish look at having been caught not giving her his undivided attention.

"Seriously, Alejandro," she said with a heavy sigh. "I'll never wear half of these outfits. You shouldn't listen to Jeremy when he tells you I need so much." She riffled through several more items on the rack and sighed. "Truly, he needs to stop wasting so much money—our money!—on having you buy me clothes just for the sake of buying."

Alejandro raised an eyebrow. "Most women would be thrilled to have their own fashion designer, sí?"

"And most men would be thrilled to have a wife who detests shopping," she pointed out.

He laughed and returned his attention to his cell phone.

On the large upholstered bench in the middle of the room, there were rows of shoes waiting for Amanda's approval. Numerous dresses, skirts, and tops were already pulled from the racks, each one with a tag hanging from the padded hanger to identify at which event she was supposed to wear it. She selected one of the more colorful outfits and put it back on a rack before she withdrew a black dress to replace it.

"Isadora has become addicted to technology," Amanda commented. "She's hardly ever off that cell phone."

Alejandro gave another short laugh.

"Hmm," Amanda said, casting a glance over her shoulder in time to see him look guilty as he slid his phone into his back pocket. "I wonder where she gets that from, *ja*?"

His blue eyes flashed at her, and he crossed his arms over his chest. With his short-sleeved white shirt and khaki shorts, he looked tan and fit, hardly changed at all since they had met almost ten years ago. "There are worse things," he teased. "Such as having to put up with *mi madre* for a week!"

She tried to not react to his comment.

She had waited until he returned from his trip to tell Alejandro about his mother's intentions to accompany them to Pennsylvania. His initial response had been stunned silence, and then he'd laughed, thinking she was playing a silly joke on him. But after she repeated the conversation from the previous week, as well as her subsequent attempts to dissuade Alecia, Alejandro finally realized that she was serious.

For over an hour, he argued on the phone with his mother. Their heated conversation, spoken in rapid Spanish, hindered Amanda from understanding what they discussed. However, from the tone of his voice and the expression on his face, Amanda figured that she was better off not knowing. Amanda knew that when tempers flared between her husband and mother-in-law, it was better to step away.

When he'd hung up the phone, he'd stared at the wall for a moment, the color all but drained from his face. Amanda held her breath and waited anxiously while he collected his thoughts.

He had finally looked at her, and she could instantly tell by his expression that the conversation had not ended in their favor. Shutting his eyes and shaking his head, he simply said, "She's determined to do this." Then he'd crossed the room to the bar and poured himself a drink.

That had been two days ago.

Now, accepting that only a miracle would stop Alecia from joining her grandchildren on what should have been a sweet, rare visit with their Amish family, Amanda tried to focus on packing and maintaining a positive attitude.

"Mayhaps it won't be so terrible," she offered generously.

Alejandro grunted.

She knew that Alejandro had spoken with Alecia the day before, instructing her that this wasn't a typical Christmas vacation. Celebrating the holidays with Amanda's Amish relatives would not include ostentatious gift-giving or endless celebrations. But his attempts to dissuade Alecia only strengthened her resolve. So Alejandro had simply made it clear that he didn't want any problems from her—and neither did Amanda.

"Alecia might find it interesting, don't you think?"

He simply stared at her with a blank expression on his face.

"And the children do love her so. Especially Nicolas. If he starts to act unruly, she can help calm him down."

Once again, he gave a slight shake of his head. "I don't see this ending well, Amanda. We already know we'll have our hands full dealing with the children without their precious television and Internet."

Amanda stood still for a moment, still looking through the rack of clothing. While all of her outfits for the work-related cities were already selected by Jeremy and would somehow magically appear in her hotel room, she'd also need to pack some things for Pennsylvania. She knew that when they returned to Miami for the Jingle Ball concert, she'd have neither the time nor energy to do it.

"Isadora will survive," she said as she reached out for another black dress and added it to her pile. "She has her entire life to be plugged into social media. And Sofia . . . those apps are just too mature for her. I don't need to remind you of the horrible comments people post."

Alejandro nodded. "And hopefully, the media will stay away."

It was a constant battle trying to keep her children out of the lime-light. After Sofia was born, the media had given the new parents a wide berth for a few weeks. But then the battle began for who would score the first photo of Sofia Diaz, daughter of Viper and La Princesa.

Vanity Fair won.

Reluctantly, and only after Alejandro and Geoffrey convinced her, Amanda had agreed to *Vanity Fair* writing an article about how her life had changed from that of an Amish girl to the wife of an interna-tional celebrity, all within such a short period of time. Amanda was very aware that the public hungered for more of her story.

But she hadn't wanted to include her children in the spotlight so Amanda had allowed only one photograph to accompany the article: Amanda holding her newborn baby, with Isadora standing on her tippy-toes to peer at her sister while proud father Alejandro looked on. Unfortunately, it had gone viral. Instead of quelling the public's inter-est, it had only fed it more.

Eight years later, Amanda was still trying to protect her children from the invasive cameras and the hordes of people that lingered near places that Amanda was known to visit with her children. The media interest in the lives of her children severely limited where Amanda could take them, at least not without security. News outlets vied for coveted photos of the Diaz children, some photographs bringing in six figures for the photographer and the agency that sold them to the news outlets.

And now there was the issue of social media. The very applications that Alejandro's team used to keep "Viper" at the top of the entertain-ment industry undermined Amanda's attempts to shield her children.

"*Ay,* Amanda!" He sounded exasperated. In truth, she hadn't expected that he would agree with her. With a shake of his head, he stepped forward and took the black dress off the top of the pile. "Enough with the black. People will think you're a widow," he said and returned it to the closet. "Isadora is fine. She's an American teenager."

"Fourteen, Alejandro," she said with careful reproach.

"A teenager." He put his hands on her arms and turned her so that she had no choice but to face him. "She barely even uses Twitter or Instagram. She likes that other application anyway, that Snapchat."

Amanda exhaled as she repeated, "Fourteen."

"You worry too much."

"A mother can never worry too much."

He laughed and pulled her into his arms, gently holding her so that her cheek pressed against his shoulder. "You, Princesa, are the exception. There are no children better protected than ours, *sí*?"

But that's the problem, she wanted to say. The security and lack of privacy created a bubble of isolation around her children. She knew what they were missing: afternoons in the park, playdates with friends, lying in the grass and watching the clouds. Her children did not have any of that. Instead, guards escorted them to play with friends who were vetted by security.

Unfortunately, Alejandro merely brushed off Amanda's concerns, reminding her how lucky their children were to have such luxuries and opportunities in their life. Long ago, she'd abandoned pointing out the downside of easily gained luxuries. Luxury and unearned opportunities were two things that neither she nor Alejandro had when they were growing up—and those were the very two things that had contributed to their appreciation for hard work's rewards. But it was an argument she never won.

"Now," Alejandro said, "finish your packing. We have to meet with Geoffrey in thirty minutes."

She sighed.

He tucked his finger under her chin and tilted her face so that she was forced to look at him. "He's one of the good guys. Besides, it's important, Amanda."

Averting her eyes, she nodded her head. There weren't many "good guys" in their lives; too often the people around them seemed most focused on what they could take from them. Amanda found herself turning the other cheek far too often—and limiting the people she considered friends. Alejandro was much more accommodating, although he was also well aware of unethical people, especially after his previous manager had tried to stage a media scandal involving another woman and Alejandro. With experience comes wisdom, Alejandro had repeatedly reminded Amanda.

But Geoffrey had helped Alejandro transition from an international music sensation to a worldwide business mogul, advising him to invest in developing new talent while continuing to build his own brand. Additionally, he had encouraged Alejandro to finance several new companies and endorse their products, the result being a financial windfall that benefited all of them.

Yes, Amanda thought, Geoffrey is definitely one of the good guys.

"*¡Bueno!*" Alejandro kissed her forehead before he turned and started walking toward the door. "And don't forget! Enough with the black clothing. Add some color, *mi amor!*" He did a quick dance move, his hips moving in the fluid way that only Alejandro could achieve, as he sang, "Red! Add some red to your tour clothes!"

"Red!"

He pursed his lips, giving her a playfully seductive look. "Umm. *Sí*, Princesa. Red is hot. Like you, *mi amor*."

She couldn't help but smile. When Alejandro acted so mischievous, Amanda remembered exactly why she'd fallen in love with him. He always had that ability to give her a single look that made her heart flutter and pulse quicken. He knew when to be playful and when to be serious. And most important of all, he knew how to make her feel like a woman—the only woman for him.

"Oh, and I forgot to tell you," he said with a quick wink, which led Amanda to believe that, perhaps, he hadn't really forgotten at all, "my mother is coming for supper tonight with Tío and Tía."

"Alejandro!"

He held up his hands as if making a peace offering and backed out the door. "I'll leave you to work out the details with Señora Perez."

Once he'd disappeared, Amanda turned back to the rack of clothes. She sighed, reached for one of the black dresses she had previously set aside, and replaced it with a red dress.

She felt frustrated that, once again, Alejandro hadn't warned her in advance about his mother coming for dinner and bringing some of her family. Yet, despite not wanting to entertain the night before they left for Michigan, Amanda appreciated Alecia's commitment to her family. She could only assume that Alecia had insisted on bringing her extended family to the house for a pre-holiday gathering before the upcoming trip to Pennsylvania.

Perhaps she wasn't that different from Alecia, Amanda thought. After all, wouldn't she do whatever she could to keep her husband happy and her children safe? The only difference was that Amanda only now realized how important it was to show her children the true meaning of Christmas. She wanted them to experience a *plain* Christmas—a Christmas without all the trappings and distractions that came with their life of privilege. Above all else, she wanted them to experience it as a part of the other side of their heritage: the Amish.

Chapter Seven

With its streets lined with small shops and restaurants, Grand Haven, Michigan, reminded Amanda of the tourist town of Intercourse in Lancaster County, Pennsylvania. The only thing missing in Grand Haven were Amish people driving their horse and buggies down North Harbor Drive.

Earlier that morning, they had flown from Miami to the Muskegon Airport in Michigan. Dan, an editor with Brilliance Audio, had been waiting for them outside the security check. When he spotted them, he waved enthusiastically and hurried toward them.

"Alejandro! Amanda!" His light-brown eyes lit up behind his black eyeglasses as he gave them a contagious smile and shook their hands. "I hope your flight was good?" he asked as he offered bottles of sparkling water to each of them. Amanda had laughed, immediately deciding she liked this Dan, and not just because of his thoughtfulness. Although she was impressed that he'd taken the time to find out she preferred sparkling water to still, she found his positive energy contagious.

They had a long day of work ahead of them, and it had already been a long morning. There had been a conflict in scheduling the charter jet, which meant Alejandro and Amanda had to fly commercial. That also meant that many fans recognized them at the airport. Security had gotten involved to move them through the checkpoints and then to a private lounge, where the prying eyes of the public couldn't bother them.

Dan had arranged for them to stay in a small private cottage at an inn on South Harbor Drive. He had driven them through town, showing them some of the local sights and stopping at the inn for Alejandro and Amanda to take a moment to freshen up before he took them to Brilliance Audio.

"So we have a full itinerary today," Dan said as they walked toward the front doors of the Brilliance Audio building. "Our publisher, Mark Pereira, will join us for the tour of the facility and introduce you to some of the people who work on the production and distribution teams for the audiobooks." He opened the door for Amanda and Alejandro. "You have no idea how excited everyone is that you're here!"

Amanda suddenly felt nervous. She had no idea how audiobooks worked and began to wonder why she had said yes to doing this. It had taken her years to adjust to speaking in public, and even now, the butterflies still formed in her stomach anytime she was asked to speak in front of a large crowd. Knowing that thousands of people would hear her voice was enough to make her want to turn around and get on the next plane back home.

"And the interest we have had from so many groups that support the children is just . . . overwhelming," Dan continued excitedly as if reading her mind.

He must have sensed her anxiety. Was it that noticeable? she wondered.

He pushed his slipping glasses back up on the bridge of his nose, his brown eyes sparkling as he spoke about the project. "Hospitals, too. They want to gift their patients with this audiobook, especially since so many of them are too young to read the printed version."

"Oh?" she whispered, suddenly feeling ashamed for even *thinking* of leaving. How could she disappoint all of those children? Her thoughts quickly turned to her own children. She was blessed with their good health, but what if one day she wasn't? Even the best health care that money could buy meant nothing without research and good facilities to tend to them. She would do anything for her own kids. She had to try to do the same for others'.

Dan nodded as they entered the lobby. "Oh yes! No one has done anything like this. It's just an unbelievable gift you are giving to these children."

Her nerves began to abate, especially when she saw a black sign with "Welcome Princesa and Viper" in white letters. The simple sign said more to her than any of the usual greeting signs could, despite their flashing lights and over-the-top graphics.

She liked this down-to-earth company. Besides their genuine interest in supporting her vision of helping sick children, she also liked that she and Alejandro were treated like regular people. Well, almost. Complete normalcy was impossible when in the company of Alejandro, unless, of course, they were in Lancaster County. The thought of home gave her comfort. Soon she would be free to roam the countryside without the prying eyes of the world. She would have the chance to feel normal, and more important, her children would know what life was like outside of the fishbowl.

"Let's see if Mark is available yet. He would have greeted you at the airport, but he had a phone meeting with his colleagues in Seattle that he couldn't change," Dan explained as he led them through a door and down a short corridor.

Unlike the offices of the high-powered executives Amanda often met with, offices intended to both impress and overwhelm, Mark's office was simple but inviting. When they walked in, he stood up and greeted them with a firm, friendly handshake. Amanda felt instantly at ease. A firm handshake spoke volumes to her—her father had had a firm handshake, as did Alejandro. It was a sign of a strong character.

"Alejandro. Amanda." He leaned against the edge of his desk and smiled, seeming as genuinely happy as Dan was. "What an honor it is to have you here in Grand Haven! We're all very excited about this project."

"When Amanda told me about it, we both knew that it was something we wanted to support." Alejandro glanced at her and smiled. "It's important to give back, no?"

She felt shy under Alejandro's steady gaze as she nodded in agreement.

Alejandro was in an unusual mood. All morning he had been pensive and quiet. Even during the flight, Alejandro had been lost in thought, quietly staring out the window as he drummed his fingers on the armrest of the plush leather seat. She hadn't wanted to disturb him, knowing that he was probably thinking of lyrics to a new song or mulling over a business idea. But when he had reached out suddenly and took her hand in his, raising it to his lips for a gentle kiss, she had wondered what, exactly, was on his mind.

Now, as they met with the people from Brilliance Audio, Alejandro seemed even more reflective. From the numerous occasions when Amanda had attended business meetings with Alejandro, he was usually direct, to the point, and eager to conduct business. The serene mood emanating from him took her by surprise. Once again, she wondered what was making him so tranquil.

"And we have exciting news," Mark went on. He gestured toward the phone on his desk. "I just confirmed that corporate has committed to matching your donations from the sale of the audiobooks to the Princesa Cancer Center."

Amanda gave a little gasp. "That's unbelievable," she said in a breathless voice and glanced at Alejandro.

He smiled but said nothing. Surely he, too, was thinking about how there was so much greed in the music industry that such a generous offer would never be extended. Over the years, she had witnessed that time and time again. Alejandro had once commented that there was no such thing as pure philanthropy. People only did things for others if there was something to gain. She had been quick to remind him of the way the Amish donated quilts and food to charity auctions. But while he might concede on that one exception, she knew what he meant. In his world, giving for the sole purpose of giving was a very rare occurrence.

Dan glanced at his cell phone and cleared his throat. He looked at Mark and said, "Shall we start with the tour? We have a tight schedule with the recording this afternoon. I don't want to run late with anything, especially since Alejandro and Amanda's flight tomorrow is at eleven thirty."

Mark and Dan led them out of the office and through a series of large spaces filled with cubicles as they headed toward the back of the building, where there was an expansive production facility and product warehouse. Mark explained the different departments as they walked, pausing to greet a few people along the way. Amanda could sense that people were peeking over their low cubicle walls, eager to catch a glimpse of the famous couple.

As they started to turn a corner, Amanda paused to read a small sign that was pinned on the wall of someone's cubicle: "Proper punctuation can make a world of difference: Let's eat Grandma vs. Let's eat, Grandma."

She smiled as she read it.

"¿Qué, Princesa?" Alejandro asked when he noticed she had paused.

She pointed at the sign. "I never thought of grammar as being funny."

He stopped for a minute as he read the sign, and then he, too, laughed. "Clever."

"I like this place," she whispered, tucking her arm into his.

"I'd imagine you'd like any place surrounded by books or the idea of books, no?"

She gave him a soft smile as if to confirm his observation. He knew her so well. Despite her busy, hectic life, nothing made her more content than when she was able to settle down for the evening with a good book in her hands. But that hadn't been what she meant.

"It's more than that, Alejandro," she said in a quiet voice so that no one could overhear her. "It just feels"—she hesitated as if trying to find the right word—"real."

He raised an eyebrow. "Real?"

Amanda nodded. "Yes, real. Real people, real joy, real life."

"And our life is not real?"

She laughed at the quizzical look he gave her. Reaching out her hand, she pressed it against his cheek. "Our life is real to us, but it's a fantasy to everyone else, Alejandro. We both know that by now."

Leaning over, he gently brushed his lips against her forehead, a gesture that surprised her, as public displays of affection were uncommon when they were working together. "*Sí*, Princesa, I know what you mean. Sometimes we forget that there are more 'real' people out there than there are 'fantasy' people. It's nice to be with genuine, honest people, no?" Then, without waiting for her response, he took her elbow and guided her toward the place Mark and Dan stood, waiting for them.

With another smile, Dan gestured toward a door. "Let's go into the warehouse. I want to show you where we produce the actual CDs for the audiobooks we publish." He led them through a doorway at the back of the building into a well-lit warehouse, where workers looked up as soon as Alejandro and Amanda entered. The hum of the machines created a buzz that filled the air, but after a few seconds, Amanda barely noticed it.

"We produce so many titles that we have different shifts running throughout the day and night," Dan explained as they walked on a thick black rubber mat next to large, boxy machines with green lights on top of them. "Oh good! Lisa's here today." He slowed down.

"Lisa normally works at night, but she wanted to come in early on the small chance she might be able to meet you," Dan explained as they approached a woman who stood up straight as they neared. He whispered, "She's a really big fan of yours. I hope you don't mind."

Amanda could tell. Long ago, she had learned to recognize what she called "the look." The color seemed to drain from the woman's face as Dan led them over to her station. From behind narrow glasses perched on the middle of her nose, her blue eyes blinked as she watched them coming toward her. She had long, straight brown hair with a red streak at the front.

While Dan introduced Alejandro to Lisa, Amanda's eyes wandered up to the high ceilings and bright lights, then down the long counter and equipment in front of her. She noticed that each machine was numbered and whirring as it burned discs with audio recordings created in the nearby studios. Underneath the counter in front of her were boxes and packaging material, and farther down at the end of the aisle there was a four-shelved rolling cart stacked high with what Dan described as the finished discs.

It was just one more new experience for Amanda, one of many in an endless parade since she'd married Alejandro. She had never really considered how the books she purchased were created. And she had never given a thought to audiobook production. She knew that Isadora preferred to listen to her books, being an auditory learner rather than a visual learner. It was strange to think that she was standing in the spot with a woman named Lisa who produced some of the audiobook CDs Isadora so often checked out from the library.

Alejandro glanced around the warehouse. "So this is how it's done," he said, sounding very impressed. "I know that Amanda loves her books."

Lisa's eyes opened wide, and Dan said, "All kinds, I hope. Print books, audiobooks, and e-books."

Alejandro laughed. "*¡Claro!* She always brings her Kindle, especially that small one that she can read while outside. Gets a lot of use out of that at home."

"Ah yes!" Dan said with a good-natured laugh. "The hazards of that Miami sun."

"If only we had some of that sun here!" Lisa quipped and met Amanda's eyes, her voice wavering nervously.

"Miami winters are nice," Amanda said, hoping her casual comment would put the woman at ease. After all, she knew only too well what nerves could do to a person. Over the years, Amanda had learned how to soothe the nervousness that fans tended to exhibit when they met her. She knew that simply talking to them often helped them relax.

"Winters here are brutal," Lisa admitted in a friendly tone.

"It *is* cold, for sure and certain."

"Driving is terrible. Especially at night. Black ice," Lisa explained. "Doubt I'll ever get used to it."

Amanda nodded but didn't reply. She was remembering winters in Pennsylvania, how just stepping outside and breathing in the cold air could sting her lungs. In some ways, she was looking forward to it. Without the brutally cold weather, it never seemed like Christmas to her. She wanted her children to experience the same Christmas feeling she had known as a child. In Miami, the blue skies and palm trees felt too tropical for the season.

There was a small awkward pause between the two women, especially while Dan and Mark took Alejandro farther down the aisle to meet another Brilliance Audio employee, which meant Amanda was left alone with Lisa.

"My daughter likes audiobooks," Amanda said at last.

At this comment, Lisa lit up. "Oh? Isadora or Sofia?"

It never ceased to amaze Amanda when people she had never met before knew so much about her. The fact that Lisa knew her daughters' names wasn't unusual.

"Izzie," Amanda admitted. "We call her Izzie. Do you have children, Lisa?" She had seen a wedding band on Lisa's finger and noticed she wore a silver necklace with a heart pendant and the word *Mom* engraved at its center.

Lisa nodded. "Yes, a son and a daughter." She proceeded to show Amanda several photos of her children, laughing at the one of her daughter making cookies—and a big mess—in the kitchen.

Amanda recognized the happiness in Lisa's expression. A mother's joy. Clearly, she, too, took great pleasure in her children. Amanda thought if given the chance, they could probably share similar stories about their respective children, reveal their hopes, and confide in each other their deepest fears for their future. After all, every mother wanted only the best for her children. It was a universal feeling.

"If you don't mind," Lisa said, "I have something I'd like to give you."

Amanda frowned for a second. It was the most uncomfortable part of being a celebrity: receiving gifts. She appreciated the thought behind such gestures, but she still had not grown accustomed to receiving things from people she had just met. Alejandro always tried to convince her that accepting the gift was a gift in and of itself. "They will tell the story over and over again, *mi amor*," he always told her. Still, it didn't help to ease her conscience.

Lisa reached behind the black computer monitor on the counter of her workstation and pulled out a small red gift bag adorned with silver ribbons on its handle.

Carefully, Amanda untied the ribbons and looked inside while Lisa waited with a glow in her eyes. Amanda pulled out a candle and admired it. It was tall and red, decorated with diagonal silver stripes. There was a piece of raffia tied around it with a paper note that quoted a well-known Scripture. "'For unto us this day our Savior is born,'" read Amanda. "That's lovely, Lisa. I'll think of you whenever I use it. Thank you so much!"

"It's my favorite time of year, and I collect candles," Lisa explained, a new enthusiasm in her voice. "Everybody loves candles! And they light up every room, and not just because of the flame. I always think of Jesus being the light of the world when I see a burning candle."

For a moment, Amanda didn't respond. She was struck by Lisa's strong sense of faith. The meaning that she attributed to the gift touched Amanda even more than the kindness of the gesture. Even though it was a small gift, plain and without any frills, it came from the heart of a woman who clearly enjoyed the act of giving without expecting to receive something in return. And the fact that she mentioned Jesus in connection with the candle made Amanda realize that she probably would never look at a lit candle in the same way.

"I never thought of it that way, but you're right!"

"Amanda!"

She looked up and saw Alejandro approaching her from the far side of the aisle, where he had wandered with Dan and Mark. He greeted Lisa with a smile and handshake but immediately turned his attention to Amanda. "They want to get started, Princesa," he said, glancing at the candle in her hand. "Pretty."

Amanda nodded and turned her attention back to Lisa, noticing that the woman was staring at her husband, a slight blush on her face. Amanda would have liked to spend more time with her. She was a real person, not just a fan or someone who hoped for a quick selfie to post on her social media. In fact, Amanda realized, no one had taken any photos of them since they had arrived. For the first time in a very long while, Amanda felt like a regular person.

"Merry Christmas, Lisa," Amanda said cheerfully as she grasped Lisa's hand in her own. "And thank you so much for such a thoughtful gift."

As they walked away, Dan offered to hold the small bag for her, but Amanda shook her head, waving him off, preferring to keep the gift close to her. Alejandro gave her a quizzical look, but Amanda merely smiled. How could she explain to Alejandro how much the candle meant to her? Amanda couldn't really understand it herself, but Lisa's words brought her a sense of calm, and she needed all the peace she could muster heading into the recording studio.

The tour of the building ended in a narrow corridor near the front entrance. Along the hallway were doors with glass panels. Amanda peered inside and saw that each room was divided into two by a large window. In the front room was equipment with so many buttons, switches, and lights that Amanda wondered how anyone could remember what each did. Alejandro's recording studios had similar equipment, even more of it.

And, just like Alejandro's recording studios, the second room had a large microphone. She had seen Alejandro in the recording booth many times, but this was the first time she, not her husband, would be behind the microphone.

"We have you each scheduled to record separately," Dan explained. "With the short amount of time we have, we thought it would be more efficient."

"I've never done this," Amanda said in a soft voice. She lifted her eyes to look at Alejandro.

He gave her a reassuring smile. "And I have no doubt you will be a natural." Alejandro leaned over and placed a soft kiss on her forehead. Without thinking, she reached over and grabbed his arm as he was walking away.

"Could you stay, please?" she pleaded with him. Alejandro gave her a thoughtful look, trying to read her expression. He must have seen the anxiety etched across her face because he gave a slight nod and called over his assistant, whispering in his ear, most likely instructions to delay his recording. The assistant nodded and headed out the door. Then Alejandro turned to Amanda and gave her a reassuring smile.

"I'll be right here watching you, Princesa," he offered gently.

She looked over to Dan, who was waiting for her patiently, and turned her attention back to Alejandro, unsure of herself. She knew she was helping with a very good cause and was aware the audiobook would raise a lot of money, but at the same time, it was overwhelming to her. Even after their many years together, she'd never gotten used to all of the attention bestowed on her just because of her husband's fame.

Alejandro, sensing her inner turmoil, leaned over to her, brushing his hand gently across her arm. Amanda felt his hot breath against her skin as his lips pressed again her ear in a whisper. "I'm not going anywhere. All you have to do is imagine that you are telling me the story. No one else, just me."

Amanda smiled, feeling the courage well up inside of her. She closed her eyes and nodded. This would be easy to do, if she could imagine reading the lines to Alejandro only, as if he were the only person there with her.

"And remember all of those children who you are helping. Read to them, Amanda, like you would to our own children," he reminded her. Of course, she would. Why hadn't she thought of it that way? So many countless nights of bedtime stories. Endless adventures and magical places. She cherished those quiet moments with her daughters and son and would now read with the same passion for all those children in need.

Dan accompanied Amanda into the recording room, Alejandro following them at a distance, as if respecting that this was her show, not his. Dan introduced her to John and Sandra, the audio engineers who were seated in front of the equipment that looked so similar to what Alejandro used at the small studio he had at their home. They stood up and greeted her with firm handshakes and awkward smiles.

The introductions over, Dan ushered her into the isolated recording booth just behind another large glass window. It was a simple room with bare off-white walls. In the center of the room was a small table with a computer and large microphone on top of it. When she glanced up at Dan, her eyes caught sight of the people gathered in the first room. Mark had joined the other two people and Alejandro in the first room. Everyone was watching her.

She felt uncomfortable with everyone's attention focused on just her. While she had been the special guest at many events over the years, somehow this was different. With so many people staring at her while she sat alone in the recording room, she felt like a fish in a bowl.

"Don't worry about them," Dan said as he gestured toward the leather armchair in front of the desk. "You won't even notice them. At least not after a few minutes. You'll be focused on this. The text that displays here on this screen," Dan said, pointing to a computer monitor right behind the microphone. "You simply need to read the text in your own voice."

She sat down in the chair and looked at the monitor. "And scroll down with the mouse to keep reading?" she asked.

"That's right. See? You already know what to do!"

She laughed, starting to feel a little more at ease. She looked up and saw Alejandro standing and watching her as he promised he would. She could see his assistant's impatient face behind him as he fidgeted with his phone. He was no doubt upset at the fact that this would set back their already jam-packed schedule, but it didn't seem to bother Alejandro at all. Instead, he gave her a playful wink, and she felt her heart soar. He always had a way of making the impossible seem possible, the difficult an easy task. He made her feel as if she were the most important thing in his life.

"And I'm sure you know that you speak into the microphone, but just not too close," Dan said, interrupting her thoughts. "We'll go through a few trial recordings to help you unwind and find the proper distance from the microphone. And don't worry if you make a mistake." He gestured toward the window that separated the two rooms. Both John and Mark were still watching them while Sandra had turned her attention to a piece of the recording equipment. "It's their job to edit it."

Just like Alejandro's production team, she thought.

"There's bottled water on the shelf right behind you," he added as he started to head to the door. "You'll be able to hear us through the headset," he said, gesturing toward the headphones that were hanging from a large hook on the side of the table. "Just in case we need you to repeat a line or two."

She nodded as he left the room. She glanced at the window as he left the booth, keeping her eyes focused on the outer door where Alejandro still stood. He mouthed words of encouragement as she lifted the headphones and began to place them on her head. With everyone staring at her, she couldn't help but wonder if this was how Alejandro felt when he recorded his songs.

"Just remember, Amanda," Dan said over the closed line to her headset. "You have as much time as you need. Get comfortable, relax, and think about the children who will hear this story. Pretend to read it to them."

Amanda looked at the computer screen and the words that stared back suddenly came to life. She was no longer doing a project—instead she imagined herself in her bedroom, reading to Alejandro in the still of the evening. She imagined reading to her own children right before bedtime. She imagined reading to the thousands of children who were fighting cancer from hospitals or recovering at home. She saw the face of Sean, the little boy Alejandro had gone to meet in a hospital so many years ago. She thought about her conversation with Lisa, who had been so warm and friendly, treating her like a real person, not a celebrity, as she shared her uncomplicated way of rejoicing during Christmas.

"You ready, Amanda?"

She nodded her head, her eyes still staring at the words while her heart filled with the joy of doing something that felt truly philanthropic for the first time in years.

"Alright then," Dan said, his voice filled with genuine enthusiasm. "I'm excited! Let the fun begin!"

And when she heard a beep in her ear, Amanda began to read the lines in her soft but clear voice, the story unfolding in her mind as the words flowed out of her mouth.

Chapter Eight

With an unsatisfied feeling, Amanda pressed the red button on her phone, ending her conversation with Isadora. The call had been short. Too short. Whenever Amanda traveled without the children, she called Isadora's cell phone to check on them every morning and again at night, making certain to call before it was too late in the evening. This morning had been no different. But what *had* been different was that neither Sofia nor Nicolas seemed very interested in talking with her, a far cry from previous mornings when she had called.

And Isadora had rushed her off the phone.

"¿Todo bien?"

Hearing Alejandro's voice, Amanda glanced over her shoulder. He stood a few feet away, adjusting the sleeves of his black shirt. Someone had already wired him with the microphone, the small black wireless receiver attached to the back of his belt. He wore a touch of makeup, and his hair had been perfectly styled so that one thick curl cast a shadow over his forehead.

When she didn't respond, he looked up and lifted one eyebrow in a silent question.

She forced a smile. *"Ja, todo bien."*

He laughed, as he always did, when she spoke to him in a mixture of Pennsylvania Dutch and Spanish.

"Viper!" A man wearing dark clothing and a headset approached them. Like everyone else on the set of the morning talk show, he blended into the darkness just beyond the stage. He didn't appear concerned that he had interrupted the couple as they shared a stolen moment to talk. Instead, he pointed toward the stage and made a motion that indicated Alejandro was not in the proper spot. "You're on in five!" He didn't wait for a response as he hurried away.

Amanda shook her head and started to comment on the interruption, but before she could, Geoffrey walked over. With an apologetic smile in her direction, he took Alejandro's arm and led him away to a group of people on the edge of the stage.

It was almost ten o'clock in the morning, but Amanda still felt groggy. She needed another cup of coffee. The previous day, their flight from Grand Haven to New York had been delayed, and there had been a layover in Chicago. Once again, Alejandro had been recognized, leading to a crowd, and security had to step in, whisking them to a more secure location before escorting them to their connecting flight. Unfortunately, when they had landed, word had spread on social media that they were arriving, and the airline had to divert the plane to a different gate at JFK in order to avoid the awaiting mob scene. And, as usual, Geoffrey had scheduled multiple meetings for Alejandro. By the time they finally arrived at their hotel, it was almost midnight.

Her eyes followed Alejandro as he interacted with the people standing next to Geoffrey. She recognized two of them as members of Alejandro's usual entourage, but the others were unfamiliar faces. From the way that Alejandro stood, his shoulders straight and his expression light but serious, she could tell that it was a business discussion. After so many years married to him, she knew when he was "on."

As she had many times before, she couldn't help but wonder if he was tired of it.

Over the years, he had reinvented his image several times. From wild playboy to international sensation to love-struck protector to devoted family man. The character of Viper seemed to perpetually evolve, adjusting to Alejandro's needs . . . and sometimes to hers. Yet, she still wondered how Alejandro remained energized enough to transform so perfectly into Viper.

"Merry Christmas, Amanda."

Amanda turned in the direction of the voice. She smiled when she saw a woman approach her. With her shoulder-length brown hair parted at the side and her dark-lensed glasses, there was something familiar about her.

To Amanda's surprise, the woman gave her a warm hug.

"I see that Viper has you back in New York City again for the holidays."

Amanda must have frowned as she tried to remember the name of the woman. Shortly after she married Alejandro, they had traveled to New York City during the winter months, first for Thanksgiving and then for New Year's Eve. Amanda knew she had met her then, but that was all she could remember. It was easy to lose track of the years in the blur of frenzied activity, especially around the holidays.

"A few years back?" The woman smiled at her, realizing that Amanda was struggling to make the connection. "Amy Church. We met when you first came to *The Today Show* with Viper for Thanksgiving and New Year's. And then again the following two summers," she said to Amanda, hoping to jog her memory.

Amanda gave a small, embarrassed laugh. "*Ach*, I'm so sorry."

Amy laughed, a delightful sound that put Amanda immediately at ease. Her smile lit up her face, and her almond-shaped eyes crinkled into half-moons. "No worries. I know that you meet thousands of people each year. It's hard to keep track of names and faces. You can't possibly remember everyone!"

Still, Amanda knew that *this* woman was someone she should have recalled better, even if they'd only met a few times. There was something peaceful about Amy, a calm that defied the typical atmosphere of live news recording studios, with workers hustling to prepare for the moment when the light on top of the camera turned from red to green.

Before an uncomfortable silence could fall between them, Amy glanced at a man passing by so quickly that his arm brushed against Amanda's. She said apologetically, "It's always hurry up and wait around here, Amanda. Just like the city. People rushing to go somewhere and then just sitting around waiting."

"That's a clever observation!" Amanda replied.

Amy seemed delighted that Amanda agreed.

"But that's no different from any other major city, I reckon," Amanda said casually. "And the entertainment industry is the same way wherever we go."

Chaos. It was always chaos. Equipment to set up. Wires to check. Sound systems to test. People to meet. Paparazzi to avoid. Dinners to attend. It was nonstop commitments that never seemed to end.

Amanda often wondered if Alejandro even noticed. He seemed oblivious to the constant demands on his time. She suspected he had become immune to it all, but she hadn't. Still, as she watched the station's staff members and interns running back and forth with last-minute preparations and adjustments for the live show, the weight of the pressure etched on their faces and in their voices, Amanda realized that Amy did not exhibit any signs of stress.

"How do you get used to this?" she heard herself ask the woman. "You seem so . . ."

"Calm?" Amy gave another little laugh. "Oh, I must just be used to it. Every holiday, people seem to get crazier at work. I'm sure it's like that in every industry."

Amanda thought about her answer for a second. Maybe there was a kernel of truth to what Amy said. Christmas was always a stressful time as Alejandro traveled to different cities to perform at holiday concerts and appear at Christmas events, often visiting several cities on the same day. He tried to keep the professional pressure away from his family life. For the most part, he was successful, but Amanda could see through his mask.

However, there was one thing Amy said that Amanda disagreed with. If she could have spoken freely, she would have commented about their visit to Michigan and how everyone at that company had seemed relaxed despite their deadlines and the upcoming holidays. Clearly, not *every* industry valued professional success over personal satisfaction.

Instead, Amanda responded simply, "Christmas is a busy time of year, for sure and certain."

"I imagine you won't be staying in the city for Christmas, will you?"

"No, the children are . . ." Amanda had almost slipped and told her that after the Miami concert, the children would join them to celebrate the holidays in Lititz, but she caught herself just in time. Because they lived in a world where the spotlight was always shining on them, both Amanda and Alejandro were protective of their children. Trying to fly into Philadelphia without being recognized would be hard enough. Amanda certainly didn't want the paparazzi staking out the farm in Lititz and harassing her family. She had put her family through that ordeal once before, a long time ago, and she had sworn never again to expose them to that type of microscopic attention. "They are back in Miami, waiting for us."

Amy glanced down at her phone, checking the time before she slid the phone into her back pocket. "I'm surprised they aren't with you today. With all of the lights and the beautiful tree at Rockefeller Center, they might have enjoyed a visit."

"Travel's too hard on the little ones," she heard herself reply. What she really meant was that travel was too hard on *her* and, if he paused long enough to admit it, on Alejandro, too. "Although my older daughter wouldn't have minded. She loves shopping," she replied with a faint smile.

"Ah yes!" Amy gave another little laugh. "Of course! Let me guess—Forever 21?"

For a moment, Amanda laughed with her. It felt good to have a casual conversation with someone who, like Lisa in Grand Haven, talked to her as if she were a regular person, not an iconic celebrity. For that short period of time, the noise and mayhem that surrounded them disappeared, and Amanda was merely standing to the side and talking with a friend.

But the moment was quickly over.

Geoffrey approached them, an exasperated look in his eyes. As he asked them to forgive his interruption, Amy took a step backward and gave her a look of understanding. "It was great to see you again, Amanda," she said in parting, then walked to the other side of the studio.

"Amanda, Charlie's been trying to reach you and says you're not answering his calls," Geoffrey told her. "He's lined up a radio interview for you this afternoon and two other interviews with newspapers before the concert. He needs you to confirm."

A small sigh escaped her lips as she turned her phone over in her hand. Sure enough, three missed phone calls and ten text messages from Charlie had magically appeared in just the short time while she had silenced her phone. "Oh help," she muttered as she quickly glanced through the messages. "I thought he was supposed to meet us here."

He reached out and touched her arm. "Mmm, sorry," he said, his mind clearly on something else. "I gotta run. But can you give him a call, please?" Like everyone else, he was stressed and anxious, rushing to cross off the next most important item on his list of things to do.

Slipping behind the set and into the privacy of the greenroom, she scanned the text messages from Charlie. They had started out calm and enthusiastic but quickly had become frantic and misspelled. All of this in less than ten minutes!

The phone rang once and a panic-stricken voice met her reply. "Amanda! Why don't you answer when I call? Dali is breathing down my neck!"

She fought the urge to roll her eyes. "I was in the middle of a few things myself."

He coughed into the other end of the phone. "Darlin', I have your schedule, and I know exactly what you are in the middle of doing . . . which should be answering my phone calls and text messages!"

This time, Amanda did roll her eyes. "Technically, I wasn't even planning on being here, Charlie. Alejandro asked me to come with him only a month ago."

"And your point?" he commented in an exasperated tone of voice. Amanda could clearly hear the clicking sound of call waiting on the other end. No doubt, he was already committing her to more interviews. If he had his way, she would be booked through and including New Year's!

She took a deep breath and quickly counted to ten. "Why are you lining up interviews for me, Charlie? It's the holidays."

"Again, your point?"

Silently admitting defeat, she shut her eyes. Like Dali, her former publicist, Charlie was relentless when it came to scheduling appointments, squeezing the most out of Amanda that he could. She knew there would be no arguing with him. It was what he had been hired for. The two important Ps: Publicity and Promotion. If she had issues with any of it, Amanda should take it up with Alejandro. While very efficient at his work, Charlie never dared contradict anything Viper said. "Where are you anyway, Charlie?"

"That's not important. But what is important is where you will be at one o'clock. I've already e-mailed you an updated itinerary." He paused. "E-mail. You know what that is, right?" he asked with a hint of sarcasm.

"Charlie—" she started, annoyed at his tone.

"Because I wouldn't know that you *do* know what e-mail is, given that you haven't responded to any of my messages since you left Miami."

"I . . ."

A noise in the background on Charlie's end interrupted him from continuing. There was a muffled noise, as if he had covered the mouthpiece of the phone for a second. "I have another call coming in. Please, please, Amanda, just promise me you'll keep checking your e-mail in case I have any changes to your schedule, OK?" he asked in a more considerate tone.

He didn't wait for her to answer before she heard him yell to someone as he hung up the phone.

Without realizing it, Amanda was counting down the hours until she'd be traveling to Lititz, where people were not so hurried or distracted by the commitments they had made. Commitments that, however important, would not prevent them from just enjoying the moment. She hadn't realized how much she was looking forward to that week away from all of these people living their lives consumed by stress.

She only needed to survive the next couple of days. "I can certainly do that," she said to herself in encouragement. "At least I hope I can."

"I noticed something today," Amanda announced to Alejandro as they sat at a private table at Taos Restaurant in Manhattan.

After a long day of being chauffeured to different places in Manhattan for interviews and meetings, Amanda was relieved to finally have a chance to sit down with Alejandro, even if it was in a public restaurant. Despite the security lingering nearby, just in case there were any problems, it felt as if they were alone.

Well, almost alone, she thought as she felt the heat of people staring at them. She tried to ignore them, focusing her attention on Alejandro, but because she never knew when someone might take a photo of them, she had to remain "on." There was nothing worse for a celebrity than being caught off guard by a photographer and ending up in a tabloid with disheveled hair or wearing a baggy sweat suit. That was one of the reasons why, no matter where he went, Alejandro was always dressed in a properly tailored suit or at least slacks with a collared shirt. That was part of the reason why he always made certain that she, too, had access to a proper wardrobe.

He swirled the ice in his drink as he casually glanced around the room, noticing several people watching them. "What is that, Princesa?" he asked, slowly returning his eyes to focus on her.

"Everyone thinks that what *they* do is the most important thing. But because they are so focused on themselves, they never really notice what anyone else is doing. It's a little self-serving."

He laughed. "*Ay*, Princesa!"

She tried to not look offended. "It's true, though!"

Sobering, he leaned forward and, with his free hand, reached out for hers. "I'm sorry, Amanda. Now tell me. I want to know what made you come to this important realization."

She shared with him her experiences of the day, starting with her observations of the frenzied activity behind the scenes at *The Today Show* and then how Charlie had whisked her away to four back-to-back interviews and two meetings in just over five hours.

"Everyone is always in such a hurry and always full speed ahead. I don't think any of them take a moment to breathe."

He sipped at his drink, trying not to smile. "And your point?"

"It wasn't like that in Grand Haven," she finally said, after thinking for a minute. "In fact, the way the people at Brilliance acted almost reminded me of Lititz. We always worked, but we still enjoyed life. Work did not consume us."

"And this makes you upset because . . . ?"

"I wouldn't quite call it *upset*," she slowly replied. "But, after enjoying our time in Michigan, I realized that it was nice to feel like a real person, even nicer to contribute to a truly philanthropic project and to be surrounded by people who are not constantly rushing around as if on the verge of a nervous breakdown. Is what they do truly so important that they can't take a moment to simply . . . be?"

The waiter interrupted their conversation, setting their meals before them. He paused to see if there was anything else that they needed before backing away from the table and then he walked hurriedly back to the bar area to fetch drinks for another couple.

"See?" she whispered.

"*Pero*, Princesa," he said, teasingly whispering back to her, "he's working. Trying to earn more tips."

She sighed. "That's exactly my point. Would the world stop if he chatted for a moment with his customers? Wouldn't he earn larger tips? So what if someone's drink was delayed another minute or two?" She looked down at the salad on the plate before her. "When did work become so consuming that it takes on a life of its own and people stop being people? Stop noticing other people?"

With a smile on his lips, he shook his head as if in disbelief. "*Ay*, Princesa," he said. "That's far too complicated a subject for tonight." Pulling the black linen napkin off the table, he shook it out and laid it on his lap. "Now, let's talk of things that don't make my head hurt, *sí*? Besides"—he picked up his fork and knife, getting ready to cut the veal *française* on his plate—"I want to get back to the hotel early tonight. We have a long day of work tomorrow. You know"—he winked at her as he teased—"so we can focus on what *we* do and hope that someone takes a moment to notice it."

Chapter Nine

Amanda kicked off her high heels and crossed the plush white throw rug of her dressing room. Sinking into the cream-colored sofa, she leaned back and sighed, feeling the throbbing of her toes as they nestled into the carpet.

Three hours earlier, their private jet had landed at Miami International Airport. After a brief hold-up due to traffic, they had arrived at the Miami venue. Within minutes of their arrival, Geoffrey and his team of assistants had pulled Alejandro away from her so that he could attend a quick sound check before the doors opened.

Likewise, Charlie and two of his staff had greeted Amanda, eager to hurry her along to her own appointments.

"There you are!" Charlie had exclaimed, as if she were a lost little girl finally found by her parents. "There are so many *important* people waiting to meet you." He stressed the word *important* as if she should be thoroughly impressed with his handiwork. With unspoken urgency, Charlie had ushered her down a corridor of hallways to the dressing room so that she could freshen up before her meeting with several scheduled guests, including the governor's wife and the media.

Now, finally, she had a minute to take off her shoes and relax, even if she knew that it would not last long.

Travel always made her tired. She had forgotten how exhausting it was to always be "on" for the public: smiling, laughing, posing for photographs. Backstage at concerts, there was a never-ending throng of people, all of them eager to have a moment of her time. Even when she felt exhausted, she needed to make each person feel as if they were the most important person in the world. Amanda worked hard at being genuine when she met people, knowing that each person *was* important. But it drained her to maintain that level of focus.

"Mami?"

Amanda looked up as Isadora peeked through a crack in the opened door of her dressing room. With her big blue eyes shining, Isadora's excitement exuded from every pore.

With a weary smile, Amanda beckoned her daughter to enter. After a late night in New York City followed by an early-morning interview at a radio station, Alejandro and Amanda had been shuttled to JFK Airport to fly back to Miami for the concert. Neither one of them had had a moment to go home and freshen up. The days of concerts were always crammed with promotional activities, and Amanda was exhausted. But she always had time for her children.

"Did you just arrive, Izzie?" she asked, knowing that Geoffrey had arranged for Isadora's transportation from their house to the arena.

Isadora stepped into the dressing room, shutting the door behind her. She nodded and tried to mask her excitement. She glanced in the mirror and touched her hair. "Did you see all of those people?" she asked with another poor attempt to act nonchalant. Amanda, however, could see through Isadora, especially as she continued preening in the mirror. When her eyes caught Amanda's in the reflection, her daughter blushed. "What?"

Nodding her head, Amanda couldn't help but laugh. Isadora had attended other concerts and had been backstage in the past. But while there were always a lot of people behind the scenes, both working and lingering, the Jingle Ball was different. Ten headliners in each city meant nine more entourages than usual. And for Isadora, seeing several of her favorite bands and singers in the same place was a teenager's dream come true.

Her face shone with joy. Amanda could only imagine how her daughter felt, likening it to when she had first attended Alejandro's concerts. There was a palpable energy in the air, an excitement that Amanda never could quite describe, even though she had tried to explain it to her sister and mother in the beginning of her relationship with Alejandro. Between the backstage workers rushing around completing last-minute tasks or attending to minor emergencies and the constant background noise of fans cheering, it was exciting to be behind the curtain at concerts. Over the years, Amanda had grown to appreciate that feeling, although she'd never grown completely comfortable with the fans' adoration of her husband.

Now, for just a split second, Amanda felt as though she were peering into the future. With a momentary sense of panic, Amanda realized this was the first of many such experiences Isadora would have interacting with celebrities, not as a fan but as a fourteen-year-old with unusual access to them. With her dark coloring and thick black hair, Isadora was turning into a beautiful young woman. And that could attract a lot of unwanted attention.

"Come sit next to me, Izzie," Amanda said, patting the seat beside her.

Isadora hurried over to the sofa and sank into it, curling up next to Amanda and tucking her legs underneath her. She leaned back, her elbow on the back of the sofa so that she could rest her cheek against her hand. "Mami, you'll never guess who I saw when I arrived! Like literally walked into!" She gave a happy eye roll and lifted her shoulders in a gesture of excitement. "I could just die!"

"Well, I certainly hope you don't do that!" Amanda laughed, the moment of anxiety over Isadora's future dissipating as she found herself caught up in her enthusiasm. "I can't imagine *anyone* is *that* important."

Isadora made a face. "Mami! You know what I mean. Now get back to guessing!"

Amanda reached out and smoothed a stray piece of Isadora's hair. "Let me see . . ." It wasn't too hard of a question. After all, Amanda knew Isadora's favorite performers as well as the scheduled lineup for the show. But she took a moment anyway, pretending to think of an answer. "Hmmm. I suspect it was either Victor or that singer from Banff."

"Banff?" With an overly dramatic look of surprise, Isadora rolled her eyes. "That band is so not popular anymore!"

"Really? Wasn't it only this past summer that you wanted Papi to take you to their concert to meet them?"

A little blush traveled up the fourteen-year-old's cheek. "Well, that was almost six months ago," she said in a tone that indicated she was embarrassed.

"Oh my," Amanda teased gently. "And here I thought you were so excited to see them!" But she knew that for a teenage girl, six months felt like a lifetime.

The dressing room door opened again, and the quiet of the room seemed to explode with noise from outside. Their conversation interrupted, both Amanda and Isadora looked up to see Alejandro walk into the room. Two of his assistants followed him, both bent over their cell phones and frantically responding to text messages. But it wasn't the assistants that made Amanda catch her breath.

It was Alejandro.

He wore a black suit with a red shirt, his hair pushed back with a few loose curls hanging over his forehead. His sunglasses were propped on top of his head, and the hint of a five-o'clock shadow brushed his cheeks.

When she saw him, it felt as though the years melted away. She could remember everything about their accidental meeting, short courtship, and their first year of marriage: the good and the bad. Even more, she remembered how they had done everything together. Their love had been so strong that being apart from one another felt physically painful. Even when she had left him during that South American tour to take Isadora away from the seedy nature of tour life, she had done it only because God had chosen to put Isadora in their lives. It had been a difficult choice at the time, but Amanda never regretted that decision.

Over the years, while their love remained strong, things had changed. Amanda no longer accompanied her husband on tours, preferring to stay home to raise their young children. Alejandro was now a seasoned veteran in the music industry and, as such, was treated accordingly. It seemed that the bigger the star, the bigger the fanfare, and while Viper didn't need to tour as much anymore, he still spent almost half of the year traveling. Whenever he returned to Miami, he always made time for his family—spending days on the yacht or taking them to the beach. But the old Alejandro, the one who doted so lavishly on his Princesa, seemed far too distracted with the complexities of adult life and the serious responsibilities that came with managing a music empire worthy of the Viper brand.

Seeing him now, in that momentary flash of the past, stirred something long forgotten in Amanda, something she had buried deep inside of her. Amanda realized how much she missed the simple things in life. She missed so many aspects of her former life and desperately wished that she could introduce her children to them. Weeding the garden, milking the cows, even hanging the laundry outside on the white rope clothesline.

Her children lived a life that during Amanda's youth she had never dreamed existed. And while most kids their age would envy Isadora, Sofia, and Nicolas, Amanda knew that the fame and fortune that came with being Viper's children robbed them of much of the innocence and freedom they would have experienced if they'd been raised among the Amish.

"*¿Qué, mi amor?*" Alejandro's words jarred her back to the present.

The way the word *amor* rolled off his tongue brought a smile to her face. He had noticed her watching him and, like always, could tell that she was deep in thought. There was a connection between the two of them that time only strengthened. Even when he traveled, he seemed to know when she needed to hear his voice, and the phone would ring. And if Alejandro was upset, Amanda always knew the exact moment to text him.

But she didn't want to trouble him with her concerns about the children. Not here and certainly not now. She knew better than to divert his attention from his upcoming performance. It was a short set for him, only two songs, so she would have plenty of time with him later.

Instead of confiding in him, she lowered her eyes and merely said, "Nothing."

"Are you sure?" He gave her a look, one that told her how little he believed her.

"Nothing other than thinking how handsome my husband looks tonight," she replied with sincerity. It was true. There was no other man who could take her breath away like he did.

"It's you, Princesa, who outshines every other woman."

And he was the only man who could make her feel as if she was the most desired woman in the world.

Alejandro then turned his attention to his oldest daughter, who was clearly embarrassed by her parents' overt display of affection. "Isadora, you should come out. That singer from the Banff band was asking for you."

Isadora flushed, and Amanda couldn't help but teasingly say in an overdramatic way, "Dear husband, Banff was *so* six months ago."

"Mami!" With a roll of her eyes, Isadora spun around to face her with a look of mortification.

Alejandro raised an eyebrow and glanced at Amanda, who merely shrugged innocently.

"I'll have security take you over to them." He glanced over his shoulder at one of his assistants, who had overheard the conversation and, without being asked, quickly escorted Isadora outside to find a security guard.

"And keep an eye on her, *sí?*" Alejandro called out before the door shut. "What's that about?" he asked Amanda after Isadora was gone.

"A little secret between mother and daughter." She chuckled, still recalling the look on her poor daughter's face.

He shook his head, dismissing her cryptic comment. He glanced back at the door Izzie had walked through. He looked pensive as he muttered, "She looks *so* grown up."

"Yes, she does," Amanda answered matter-of-factly. Isadora was as beautiful as her father was handsome.

"Too grown up," he grumbled in protest. "She's only fourteen!"

Amanda laughed as she stood up and crossed the room toward him. "A teenager, isn't that what you said last week?"

He grunted in response as she patted him gently on the shoulder. She knew how he felt about Isadora's new popularity with the young men who circulated in their social settings. As a father, he worried. But Amanda knew that Isadora wasn't like typical teenage girls, overly seeking the attention of the young men who performed onstage. Of course, having access to the heartthrobs of America certainly didn't make her unpopular with the few friends that Amanda and Alejandro allowed into her inner circle.

Amanda leaned forward and kissed him. "I better go keep an eye on Izzie, *ja?*" She could already see her daughter, standing with those young men and taking photos. Selfies. Usually, Isadora only posted them to her private social media sites, but someone constantly monitored even those accounts to make certain nothing less than acceptable was posted.

"Security will," Alejandro said.

But Amanda knew better. Isadora still needed a parent to chaperone her, and that responsibility usually fell onto Amanda's shoulders. She didn't mind. After all, she knew far too well from her own experiences how easily security could be distracted or even tricked. Her friend Celinda had taught her that almost nine years ago in Paris, when the two young women had played a lighthearted prank that led to an uncontrollable mob scene.

"There's nothing better than a mother's watchful eye," Amanda said over her shoulder as she opened the dressing room door. "Besides, I'm sure you'd like a few minutes alone before your set."

Amanda made her way through the dark hallway toward the gathering area, one of several greenrooms where the entertainers and staff could grab a water or something to eat. She passed a few people who smiled at her, obviously recognizing the wife of Viper, a celebrity in her own right. No matter how much Amanda tried to avoid calling attention to herself, the paparazzi and the public still considered her akin to royalty. Over the years, she had traveled to big cities for interviews, sometimes without Alejandro and on a few occasions without the children. Being away from them made life in the spotlight even more distasteful. But she always remembered that she had a choice. Choosing Alejandro meant choosing Viper, and with Viper came fame.

Despite her feeling about her celebrity status, she would never have changed her decision, for Alejandro completed her.

Standing in the doorway, she recognized several people. Her eyes drifted through the gathered group until she saw Isadora standing in front of the lead singer of Banff, the current boy band phenomenon. At fourteen, Isadora was petite, but she was beautiful enough to attract attention. Amanda knew that much of the attention was because of her parents. Her sweet disposition and youthful shyness was no match for most of the people in the industry, so Amanda kept her well within her sight at all times. But she also knew that many of the singers and band members respected Viper enough that Isadora would be safe. The Banff band fell into that category.

It was harmless enough, Amanda thought, as Isadora took some selfies with the band, and the smile broadened on her daughter's face when the band members kept talking with her, not just because she was Viper's daughter but because they genuinely enjoyed her company. Long ago, Amanda learned to watch the interaction of superstars with their fans. How celebrities treated the people who adored them spoke volumes about their moral fiber.

Isadora sensed Amanda's presence and, turning slightly to face her, gave her a small wave of acknowledgment. Her eyes widened, signaling to her mother how excited she was to be in the company of her teenage crush. Six months may have come and gone, but clearly, Isadora still felt excited about being in their presence.

Soon Isadora would transition into adulthood, and eventually, that meant finding someone to share her life with—a relationship that would go far beyond the playful flirtation of an innocent romance. Amanda couldn't help but think how different Isadora's courtship would be if they lived in Lancaster County instead of amid the bright lights and alluring nightlife of Miami, Florida.

As she watched her daughter, Amanda thought back to her own teenage years, when she had turned sixteen and started her *rumschpringe*. While some Amish girls keenly anticipated their birthdays, looking forward to finally attending youth gatherings, Amanda hadn't been one of them. When her friends sat around whispering about which boy might ask them to ride home in a buggy, Amanda had merely smiled and nodded her head, but never contributed. They thought she was being secretive, but, in truth, she wasn't interested in dating. Not yet, anyway.

Most nights, she walked home from the singings by herself. On a few occasions, she had accepted an offer to ride home with a young man, but she was never courted by anyone. Not like Anna.

Everyone had thought that Menno Zook would marry Anna. That spring, even their mother had begun planning her garden with the idea that they might have a wedding in the autumn. But the sudden death of their younger brother, Aaron, had thrown everything into a tailspin. After the accident, a dark cloud of gloom hovered over the Beiler farm, and to everyone's surprise, Menno had married another Amish girl, leaving Anna to balance the heartache of the loss of her brother and the loss of her suitor.

It was an unusual situation. Usually during courtship, a young man and woman who rode home from the youth gatherings together for an extended period of time eventually married. Unlike the world in which Alejandro lived, dating was done with the sole intention of finding a life partner, not a one-night companion.

With a start, Amanda realized that it was just that world that Isadora was so innocently standing in. She suddenly looked at the Banff band members in a different light. Regardless of how nicely they treated Isadora now, within a few short years, the general respect shown for the fourteen-year-old daughter of Viper would turn into something more sinister.

Amanda fought the feeling of rising anxiety. She knew that while no one was immune to receiving a broken heart—even when living in an Amish community—Isadora was at risk of experiencing something far worse: a broken spirit.

And *that* was something Amanda knew she couldn't allow to happen.

Chapter Ten

Even though the drive from the Philadelphia airport to Lititz, Pennsylvania, was less than two hours, all three children had fallen asleep in the back of the large Escalade that Alejandro had arranged to pick up at the airport. Amanda fought the urge to doze while Alejandro drove along the highway toward Lancaster. Alecia, however, sat upright in the backseat, her alert eyes staring out the window as the scenery changed from urban to rural.

Earlier that morning, when they had left for the airport, the two younger children had practically stumbled out the front door, half-asleep. Once inside the car, both Sofia and Nicolas had curled up beside their grandmother. Isadora, however, was still exuberant from the previous evening. She stared at her phone, scrolling through the photos and monitoring her social media accounts until they arrived at the airport. But even she had slept in the private jet as well as during the car ride from the airport to the farm.

Now, as the landscape began to look familiar, Amanda couldn't help but wake them.

"We're almost there," she said in a gentle whisper.

Slowly, there was movement. Nicolas was the first to shift in his seat and press his nose against the window. "Why are the trees so ugly?" he asked. "Where are their leaves? Why is everything gray and yucky?"

Alejandro stifled a laugh as Amanda frowned. "It's winter, dear heart. Seasons change here."

Nicolas gave a slight scoff, clearly not in favor of bare trees and overcast skies.

Alecia inhaled loudly, as if to make her presence known. "And to think," she said in a tight voice, "it was so sunny and warm all day yesterday."

Beside her, Alejandro stiffened, and Amanda quickly placed her hand on his thigh, hoping that he wouldn't comment. To Amanda's surprise, Alecia had remained steadfast in her determination to travel to Lancaster County with them. Right up until they boarded the plane, Amanda had doubted whether her mother-in-law would actually make the journey. But Alejandro had told her that Alecia would be unlikely to change her mind, even though he didn't seem thrilled with the idea that she would join them.

Amanda glanced over the seat toward her mother-in-law. "Oh, Alecia," she said in a cheerful voice. "One week of change is good for all of us. We'll surely appreciate Miami's winters when we get back."

Isadora made a face. "I already appreciated them," she mumbled, and Amanda gave her a look of disapproval.

"Please, Isadora," she said in an exasperated tone. "I'm counting on you to be positive."

"Okay. I'm positive that I'd much rather be on the beach, tanning."

Amanda gave her a warning look, and Isadora lowered her eyes in understanding.

"Fine." Somehow, Isadora had a way of making the word into two syllables.

Amanda looked out the window, and her heart skipped a beat. As Alejandro pulled into the driveway past the old, beat-up gray mailbox and a new white fence, she caught her breath. There it was, right in front of her—her childhood home. The farm appeared smaller than Amanda remembered it. She glanced at Alejandro, but with his eyes hidden behind his dark sunglasses, she could not read his expression. In the backseat, the children had stopped talking and now peered out the windows. Isadora seemed more relaxed than Sofia, and as usual, Nicolas took his emotional cues from Sofia.

"Is this Grandma's house?" Sofia asked, the slight Sofia asked, the slight inflection of her voice hinting at her shock.

Alecia mumbled something in Spanish and Alejandro responded just as quickly, which brought silence to his mother.

"It smells," Nicolas added, pinching the end of his nose.

Alejandro cast a stern look over his shoulder at his son. "*¡Basta, hijo!*"

Scowling, Nicolas crossed his arms over his chest and sank farther into his car seat.

"I think I remember . . . ," Isadora said in a quiet voice, her expression changing from sour to excited.

Amanda reached over and touched Isadora's leg. "Do you, now?"

Slowly, Isadora nodded her head. "It's a happy place. I . . . I remember that much."

Her daughter's words warmed Amanda's heart. Of all the children, Isadora had spent the most time at her family's farm. But she had been so young that Amanda worried that Isadora would have no memories—or even worse, unhappy ones!—regarding that period of her life. Nine years ago, Amanda had left Alejandro's South American tour with her newly adopted stepdaughter, seeking a calm place for Isadora to adapt to her new life. It had been a hard time for both of them: Isadora having lost her mother and her grandparents and leaving her home country, Brazil, and Amanda having to leave her new husband, not knowing what would happen to their marriage.

Hearing Isadora refer to the farm as a happy memory meant that Amanda had done the right thing when she'd brought the child away from the rowdy tour to adapt to her new life in the peaceful surroundings of Amanda's own Amish upbringing.

Now, she thought, if I can only reach the other two.

"Look!" Amanda said in an excited voice. "They've painted the barn red!"

"So they did," Alejandro replied as he slowed the car. "I wonder why. You don't see many red barns out here."

"I bet that was Jonas's doing. I remember Ohio had so many red barns." Amanda gave a slight sigh. "So much has changed, yet it all seems so familiar."

"Who's Jonas?" Nicholas asked.

"Your uncle, goose!"

Amanda turned to reprimand Sofia. But she was already leaning forward, her hand on the back of Amanda's seat. "Mami, is this really where we are staying? Nicolas is right. The air smells bad."

"That's from the cows, *mija*," Alejandro answered for Amanda. "You have a week to get used to it."

"A whole week?" Sofia wrinkled her nose in disgust.

Amanda covered Sofia's hand with her own. "You won't even notice the odor after an hour or so. Trust me."

"Do *you* smell it?" Sofia asked.

Amanda shook her head. "*Nee*, not the same way you do." She smiled at her daughter. "To me, the air doesn't smell bad at all. Instead, it smells like I've come home."

Nicolas made a face, and Sofia's eyes opened wide at Amanda's comment. "This doesn't smell like home to me," she said softly.

Isadora nudged her sister with her elbow. "Stop, Sofia. You'll make Mami feel bad. This is where she grew up." She looked out the window at the empty cornfields. "It's a good place," she said in a soft voice, a distant look in her eyes.

No sooner had the car stopped than Amanda unbuckled her seatbelt and opened the door, not waiting for the rest of her family. She stood next to the car for a long moment and stared at the different buildings: the house, the stable, the dairy barn. All of them were in need of a good paint job, especially the dairy. Or had it always been like that, patches of chipped paint in various spots? She couldn't remember.

Like the farm, the house looked smaller than Amanda had remembered. She had tried to explain to the children that it was actually two houses: a main house for Anna and her family and a smaller house for Mammi Lizzie. Like all Amish houses, they were connected so that both sides could have privacy if they wanted it, as well as easy access to each other if they needed it. It was common on Amish farms for several generations to live on the property.

The front door of the main house opened, and a young woman in a brown dress emerged. She tossed a heavy black shawl around her shoulders as she hurried down the steps. Anna. Behind her sister, a young girl stepped outside. She looked to be around Sofia's age, and Amanda immediately knew that the girl was Hannah, Anna's first child, who was born just months before Sofia. Now she stood on the porch, a perfect replica of Anna. She held her baby brother, Samuel, while her younger sisters, Rachel, Sylvia, and Elizabeth, peered out the door, their eyes wide with curiosity. Each of the girls had their hair parted in the middle and pulled back away from her face. Of the children, only Hannah wore a scarf over her head.

"Amanda!" Anna called out.

Amanda recognized the large dark-olive-green boots on her feet as the kind her father used to wear when mucking the dairy. Over her head, Anna wore a plain navy knit scarf that was tied under her chin. Amanda glanced at the clock in the rented SUV and saw that it was almost one o'clock. Her sister must have just returned to the house after working in the barn.

"Is that really you?" Anna said, still smiling despite the tired look on her face.

Amanda glanced at the open car door and saw that Alecia was struggling to help Nicolas put on his coat, while Sofia and Isadora waited for Alejandro to put away his phone and get out. Amanda decided not to wait for them and quickly walked toward her sister. Her heart felt as though it would burst with joy. She had only met two of her nieces, Hannah and Rachel, just after Anna gave birth to Sylvia. Now, Amanda couldn't wait to get to know her other niece and her nephew. Still, the years had passed far too quickly and Amanda realized that one week wouldn't be enough.

"Hurry along, then!" Anna said in a cheerful voice, gesturing with her free hand, the shawl slipping over her shoulder. "It's cold enough out here!"

And then Amanda paused, frozen in place for just a moment. Even from a distance, the large shawl draped around Anna's shoulders could not hide the fact that she was pregnant. Very pregnant. Why hadn't her mother mentioned that in the letter? Six children in eight years was a lot for anyone to handle. No wonder her sister had dark circles under her eyes.

Amanda reached out to embrace her sister. "Oh, Anna! I can't believe we're actually here!" she said.

"Oh, *ja*, we can't, either!" The thick Pennsylvania Dutch accent on her sister's words caught Amanda off guard. It sounded so singsong, a little lilt at the end of every other syllable. Amanda had forgotten about how pretty the Amish accents were.

She had also forgotten the Amish disinclination toward physical affection. While her sister's face and words expressed joy at seeing Amanda and her family, Anna didn't return her embrace.

Amanda pulled back, embarrassed. Hugging her sister had seemed natural to her. Her years of living among the Englische and dealing with adoring fans had clearly changed her. Embracing other people was so much a part of her life that she barely remembered her youth and how her parents rarely hugged her.

The screen door moved as Sylvia nudged it with her bare feet. The movement caught Amanda's attention. "Oh help!" Amanda laughed as she hurried to the porch and gently touched the smallest girl's head. "Who have we here? I don't recognize any of these lovely young ladies!" she teased.

"Those are your nieces!" Anna gave a little laugh. "And your nephew, Samuel! Let's go on inside," Anna said, waving her hand toward the house as she stepped toward the door. "Save your greeting for the warmth, 'Manda. It's too cold for hellos out here."

Upon entering the house, the first thing that Amanda noticed was that the main room was cloaked in darkness. There were no kerosene lamps burning yet, and the hunter-green shades were drawn down to the middle, allowing only enough light into the room so that it wasn't completely dark. As her eyes adjusted, Amanda quickly glanced around and noticed how untidy the house was. The counter was covered with dirty pans and bowls, and the table looked as if Anna had been starting to make bread.

Hadn't Anna known that they were coming? she wondered. While they were growing up, her mother insisted on keeping the house tidy, saying there was no excuse for a messy or dirty house. Anyone could have stopped in, expected guest or surprise visitor, and that kitchen would have been spotless. Clearly, Anna didn't follow their mother's practice.

"Now, don't you mind the mess in here," Anna said, as if she read her sister's mind. "I wasn't certain of what time you were arriving and needed to make some more bread for church tomorrow."

There was no malice in her sister's voice, but Amanda knew that she had been caught judging the condition of the kitchen. Embarrassed, Amanda felt the color rise to her cheeks and was thankful that the room was not illuminated so that her sister couldn't see her reaction.

"Go on and sit down." Anna smiled as she took the baby from Hannah and sat in the rocking chair. "We have all day to clean up, don't we now?" She addressed this last question to Hannah, who grinned and nodded. "There's an awful lot of catching up to do, and that's much more important!"

Quickly, Amanda turned her attention to the children.

Each of them wore the same style of dress but in a slightly different shade of green. Not one of them wore aprons, another surprise for Amanda since Lizzie had always insisted they wear something to cover their dresses. While Hannah's and Rachel's dresses were clean, the smaller two girls' both had stains down the front. Despite it being winter, their feet were bare and dirty, typical for an Amish child. Only the little one wore a sweater, the buttons mismatched with the buttonholes.

And they were shy. Amanda couldn't help noticing that, except Hannah, they all stared at her with large, dark eyes from round faces that could use a good washing. They tried to hide behind each other, Hannah winding up in the front with the younger three peeking around her at the strange woman who stood before them.

"Let me see," Amanda said. She focused her attention on Hannah. "I bet you don't remember me," she said. "The last time I was here, you were just about the size of your younger sisters. Do you remember that, Hannah?"

She smiled and shook her head.

Kneeling down, Amanda faced the younger girls. She reached out and touched one who looked to be about seven years old. She surmised that she was only a few months older than Nicolas. "You must be Rachel."

At the sound of her name, Rachel seemed to brighten, just enough to nod her head. But there was something in her large chocolate-brown eyes that, despite looking so much like Anna, made Amanda see herself. The little girl had an energy about her that shyness could not hide.

"You've grown into quite a big girl," Amanda said, and Rachel giggled.

As Amanda talked to them, pausing to make a fuss over five-year-old Sylvia and three-year-old Elizabeth, she felt their uneasiness slowly shift to genuine curiosity. Amanda remembered well her own fear of strangers when she was a child, especially of people from outside the Amish community.

Englischers, she thought. Like they think I am.

The thought startled her. She hadn't considered what her nieces would think of her—their mother's sister who had refused to accept baptism and join the Amish church, instead marrying Alejandro. The aunt who had traveled the world in order to help build her husband's empire. The woman who stood before them now in a simple black wool dress with pearl jewelry adorning her throat and ears.

When Amanda was a child, her parents tried to shield her from the Englischers who stared at the Amish people, pointing fingers and taking pictures with their bulky cameras. She had been sheltered from the outside world, just like Anna's children were. It was so very unlike her own children. *They* barely noticed—and in some cases expected!—turned heads and stolen photos whenever they were in public.

The loud noise of yelling from outside and then stomping on the porch stairs broke her train of thought.

"*Ach,*" Anna laughed. "That must be your Nicolas!"

Amanda glanced toward the door. "He's a ball of energy," she said. "And all boy."

When the door opened, Jonas walked in first, carrying one of the suitcases. He looked across the room and saw Amanda kneeling before the children. With a broad smile, he raised his hand and greeted her, almost as if she were a regular visitor at the house. "Hello, there!" He paused and kicked off his muddy boots. They landed to the side of the door, leaving a few clumps of dirt on the floor. "I found some people that belong to you!"

Quickly, Amanda stood up and crossed the room to give him a proper greeting. But she didn't care; she embraced him anyway.

Behind him, Alejandro entered, his tall frame filling the room, especially when he stood next to Jonas. He set down the luggage that he had carried into the house. "Anna. Good to see you," he said as he removed his sunglasses and hung them on the front of his shirt, barely visible under his black leather coat. He walked over to her and leaned down and forward to press a kiss on her cheek. "Merry Christmas." He paused.

"Why, I don't think you've changed at all!" Anna said, her eyes glowing with delight. "It's so right *gut* to see all of you! I just can't believe my eyes!"

"And I see you're expecting!" He glanced at Amanda and raised an eyebrow. "You never told me, no?"

"Had I known, I would have," Amanda said, wondering if he was thinking about their small family. While the decision to not have more children had been mutually agreed upon, he had been the driving force behind the matter. She wondered if he had any regrets. Seeing Anna cuddle Samuel in her arms made Amanda long for the sweet smell of a bundled baby.

Jonas leaned against the counter and crossed his arms over his chest. Like Anna, the joy on his face was unmistakable. "I reckon Anna was keeping it a secret from all of you!"

Anna laughed as she waved her hand at him, as if dismissing what he said. "Oh now," she said in a teasing tone. "I don't have no secrets! You know that, Jonas." She looked at Amanda. "He's just playing with you."

"Why didn't you tell us?"

Anna shrugged. "Why, you both have so much going on. I didn't even think to bother you with the news until the baby comes!"

The door opened once again. This time, Isadora walked in with Sofia and Nicolas struggling to push past each other. When Nicolas squeezed through, he tumbled inside and tripped over the wayward boots that Jonas had kicked off.

"Nicolas!" Amanda hurried over to him and helped him back to his feet. He was a mess already, with dirt on his knees and his shirt untucked. Quickly, Amanda brushed off his pants and ran her fingers through his hair. "Children," she said, pausing to give him a warning look, "come meet your cousins."

Grudgingly, the three walked into the center of the room, staring at the four little girls in their plain Amish dresses. Each group of cousins stood in a line, waiting for the others to make the first move. For a long moment, no one said anything. Amanda could see that they were sizing each other up, wondering about these strange relatives looking at them.

Nicolas took a step forward and squared his shoulders. Amanda thought he was going to extend his hand and shake hands like he had been taught. Instead, he hooked his fingers under his belt and tugged his pants upward. "Well, howdy, y'all!" he said in a silly voice and then scampered away, shuffling his feet like a penguin.

Horrified, Amanda's mouth dropped open, and Alejandro stepped forward before Amanda could say another word. "Nicolas!"

Before Nicolas could be reprimanded, Sofia turned and looked at her mother. "Mami, there's a three-legged baby cow in the barn! He can run darn fast!"

This time, it was Amanda who cried out. "Sofia!"

"What?" Sofia blinked her eyes, genuinely confused as to what she had said that was wrong "It's true. Oh, and Nicolas stepped in cow poop." She jerked her thumb in the direction of her brother. "He smells terrible now."

"Aw, that's not me. It's the barn!" Nicholas pinched his nose. "It stinks something awful!" he said, waving his hand in front of his face.

"That's it!" Alejandro said, using what Amanda recognized as his I've-had-enough voice. The muscles along Alejandro's jawline twitched as he clenched his teeth. His hand came down on his son's shoulder. "You, young man, help me find Abuela. I think she was headed toward the barn when we came inside."

Nicolas scowled as his father dragged him back outside.

Appalled at the scene just created by two of her children, Amanda didn't know what to say. She stammered as she tried to apologize. "I . . ." The words wouldn't come. She bit her lower lip and felt a tightness in her chest. Her mother and father never would have accepted such horrid behavior! How on earth had her own children become so ill-mannered?

"Aw, don't you worry none," Anna said, obviously noticing her sister's discomfort. She gestured for Hannah to take the baby so that she could get up. "They're probably just excited, *ja*? Now, let me see Izzie." Walking across the room, Anna stood before Isadora. She gave a little gasp as she examined her oldest niece. "Oh help, girl! Look. At. You!"

Isadora smiled and lowered her eyes.

Anna clicked her tongue. "Why, I don't believe what I see! Where is that little girl who loved sugar cookies so much that I had to make them every day?"

"I . . . I think I remember that!" Isadora whispered in a soft voice. When she looked up, there was a quizzical look on her face, as if she were trying to fit the pieces left to an unfinished puzzle. "I stayed here a lot, didn't I?"

Delighted, Anna clapped her hands. "*Ja*, you sure did!"

"While Papi and Mami traveled?"

Anna reached out and pulled Isadora into her arms, giving her a quick but warm embrace. "What a special time that was for us! Wasn't it, Jonas?"

"It was, *ja*!"

Outside, Amanda could hear Alejandro talking with Alecia in Spanish as he helped her into the house. With such a disastrous beginning to their visit, Amanda wondered what else would go wrong. She shut her eyes and quickly said a prayer that Alecia would behave herself in Anna's house.

"Mami," Alejandro said when they finally entered. "This is Anna and Jonas." He guided her over to greet them, his hand gently pressed against her back. "And this," he said, gesturing to his mother, "is my mother, Alecia."

Alecia appeared to stiffen as she accepted their handshakes and leaned forward to kiss their cheeks. Her eyes took in Anna's enlarged stomach, and she raised an eyebrow at Alejandro. And then she began to look around the room.

"¡Ay, Dios!" she mumbled, making the sign of the cross with her hand, and Amanda braced herself.

Anna did not give Alecia a chance to say anything. Still smiling, Anna addressed her husband. "Mayhaps we should let them get settled in." She turned to Amanda. "Mamm thought it best if Alecia stayed in the *grossdaadihaus*. It'll be quieter over there, you know. And we have your old room made up for the two of you. Jonas even painted it when we heard you were coming!"

Amanda caught her breath. "My old room?" In the past, they had always stayed in the *grossdaadihaus*. She couldn't even remember the last time she had been upstairs in the main house, never mind to stay in her old bedroom. "Oh, Anna . . ."

"And the *kinner*," Anna continued, visibly pleased with Amanda's surprised reaction but not wanting to give her a chance to fuss, "they'll stay in Aaron's room."

"Who's Aaron, again?" Sofia asked.

Isadora nudged her. "Mami's brother," she hissed under her breath. "He died, remember?"

For just a moment, a shadow passed over Anna's face. Amanda wasn't certain if it was because she was remembering their younger brother or because she was thinking about the dark period of time following the accident in the barn.

Alejandro cleared his throat, reaching for Amanda's hand and giving it a gentle squeeze. Amanda's eyes met his as Alejandro nodded, letting her know he was right there beside her.

The shadow disappeared, and once again, the smiling, happy Anna returned. "Rachel, you go on and show your cousins to their room, *ja?*"

Amanda let Alejandro take his mother next door. Amanda had suggested that Alecia "freshen up" and unpack, although she suspected her mother-in-law would waste no time calling her friends in Miami to tell them all about the farm and the living conditions she found herself in. It was a conversation that Amanda was glad she wouldn't overhear. It was one thing to imagine what Alecia thought of her family home; it was quite another to hear the actual words spoken.

Once everyone dispersed in their separate directions, Amanda stood in the center of the kitchen with her sister. An awkward silence fell over the room, although they both could hear the noise of the children walking on the hardwood floor. Nicolas gave a shout and, from the sound of it, had jumped on the bed.

Looking at the stairs, Amanda took a small breath. "I should check on him," she said softly.

"Now, now, 'Manda. Don't you worry about him." Anna redirected Amanda's attention away from her unruly son. "Remember how Aaron used to do such things? That's boys for you." She motioned to Amanda to join her in the sitting area of the kitchen. "*Kum, schwester.* Let's visit while we have a moment, *ja?*"

Amanda joined her in the sitting area, taking a spot on the sofa. "Let me hold your sweet Samuel," she said, reaching out for the child. "I didn't even spare him a glance, did I?"

Happily, Anna handed her the sleeping child.

Amanda gazed down at her nephew. His one-year birthday had been in early November, and, having been born premature, he was small for his age. But he was a beautiful boy, reminding Amanda of their brother when he was a baby. His hair was light brown, almost blond, and hung in long waves over his forehead. "Oh, Anna, he's just precious, isn't he?" Amanda whispered, doing her best to fight back the tears pooling in her eyes at the thought of Aaron.

"He is my special gift from God," she replied, beaming with joy. Just then, a chorus of mischievous screams came from upstairs.

"All this noise!" She glanced up at her sister. "I'll have to remind Nicolas to keep his voice down."

"Pshaw! Not to worry. Samuel sleeps through everything." Anna leaned over and stared at him. If Amanda hadn't known better, she would have thought she saw a look of pride on her sister's face. "Besides, he sleeps downstairs in our room."

Of course. Amanda had almost forgotten that Anna and Jonas's bedroom was her parents' former first-floor bedroom. When their father had taken ill nine years ago, the newly married Anna had moved home from Ohio with Jonas to help on the farm while Lizzie tended to Elias. After Elias died, they had stayed and taken over the responsibility of the farm.

"Where is Mamm anyway?" Amanda asked, glancing toward the door that connected the main house with the *grossdaadihaus*. "I'd have thought she'd come over by now."

Anna looked as surprised as Amanda. "Why, I rightly don't know!"

"She surprised me," Amanda said slowly. "Her letter asked us to come here. She's never done that before. Is everything going well here?"

"Oh *ja*! She's just right as rain! She helps me so much with the *kinner*, especially when Hannah and Rachel are at school. She just loves them so much." Anna paused, looking thoughtful. "Mayhaps she wrote because she just wanted to see you and the *kinner*."

There was no malice or criticism in Anna's tone, but her words caught Amanda off guard. She had forgotten how Amish people spoke candidly, never prone to sugarcoat the truth. How she wished that she could excuse her absence—blame it on the children, her commitments, or even Alejandro's schedule. But the reality was that she *could* have made the time, if only she had thought about it. She could have visited more often if she had tried harder.

"But you're here now!" Anna continued, unaware of Amanda's feelings of guilt. "And Mamm was so happy that you were coming home." She leaned forward and added, "Even with Alejandro!"

Her comment made Amanda laugh, and Anna joined her.

"She never really did warm up to him, did she now?" Amanda asked.

Anna gave a playful shrug. "Well," she said, drawing out the word and leaving the question unanswered.

They both laughed again.

"Oh now!" someone called out from the other room. "I recognize that laugh!"

At the sound of her mother's voice, Amanda lit up. She handed Samuel back to Anna before she jumped up and hurried over to the door that led to the *grossdaadihaus* as Lizzie emerged. "Mamm!" She fought the tears that came to her eyes as she hugged her mother, suddenly realizing how much she had missed being with her family. "Oh, how good to see you! I was just asking Anna where you were!"

To Amanda's surprise, Lizzie embraced her in return. "Look at you! So tall and thin!" She pulled back and stared at Amanda. "Too thin! Why, doesn't that man feed you at all?"

Amanda gave a little groan. "Mamm!" It occurred to her that Alecia and her mother were not so different.

"Oh, Mamm," Anna called out. "Don't be starting on Alejandro already! He brought her home, didn't he?"

Lizzie raised her eyebrows at Anna's comment but changed the subject. "When did you get so tall, Amanda?"

The truth was that Amanda had also noticed that her mother seemed smaller to her. Perhaps it was her girth, so typical of Amish women. Or maybe it was her age. Even though her mother had not visibly changed beyond a few wrinkles and even more gray hair, she appeared different.

"It's probably my shoes," Amanda said, lifting her foot to the side and pointing at the bottom of it. "Heels." They weren't too high, but they weren't flat, either. Nor were they the simple black sneakers that both Lizzie and Anna wore.

"Can't be milking cows in those shoes, now, can you?"

Amanda tried to hide her smile. She couldn't imagine what her children would say if they saw her sitting on an old milk stool by the side of a black-and-white cow, her hands gently tugging at the teats on its udder. "I'll leave the milking to the boys," she said lightly. "Alejandro always enjoyed that."

Lizzie made an approving noise and nodded her head. "Hard work is good for any man," she said.

Amanda wanted to respond that Alejandro was a hard worker, harder than her mother could imagine, but she knew that neither Lizzie nor Anna could ever truly understand the professional demands on both him and Amanda. She also knew that they could never comprehend the opulent lifestyle that went along with his success.

"Now, where are those *kinner* of yours?" Lizzie said, but by the noise filtering down the staircase, she didn't need Amanda to tell her that the children were upstairs.

Amanda walked to the bottom of the stairs, setting her hand atop the banister. The feeling of the smooth wood under her fingers felt comfortable and familiar. How many times had she grabbed that very spot when she was a child? "Isadora. Sofia. Come down to see Mammi Lizzie and bring your brother," she called up the staircase.

Nicolas was the first one to run down the stairs, taking two at a time. At the bottom, he almost collided with Amanda. "Mami! I like my cousins, but I sure can't understand anything those little ones are saying!"

Anna and Lizzie laughed as Amanda tried to explain. "They speak Dutch, Nicolas. Pennsylvania Dutch."

His eyes opened wide. "Oh." He frowned. "You mean they don't speak English?"

"Oh, Nicolas!" Anna tried to hide her amusement at her nephew's question. "Just a little. When they go to school, they'll learn more."

"It's no different from when you speak Spanish with Papi," Amanda reminded him.

Nicolas seemed to contemplate this.

Before he could think up another question or comment, Amanda diverted his attention. "Come now and greet your grandmother." Amanda placed her hand on his shoulder and gently guided him toward Lizzie. "She hasn't seen you since you were a baby."

For the first time since they had arrived, Nicolas stood upright, his heels together and his shoulders straight. He stood before Lizzie and stared at her before he stuck out his hand.

Delighted, Lizzie shook it. "My word! Just look at this boy!" She clicked her tongue and inhaled as she bit her lower lip. "The spitting image of his *daed, ja*?" Her compliment bolstered his confidence and he gave her a grin. "And the personality, too, I see."

"Nice to meet you, Abuela."

Quickly, Amanda corrected him. "Mammi Lizzie," she said. "We call my mother Mammi Lizzie."

He didn't respond but nodded his head.

Isadora and Sofia walked down the stairs next. When Lizzie looked up at her, Isadora's eyes lit up. She ran across the room and gave her grandmother a big hug. The greeting touched Amanda, and she had to look away, blinking her eyes to keep the tears at bay.

"Mammi Lizzie!" Isadora said in a breathless voice. "It's so good to see you!"

At that moment, she was no longer a fourteen-year-old girl struggling to find a balance between her teenage innocence and the pressures of celebrity-status popularity. Instead, she was just a girl reuniting with her beloved grandmother.

Sofia watched the scene timidly and pursed her lips. She glanced at Amanda, and when Amanda motioned to her, she approached Lizzie. When Isadora pulled away, Sofia gave Lizzie a quick hug. As soon as their greeting was over, she hurried over to her mother. Amanda couldn't help but wonder about her reaction. Sofia had never been shy. Usually, her outspoken nature made her even more visible than Nicolas.

A few minutes later, Alejandro and Alecia returned to the room. From the look on Alecia's face, Amanda knew that there had been a serious discussion between mother and son. She appeared resigned— even stoic—two words that Amanda would never have used to describe Alecia. Introductions were made, and for the next hour, the adults sat and talked in the sitting area. Isadora chose to remain with them rather than go explore the barn with the younger children, who, despite the overcast skies and chilly air, were determined to run around outside. Isadora seemed to linger between Anna and Lizzie, her eyes constantly studying the two of them when they weren't looking. Amanda couldn't help but wonder what her daughter was thinking.

Anna did most of the talking, updating Amanda on the latest news about people she remembered, as well as people she wasn't sure she'd even met. Occasionally, Lizzie would lean forward to add something, especially when it was about a distant relative or older member of the church district.

Alecia mostly remained silent.

"What is the schedule for the week?" Amanda asked at last. "And what can I do to help with preparations for the holiday?"

"*Ja*, well," Anna said slowly, "we've church tomorrow."

Alecia finally spoke up. "What time is the Mass?"

Anna hesitated at the question.

"Mami, it's not a church," Alejandro said. "It's not called Mass."

Amanda started to respond. She wanted to explain to Alecia that the manner of worship in the Catholic Church was markedly different from that in an Amish church. Over the years, no matter how many times Amanda had tried to explain her family's religion to Alecia, her mother-in-law simply could not accept that there were different ways to worship God other than Catholicism. And Amanda never commented that the Catholics were one of the main groups that had persecuted her Anabaptist ancestors so many centuries ago.

"And we've got quite the busy week!" Anna shifted the child in her arms. "Hannah and Rachel have school this week." She glanced at her husband and feigned a sheepish look. "But I did tell them they could miss a day or two."

Lizzie waved her hand at Anna. "Of course they can! Especially for the cookie swap on Monday!"

"And Tuesday we're invited to a quilting bee on the far side of Musser School Lane. And there's a horse auction that day near Narvon. Jonas thought Alejandro might want to go to that."

"Oh *sí*?" Alejandro brightened at the mention of the horse auction. "I'd love to go."

The usually quiet Jonas, whether from choice or simply because he never could get a word in edgewise, nodded. "*Ja*, and it's not that New Holland one, either. Too many Englische folk attend that one." He winked at Isadora. "They might recognize your *daed*, eh? Call those photographers again." He laughed and Isadora smiled at his teasing.

"And then Wednesday is a women's holiday lunch that we were invited to attend," Anna continued. "But I didn't commit to that, Amanda. I wanted to check with you first. On Thursday, we need to prepare for the school pageant on Friday, and then we have Christmas Eve and Christmas! Time for just the family to enjoy each other, although the bishop and his wife are coming on Christmas."

For a moment, Amanda thought she hadn't heard her sister properly. "Excuse me?"

A friendly smirk crossed Anna's face. "Oh *ja*! Why, when he heard you were coming home and having Christmas with us, he invited himself to supper. Didn't he, Jonas?"

Jonas chuckled and plucked at the bottom of his beard. "That he did. Can't ever recall him coming here for supper, never mind a holiday supper."

"What on earth . . . ?"

Lizzie cleared her throat. "Mayhaps the bishop just wants to spend the holidays with our family. I seem to recall his family gathering is on Christmas Eve. So there's nothing that needs to be overanalyzed now, is there?"

But Amanda and Alejandro exchanged a knowing look. The bishop had never been much of a fan of Alejandro and even less a fan of Amanda's relationship with him.

But Alecia had perked up when she heard their exchange. "A bishop?" Alecia said, looking very impressed that a high-ranking member of the church would come to visit her son and daughter-in-law. Amanda knew that she was envisioning a man wearing a beautiful red cassock and clutching rosary beads. It took all of her willpower to bite her tongue and not scold her husband for not preparing his mother.

"*Ay*, Mami! It's not like that," Alejandro said under his breath. "I'll explain later."

Anna gestured for Jonas to take Samuel. "So much to do, *ja*? It's always so much busier at this time of year," she said as she stood up and started toward the main part of the kitchen. "I'd much rather just sit home and visit with you, Amanda. Right, Mamm?"

"We'll just have to make do with the time that we have, *ja*?" Lizzie said before she reached over and patted Isadora's hand. "I sure do want to hear all about this girl, though. You need to update your *grossmammi* about all that you've been doing! You've grown so much since I last saw you."

Out of the corner of her eye, Amanda noticed Alecia bristle as Isadora began to share stories with Lizzie about her school and friends and the concert she had attended the previous night. When Lizzie asked about Katie Cat, Amanda thought Alecia would stand up and sit between Isadora and her other grandmother.

"So," Amanda said loudly, hoping to divert Alecia's attention. "Tell us what to do, Anna. Alecia and I are more than happy to help with anything you need."

Anna stood at the counter for a moment and tilted her head to the side. "*Ja vell*, let's see now . . ." She paused as if reviewing a to-do list in her head. "I could use some help getting ready for tomorrow," she said. "Mayhaps you might help me canning some of the beef that Jonas picked up yesterday."

"In December?" Amanda asked, dumbfounded at the request.

"Oh, I know!" Anna laughed sheepishly. "We were so busy during the harvest that I just hadn't canned enough. I didn't realize we ran out until last week." She looked over at Hannah. "Isn't that right, Hannah?"

Her daughter nodded emphatically.

"Jonas bought some home just yesterday, and I haven't gotten around to it yet. But mayhaps you might take that chore on, Amanda."

It hadn't been exactly what she was expecting, but Amanda readily agreed. Some of the best memories she had were of time spent working beside her mother and sister.

Jonas stood up and motioned to Alejandro. "We can go fetch the box of beef, and I can show you the new milking system we installed just last year yet."

"New milking system?" Amanda glanced from Jonas to Anna. "You hadn't written to me about that, Anna. How exciting!"

Alejandro walked over to her and, leaning over, gave her a soft kiss on her cheek. "Have fun canning beef," he whispered. When she looked at him, she saw that he was holding back a smile, and there was a mischievous look in his eyes. And then she remembered.

The color flooded to her cheeks, and she averted her eyes. She had forgotten about his first visit to Lititz, when he had helped her and her mother with the beef canning. When Lizzie had turned away from them, their hands had entwined, and for the briefest of moments, it was as if they were alone in the room. Later, Amanda had boldly told Alejandro that he did not belong in the world of Viper and its fast-paced lifestyle of endless partying and one-night stands. Even more important, Alejandro finally had realized that Amanda was more than just a plain Amish girl. She was a woman who observed and understood more than she let on. And that had unnerved him.

Now, more than nine years later, Amanda stood in the same room, preparing to teach his mother and his children how to can beef. She looked over at Alecia and the children, all of whom stood staring with their mouths hanging agape as Jonas returned carrying a cardboard box full of plastic bags of raw meat. As she opened it and took out one of the plastic bags, she noticed the color drain from Alecia's face while Nicolas bellowed "Gross!"

Amanda sighed. "It's not gross, Nicolas. Your father even helped me can beef one time many years ago!" She turned to Alecia. "And certainly you canned beef in Cuba."

Alecia shook her head. "We had canned beef from Russia, but I never did it myself."

Clearly, Amanda had her hands full with getting her family to assist her. But she knew that teaching them to appreciate the important things in life, such as the food that graced their table, was part of the Christmas message that she wanted to share with them. They would all be getting their hands dirty today, she thought, and hopefully learning that not everything in life had to come in pretty packaging.

In her most cheerful voice, Amanda sang out with a determined smile on her face, "Well then. Let's get started, shall we?"

Chapter Eleven

In the early-morning hours, Amanda made her way down the staircase, careful to walk softly. The last thing she wanted to do was wake the children. She knew far too well how precious the quiet moments of dawn were. Now that she was rested, she wanted to spend some quality time with her sister.

Because the sun had not crested the horizon yet, someone had turned on the propane lantern that hung over the table. It hissed and spewed forth a blinding light in that part of the room, a sound that brought back a new flood of memories. The smell of bread baking in the oven brought her back to her childhood. Almost every morning, she had rubbed sleep out of her eyes as she padded down the stairs and had been greeted by the yeasty scent of fresh bread. Today was no different.

She stood on the bottom step, bathed in the shadows the lantern created, and watched as her sister moved around the kitchen.

The scene reminded her of her mother. How many mornings had Amanda walked down those same steps to find her mother already working in the kitchen? Whether she had been baking bread or making cheese, Lizzie was always hard at work on something.

It dawned on Amanda that, like herself, her mother must have enjoyed those quiet hours before her children awoke.

"Mmm. Smells like home," Amanda said at last to break the silence.

Anna jumped at the sound of her sister's voice. As she turned around, she gave an embarrassed laugh and placed her hand on her chest. "Oh help! You startled me, *schwester*!"

Amanda walked to the table and sat down on the bench. She ran her hands across the wood top of the table, amazed that it was the same table where she had eaten every meal her mother served. Even more impressive was that her father had sat on the very same bench when he had been a child.

"Morning is my favorite time of day," Amanda said with a wistful tone in her voice. "Looks like it's yours, too."

Anna opened a cabinet to retrieve two coffee cups. "Usually, I'm helping Jonas with the milking. It is a true gift to have more time to work in the kitchen before the children are awake today." She poured some coffee into two cups, pausing for a moment as she looked over the rising steam at Amanda. "Do you really still consider this home, or is this how your Miami house smells in the morning?"

Accepting the cup of coffee from her sister, Amanda gave a little laugh and shook her head. "*Nee*, Anna, my kitchen does not smell like this."

Anna joined her at the table, sitting in one of the chairs across from her. She frowned, thinking about Amanda's response. "So you still consider this your home, then?"

The question surprised Amanda, and it took her a moment to respond. The word "home" had so many meanings. When she was younger, home was the kitchen where she used to stand next to her mother while she cooked their meals. During her growing-up years, her parents' farm was the center of her universe, the boundaries of which were limited to the little one-room schoolhouse and wherever church was being held that week.

Now, however, home did not have a physical border but an emotional one. Home was with Alejandro and her children, wherever their obligations took them.

Still, as she sat there at the table with the coffee cup in her hands and her sister seated across from her, Amanda couldn't help but feel *at home*, even if it no longer was *her* home.

"We grew up here, Anna," she said softly. No matter how she tried to explain it, she knew that her sister simply could not imagine a world that did not center around the very kitchen where they currently sat. She tried to be delicate with her words. "It will always be my childhood home. But I left here, and our lives are so . . ."

When Amanda hesitated, Anna finished the sentence for her. "Different."

Nodding, Amanda raised the cup to her lips. "It's hard to explain. The change was so gradual. And not having been home for so long . . ." She looked around the kitchen, noticing that Anna had made an attempt to tidy it. "It seems so comfortable and familiar, almost like I'm dreaming, yet I know I have to return to reality."

Anna made a little noise as if agreeing as she, too, sipped her coffee.

Hoping to change the subject, Amanda glanced at the clock. It was just after six o'clock. Surely Hannah and Rachel would arise soon and help with last-minute chores in the barn. After all, without an older brother to assist with the morning chores, the responsibility to help Jonas would fall on either their shoulders or Anna's.

"Let me help you finish cooking," Amanda said. "I can't tell you how long it's been since I've cooked a good, hearty Amish breakfast!"

Anna raised an eyebrow. If she wanted to comment on Amanda's statement, she didn't. But the expression on her face told Amanda exactly what her sister thought.

"I . . . I mean we sit for breakfast," Amanda tried to explain as she stood up and headed to the counter. "As a family, I mean. Well, when Alejandro isn't there, it's just me and the *kinner*." The mere fact that she felt as if she needed to explain the morning routine in her house just added to her guilt. "It's just that . . ."

Graciously, Anna raised her hand and said, "*Nee*, Amanda. There's no need to explain. It's a different life."

Amanda exhaled, grateful that Anna seemed to understand that much.

"But," Anna said as she stood to join her sister at the counter, "I sure do wonder how you managed to adapt from our simple Amish life to Alejandro's more complicated world." Abruptly, she paused for a moment, her hand moving to the right side of her stomach. For a moment, she didn't say anything, and then she smiled. "Baby must be awake."

"Kicking?"

Anna thought for a moment and then shook her head. "Turning, I reckon."

"Speaking of the baby, Samuel is the most peaceful child!" Amanda said as she began cracking eggs into a large plastic bowl. Two dozen eggs would make enough scrambled eggs for the people who would sit around the breakfast table, but only because Anna was also making pancakes, scrapple, hash browns, and two loaves of sliced bread.

"Oh, that he is!" Anna's delight with Amanda's compliment shone on her face. "How blessed we are to have that child."

With a quick flicking of her wrist, Amanda whisked the eggs. "I can't believe he hasn't woken yet! In fact, I don't think I've heard him cry since we arrived."

When Anna didn't respond, Amanda glanced at her. She had stopped slicing the fresh bread and was staring at the wall. The joy had disappeared from her face, and Amanda realized that Anna was deep in thought. Setting down the fork, Amanda wiped her hand on a towel and faced her.

"Anna?"

"He's our only boy," Anna said, her voice low and her words slow.

"And he's a perfect little boy."

The corners of Anna's mouth lifted into a smile, one that told Amanda there was more to the story than that. "*Nee*, Amanda, we won't be having any more *kinner* after this one," she said, gently rubbing her stomach. "And I already know it's a girl."

Amanda caught her breath. "Oh." It was all she could say. How on earth had Anna learned that she was having a daughter? While more of the younger Amish women were using Englische doctors and taking a more active role in the prenatal care of their babies, they rarely found out the sex of the baby. Even Amanda had not wanted to know, although Alejandro had tried to coerce the doctor into telling him.

With a light laugh, Anna refocused her eyes on the bread between her hands, carefully slicing the loaf with the sharp knife. "After Samuel was born, the doctor didn't want me having more *bopplis*," she said. "Something about my uterus being weak." She laughed again. "And it's not as if you can exercise that, now, can you?"

It was one thing to decide, as a couple, to not have more children. But Amanda knew that it was quite another to be told by a doctor that they couldn't have more children. Her heart broke for her sister, who apparently had wanted an even larger family.

"The doctor has been closely monitoring this little one," Anna said, pausing again to run her hand over her stomach. "That's how I know she's a girl."

"Whether you have one son or a hundred," Amanda replied, "each one is special, Anna. And God saw fit to send you Samuel."

"He did, that is true." Anna's eyes misted over, and she smiled in a wistful way. "As I always say, Samuel is our gift from God. He knew that such a special little boy needed a family to love and support him."

"Well, of course they would! Any family would!"

This time, Anna laughed, her eyes crinkling into half-moons that sparkled. "Oh, Amanda! You didn't notice, then?"

"Notice?" Amanda put her hand on her hip as she faced her sister. "Notice what, Anna? You're talking in riddles, *schwester*. What on earth was I supposed to notice?"

"Oh, Amanda!" she said, still smiling. "Surely you realize that Samuel's *ferhoodled*?"

Amanda's mouth opened, but no words came out. She stared at her sister, trying to digest what she had said. *Ferhoodled?* She hadn't heard that term in years. Even then, it usually meant someone who was confused because they were in love. But that certainly wasn't what Anna meant. "Surely you don't mean . . ." Amanda couldn't even finish the sentence.

Anna waved her hand at Amanda. "Now don't you get all flustered on me," she said in a light tone. "It only makes him more special to us. He might develop slower than the other little ones, and mayhaps he needs more care, but that just means we just can shower him with more love." She returned her attention to the food. "And the girls just love him so. Why, you saw Hannah and Rachel bickering over who was going to hold him last night after supper!" A noise outside the window caused her to look out. "Oh help! The men are coming in already! Reckon with Alejandro helping him, Jonas finished extra quick."

Still stunned by Anna's revelation about Samuel as well as by her upbeat attitude, Amanda stood still, with her fork in midair over the unbeaten eggs in the bowl. She only started to beat the egg mixture as Alejandro strode into the room and paused to kiss her cheek.

"What a morning!" He accepted the cup of coffee Anna offered to him. "*Ay, Princesa!* There's nothing like crisp air in the morning to open a man's lungs and hard work to open his mind!" He winked at her, his eyes bright and full of life.

Good-naturedly, Jonas clapped him on the shoulder. "I forgot what a right *gut* worker you are, Alejandro! Why, if I could get through those cows this quick every day, I could double the herd!"

"Mayhaps there's a farmer in you yet," Anna teased Alejandro.

"Man could get used to this," Alejandro said, more to himself than to anyone else. But Amanda heard him and felt almost as stunned by that statement as by Anna's disclosure about Samuel.

"You wouldn't miss the limelight and travel, then?" Jonas asked.

Amanda gave a soft laugh. "Of course he would!"

He sat down at the table and leaned back in the chair. He stretched his legs out before him and took a sip of the coffee. "*Ay*, Princesa! After all these years, you should know that I still have some surprises up my sleeve yet."

His playful mood warmed her heart. It had been far too long since he'd appeared so relaxed and happy. "Oh really? Surprises?"

"You like surprises, no?"

"After all these years," she teased back at him, "you should know that I am, in fact, not particularly fond of surprises at all."

He laughed and reached out for her to take his hand. When she did, he pulled her toward him and kissed her palm. "*Te amo, mi amor,*" he whispered and she felt her cheeks glow under his tender sentiment, even though she felt uncomfortable with his display of affection in front of Anna and Jonas.

The clock on the wall clicked and began to chime.

"Six thirty already, then?" Anna gasped and wiped her hands on her apron. "Oh, I was so thankful when the clocks turned back in November. I much prefer church service when it's slow time and we have that extra hour!" She grimaced. "Fast time is just dreadful, trying to get everyone ready an hour early!"

It was the closest thing to a complaint Amanda had heard from her sister.

Many Amish communities did not recognize daylight savings time and did not move their clocks forward. At least not officially. During daylight savings time, a period they called fast time, farmers arose at the same time as slow time, but it was an hour earlier than the actual clocks. Many bishops adopted the same schedule for church, which meant the worship service started at nine o'clock during the winter season.

"Best go get those little ones up and dressed, *ja?*" Anna said, directing the question to Amanda. "We need to make sure they eat. Empty bellies make for fidgety *kinner* during service."

The night before, when Alejandro and Amanda had retired to their bedroom, she had expressed her concern about the children attending church service, especially Nicolas. Almost three hours long and conducted in High German and Pennsylvania Dutch, an Amish worship service was not something most non-Amish people enjoyed. But Alejandro had insisted that they attend, refusing to give even his mother an excuse to stay at the farm.

"He's far too rambunctious," he had said as he pulled Amanda into his arms, his head resting on the pillow with hers tucked under his chin. "Might do him some good to attend an Amish worship."

She had forgotten how much Alejandro enjoyed the worship services, even though he didn't understand the hymns or the sermons. The few times he had accompanied her, she'd been amazed at how the rest of the men seemed to enjoy his company during the fellowship afterward. The question of whether Alecia would enjoy it as much as her son, however, remained to be seen.

As Amanda oversaw her three children getting dressed, listening to them complain about having to go to church, she knew that she would have her hands full keeping them from fussing during the three-hour service. Amanda hoped that she wouldn't need to placate Alecia, too. She wanted to enjoy herself. Ever since Anna had told her that they were attending church, Amanda had realized how much she had missed attending worship services. She was even looking forward to seeing the bishop, one of the main people in the community, with whom Amanda had not always seen eye-to-eye.

By seven o'clock, Amanda had managed to herd Sofia and Nicolas downstairs to join their cousins at the kitchen table. They were still seated there, finishing their breakfast, when Alecia emerged from the door that led to Lizzie's house.

"There are *mis preciosos!*" Alecia called out in a singsong way, far louder than necessary. "*Qué linda*, Sofia! Such a beautiful dress! I knew it would fit you just right!" She sounded delighted. "Come to Abuela. Let me see you up close."

Amanda paused, wondering for whose benefit Alecia intended her overly dramatic praise: Sofia or Lizzie? Either way, Amanda knew that she was clearly trying to establish her grandmotherly advantage over Lizzie.

With a sigh, Amanda turned to look at her mother-in-law, who by this time had reached Sofia's side and was twirling her so that her dress spun. And that's when Amanda noticed what Alecia was wearing.

Accustomed to the services she attended back home, Alecia had dressed in her finest wool suit, her hair perfectly coifed and makeup done to excess. She was adorned with a gold cross necklace, several dangling bracelets, and numerous rings on both hands. After all, Alecia would never attend Mass in anything less than her best church attire. To her, it was a sign of respect, as well as proof of her elevated status in her community back home. To Amanda, it was garish and ostentatious.

From the horrified look on her mother's face, Lizzie thought so, too.

"*Ay*, Amanda!" Alecia cried out, clearly impervious to their reactions. "Such a plain dress! And black? You look like you're attending a funeral, *hija!*" She gave a little laugh, as if that would soften her criticism. "Don't you agree with . . . ," she started to say as she turned toward Lizzie. She stopped midsentence when she saw that Amanda's mother was also dressed in a plain black dress. "Oh."

Lizzie pressed her lips together. If Amanda didn't know her mother better, she would say she looked like she was going to roll her eyes. But her mother would never do such a thing. Instead, she said nothing, letting her silence speak loud and clear of her disapproval.

The master bedroom door opened, and Anna walked into the kitchen, a smile on her face as she smoothed the black apron that covered her black dress. She carried Samuel against her hip. Stopping in the center of the kitchen, Anna smiled as she looked at Amanda. "Everyone ready?" When she started to the door, she caught sight of Alecia and hesitated for the briefest of seconds before continuing.

Oblivious, Alecia followed her to the door.

"Where is the car to take us to the Mass?" Alecia asked innocently as Alejandro walked around the side of the barn and joined them.

"Ay, Mami, I keep telling you it's not called Mass," Alejandro corrected her once again.

Alecia waved her hand at him dismissively. "I'm sure it's the same, no matter what you *call* it, Alejandro."

Amanda bit her lower lip, trying to hide her amusement at Alejandro's expression.

"Now, where's the car?" Alecia looked around, and when she noticed that Alejandro had not been warming up the SUV, she turned to question him, a scowl on her face. "You didn't warm it up?"

"We're not going in the car," he responded in a flat voice.

"So how will we get there?" she asked impatiently.

"Your chariot, Mami," Alejandro exclaimed, extending his hand with a grand flourish toward the horse and buggy that Jonas drove toward them. The horse's breath came out of its nostrils as little white puffs of condensation. When Jonas stopped it near where they stood, the horse snorted and jerked its head upward.

"This . . . this is how we are going to church?" Alecia stuttered as she took a step backward and stared in disbelief at the gray-top buggy and chestnut-brown horse. "I . . . I don't . . ." She looked at Alejandro, her eyes open wide. "Is it safe?" she whispered.

"*¡Claro!* Just be quick when you climb in, *sí?*"

Amanda could predict how this would end if she didn't intervene. "Alejandro," she said in a soft voice. "With so many of us . . ." She glanced toward the SUV and then back to him.

He winked at her and laughed as he took his mother's arm. "Come, Mami, I'm teasing you. Jonas will take the children, and I'll drive the rest of us." He guided Alecia toward the car, still chuckling as she swiped at his arm.

Amanda smiled to herself, watching as he helped his mother into the car before returning for Anna. He reached out and took Samuel from her, making a silly noise that made the little boy laugh. Isadora carried a box of the canned beef, walking beside Lizzie while Nicolas raced his sister and cousins toward the buggy.

By eight thirty, they had arrived at the Millers' farm. Amanda slowly opened the car door and got out. She stared at the line of gray-top buggies and the people who were walking toward the farmhouse. For a moment, she felt a sense of dread.

It had been years since she had attended a worship service with most of these people. As she stood on the edge of the driveway, Nicolas clinging to her side, Amanda felt nervous about walking into the house.

"*Kum* now, Amanda," Lizzie said in a soft voice. "No fretting."

Amanda turned toward her mother.

Lizzie gave her a reassuring look. "Take one of these boxes, *ja*? It will get your mind focused on something else."

Isadora walked ahead, holding Elizabeth, with Sylvia clinging to her side. The few words that Isadora remembered in Pennsylvania Dutch from her previous stays at the farm had endeared her to the smallest cousins. They had insisted on riding in the car with Isadora instead of in the buggy with the other children. Meanwhile, Sofia was running with Hannah and Rachel and a small group of children. Amanda hoped her daughter hadn't splattered any mud on her dress.

With the exception of Nicolas, the cousins had all found a happy balance.

"Here, sweetheart," Amanda said as she took one of the boxes from the back of their rental car. "Could you carry one? They aren't heavy at all."

Anna walked around the side of the car, Samuel in her arms. "Aw, now, Amanda," she said, smiling at Nicolas. "Big boy like him? Why, I bet he could carry two of those boxes!"

He grinned at her and eagerly took the box from his mother.

The presence of the SUV in the driveway of an Amish farm caught the eye of several of the men lingering nearby. With their broad-brimmed black hats and identical black suits, the group of men looked fierce as they stared in the direction of the Englische newcomers. Alejandro, however, raised his hand, greeting them with a confident wave. He turned back to the car to help his mother get out.

One look at her face was all that Amanda needed to see to know that Alecia was shocked.

"*¿Qué es eso?*" she asked as she looked around the farm. "This isn't a church, Alejandro!" She spun around and stared at her son, her eyes wide and a confused expression on her face. "It's someone's house, *sí?*"

He took her elbow in his hand and started to guide her toward Amanda. "Mami, I told you . . . ," he said in a low voice.

Amanda tried to intervene. "Alecia, had you forgotten that Amish worship in the homes and not church buildings?"

"I . . . I suppose I had," she stammered, letting Alejandro lead her toward the entrance.

At the door, Alejandro gave Amanda a reassuring smile and silently turned his mother over to her care. Alejandro headed over to where Jonas now stood and began shaking hands with some of the men who lingered outside of the barn. Most families arrived early for the service so that the men and the women could catch up on the latest news and the younger adults on the latest gossip.

"This is all so strange," Alecia whispered to Amanda.

"You'll be fine," Amanda said. "I promise."

Inside the house, the women, all dressed in black dresses, stood in a large semicircle just inside the kitchen, while two younger women were organizing the food that people had brought with them. The room felt very large because the partitions between two rooms had been removed in order to accommodate the two hundred people who would attend the service. Toward the back of the room, simple wooden benches were set up, two sections facing each other with a space in the middle. Amanda knew that was where the bishop and his preachers would give the two sermons.

"Amanda Beiler!"

She looked up as one of the young women hurried over to her and, with a warm smile, shook her hand.

"Katie Miller!"

"*Ach!* Look at you, now!" Katie took a step back. "Why, you haven't changed one bit!"

Amanda knew that wasn't true, at least on the inside. "No more so than anyone else," she replied, trying to sound demure as she deflected the compliment.

"When we heard that you were coming, we thought you'd bring those photographers with you again!" Katie gave a little laugh.

Inwardly, Amanda cringed. She suspected that, at some point, word would spread about their plans to celebrate Christmas in Lititz. But she also knew that if any of the paparazzi showed up, it would not be a media circus like the first time Alejandro stayed at the farm. Back then, so many photographers had camped out at the end of her parents' driveway that the road was almost impassable, and the bishop had asked Amanda to stay with relatives in Ohio until things quieted down.

"*Danke* for having us today," Amanda said, purposefully not responding to Katie's comment. "This is my mother-in-law, Alecia, and my son, Nicolas." She gave Nicolas a little bump with her hip so that he remembered to shake Katie Miller's hand.

"You won't understand much of what the preachers say," Katie said as she greeted them. "It's all in German, you see. But we're glad to welcome you."

Alecia didn't speak, her eyes wandering around the room, looking at the benches and the women.

"Come, Alecia. We must greet the others," Amanda whispered and started to walk toward the waiting line of women. "And don't worry. No one will try to kiss you."

"What?"

Amanda hadn't had time to explain that, at Sunday worship, the women greeted each other with a holy kiss based on Paul's command: *All the brethren greet you. Greet ye one another with a holy kiss.* She knew that this Scriptural practice would surprise Alecia, and she would certainly have questions later. But, for now, Amanda focused on following her sister to greet each woman with a handshake and a kiss on the lips.

Alecia followed and awkwardly shook every woman's hand, the color draining from her cheeks and her eyes wide as if from shock. As they assumed their place at the end of the line, Amanda noticed that Alecia stood close to her, as if afraid to be far removed.

Next to her, Anna held Samuel against her hip while she greeted people.

"Let me," Amanda said, reaching out for the child.

Happily, Anna passed him over to her. He gave Amanda a big smile, displaying the few teeth that he had. As usual, he did not fuss and clung to her side, his big eyes staring over her shoulder at all of the different people standing nearby.

Several of the older women greeted Amanda but continued down the line without pausing to chat. She wasn't surprised nor was she offended. It had been several years since she had been to a worship service, and she was an outsider now, not a part of the community.

Realizing this filled her with a sudden sense of sorrow. Her children would never know what it was like to have a genuine support system like the Amish. The older Isadora, Sofia, and Nicolas grew, the more they would encounter people who merely wanted something. People often tried to use Alejandro and Amanda for their own purposes, usually involving increasing their own wealth or fame. Just like Alejandro used to say to her: everyone seemed to want something from him. So why would it be any different for the rest of their family?

A few minutes later, a hush fell over the gathering. Alecia leaned over and whispered, "What's happening, *hija*?"

Amanda glanced toward the door. The bishop and preachers had entered the house, a signal that the service was about to begin. "It's the bishop, Alecia. Service will begin when they take a seat, but they have to greet the women first."

One by one, the bishop, the preachers, and the host of the worship service slowly walked down the line of women, shaking hands and simply stating, "Good morning."

With great curiosity, Amanda watched as the bishop approached her. The last time she had attended a worship service, he had been visiting another church district, and she hadn't seen him. He had aged over the past few years, his beard still white but thinning and his shoulders stooped forward. When he stood before her, she saw that his skin was light and papery, age spots covering the back of the hand that he stretched out to greet her.

He mumbled, "Good morning" before he recognized her. And then, he paused.

"Good morning, Bishop," she said. She turned to Alecia. "May I introduce my mother-in-law?"

Suspiciously, he eyed Alecia before greeting her and then looked back at Amanda. She wondered what he saw—probably a young woman who was far removed from the Amish girl she had once been, at least on the outside. But she hoped that he could see beyond that. For her heart was still faithful to God, even if she worshiped him privately instead of through a life of humility and plainness.

"It's good to see you," he said in German, before he continued greeting the other women.

Those five simple words took Amanda by surprise. She stared after him for a few drawn-out seconds before she returned her attention to the next man, one of the preachers who stood before her, waiting for her greeting so that he, too, could continue down the line.

Once the bishop and preachers finished, they walked to the benches and sat down in the first row on the left-hand side of the room. Now it was time for the women to take their seats. Since they sat from oldest to youngest, Amanda gestured for Alecia to follow her mother so that she wouldn't have to sit in the back of the room with the young mothers with children.

"Go on," Amanda coaxed. "Mamm will tell you what to do."

But Alecia did not look convinced. Lizzie gave her no choice, standing and waiting for her with an impatient expression on her face. "*Kum* now," she said in a loud whisper. "You'll be holding up the others."

Reluctantly, Alecia went with her, leaving Amanda trying to not smile at her mother-in-law's look of panic.

"Where's Abuela going?" Nicolas asked.

"With Mammi Lizzie. She'll be fine." Amanda reached down and put her hand on his shoulder. "You look very handsome, Nicolas," she said softly. "Now if you can just try to not squirm during the service, Mami will be so proud of you."

He lit up at her words and straightened his shoulders. "I'll try, Mami. But if I have to go potty, don't get mad."

She stifled a laugh, the room being far too quiet to have *that* overlooked.

The women with their children sat down on the benches on one side of the room, facing where the men would sit. The bishop and preachers sat in the center of the room, appearing to be deep in reflective thought. Once the women were settled, the men began to walk into the house from outside. Quietly, they entered the kitchen and walked single file through the benches to assume their spots. Only after they had sat did the unmarried young adults enter, women first and men second. When everyone was finally seated, as if on cue, the men reached up for their black hats and simultaneously set them under the benches where they sat. The movement was fluid, and Amanda smiled when she saw Alecia, who sat two rows in front of her, give a little jump.

Even though she was a guest and not a baptized member of the Amish church, Amanda sat beside her sister on the hard bench. Beside her were Isadora, Sofia, and Nicolas, the three of them staring at everything, taking in all the different sights and sounds of this Amish worship service. After the initial silent prayer, the bishop and preachers left the room, and the congregation started singing a hymn from the Ausbund, a book of songs that had been used in Amish worship for almost five hundred years. The hymns, written in High German, were sung in a slow, a capella style. Despite not understanding the words, Isadora seemed to follow along in the chunky black book that she held in her hands. Sofia and Nicolas, however, began to fidget by the time the first thirty-minute hymn was finished.

Amanda placed her hand on Nicolas's knee and felt him lean against her. Sofia leaned forward and glanced at her, mouthing "How much longer?" Amanda merely shook her head and looked away. Whispering during an Amish church service was simply not allowed.

As the hymn ended, the bishop and preachers returned to the room. Amanda knew that they had left to discuss who would preach the two sermons. She never quite understood why this was an on-the-spot decision, but it had been that way for as long as she could remember.

The bishop stood up in the front of the room. He had been selected to preach the first sermon, the shorter of the two. His voice seemed to rise an octave, and he spoke in a singsong manner, his words a mixture of High German and Pennsylvania Dutch. Beside her, Nicolas sighed, and she began to feel his body go limp. Like several of the other children, he was falling asleep. As the room began to grow warm from so many people sitting there, Amanda knew that others would doze off, even if only for a few minutes.

"And we are all like lost sheep, full of sin and straying from the pasture where the shepherd had led us," the bishop was saying. "It is up to us to find our way home to the pasture of the Lord and not continue wandering farther away. The Lord cannot protect us if we insist on roaming farther and farther away from his house . . ."

Amanda blinked, focusing on the bishop's words. *She* felt like a lost sheep. All of these years, she had struggled to find her way in Alejandro's world. And she had adapted. But in doing so, she had lost her ties to her roots. That realization didn't surprise her. What did give her reason for pause was how many things she missed about her life as an Amish woman. While she wouldn't have changed anything about her decision to marry Alejandro—for he was, undoubtedly, the man that God intended for her—she would change a lot about their lifestyle.

Starting with her children and how much of the world they had been exposed to and at such a young age.

Anna nudged her and startled her from her thoughts. From somewhere in the room, a cell phone vibrated. Inwardly, she groaned, knowing full well that there was not one Amish person, not even the most rebellious youth, sitting in that room who would have dared to bring a cell phone into the service. And that meant one of only three people were the guilty parties: Alejandro, Isadora, or Alecia.

On the bench ahead of her, Amanda thought she saw Alecia glance in the direction of the vibration. Thankfully, she had not drawn more attention to herself by standing up and excusing herself to leave the room so that she could answer it.

By the time the noise had disappeared and Amanda had refocused her attention on the worship service, she realized that the bishop had stopped preaching, and now the congregation was singing the second hymn, "Das Loblied." Without referencing the black chunky hymnbook in her hands, Amanda let her voice join the other members as they sang the hymn of praise to God:

> O God, Father, we praise thee
> And thy kindness glorify.
> Which thou, oh Lord, so mercifully
> To us anew has shown.
> And hast us, Lord, together led
> Us to admonish through thy word,
> Bestow on us thy grace.

As the congregation sang the last line, Amanda looked across the heads of the women seated before her, her eyes scanning the faces of the men who sat on the opposite side of the room. She located Alejandro, who was sitting beside Jonas, among the other married men. He looked so out of place among the Amish men, with their mustache-less beards and simple haircuts. Yet he also looked at peace.

He must have sensed her gaze, and he smiled, just a little. She remembered the first time that he had attended a worship service with her and her parents. When someone had teased him about not understanding a word of what had been said and sung, Alejandro had replied that music transcended the limitations of language.

It was almost noon before the service ended. By that time, even Amanda felt antsy, and her body ached from sitting on the hard bench for so long. As they stood up, she saw Anna rubbing her back as she stretched.

"Bet you don't miss those long sermons," Anna whispered as they moved to the side of the room.

Amanda tried to keep a straight face. The preacher of the second sermon had been especially long-winded today, and his monotone voice had sent her mind drifting to other things. She had been thankful when he finally stopped and the final hymn began.

The men, including Alejandro, began to convert the benches into long tables for the fellowship meal by slipping the legs of the benches into wooden trestles. The smaller boys dashed around the room, collecting the Ausbunds and setting them inside wooden crates that would be stored in the church wagon for use at the next service. To Amanda's surprise, she saw her son participating in the cleanup, helping a young Amish boy who took the books as Nicolas handed them to him.

"I think he's found a friend," Amanda said to Anna, gesturing toward the two boys.

"Oh, he's all boy, isn't he now?"

Lizzie and Alecia walked through the gathering and joined them in the back of the room. Alecia looked tired, her eyes watering, and Amanda guessed she had fallen asleep during the service.

"How'd you like the service, Alecia?" Anna asked.

"Three hours is long, no?"

Amanda bit her lower lip to keep herself from showing her amusement.

"What is happening now, *hija*?"

"They'll set up two long tables, and we'll sit for some food," she explained. "And after that, we'll return home to relax and visit."

Realizing what she had said, Amanda turned away to avoid the look of surprise that Alecia gave to her. Had she really called it home? It was an unintentional slip, but the expression on Alecia's face gave the word more importance than Amanda had meant.

Behind her, a man cleared his throat, and Amanda looked up in surprise when she saw that the bishop stood there, trying to get her attention.

"Amanda Beiler," he said. "I heard you were coming for Christmas."

She wanted to correct him that her name was Amanda Diaz, not Beiler, but she bit her tongue. "It's good to see you," she said.

He glanced at Isadora, who stood beside her, and he nodded. "Your *dochder, ja?*"

Amanda had forgotten that he knew Isadora from so many years ago.

Returning his attention to Amanda, he switched to Pennsylvania Dutch and said, "And your thoughts on the sermon? Did you enjoy it?"

If she had been surprised that he approached her, singling her out from the other worshippers, she was even more surprised at his question. "I did," she responded.

His lips twitched, just a little, as if he wanted to say something more, but instead he just said, "I'm glad," and walked away to join the men.

Amanda stared after him, even more dumbfounded. "What on earth . . . ?"

Lizzie placed her hand on Amanda's arm. "Didn't you listen to his sermon, *dochder?*"

Amanda turned to her mother, a look of disbelief crossing her face. Had the bishop's sermon been intended to send her a message? Did he consider her a lost sheep that had left God's given pasture? He had always been critical of her leaving the community, probably feeling as if she had strayed off the path that God had chosen for her. But she felt the opposite way. God led her to Alejandro. And despite what the bishop might think, she was a good wife and a good mother. More important, she always behaved in accordance with God's will.

"Did he have me in mind when he preached the sermon?" Amanda asked, more than a little irritated at the suggestion. "Was he trying to send me a message about my choices?"

At this, Lizzie merely shook her head. "Oh, Amanda, have you been in the world of the Englische so long that you only see shadows instead of the light?" And then, Lizzie smiled. "*Nee,* Amanda, he wasn't sending you a message about your choices. That was his way of saying welcome home."

Leaving her daughter at a loss for words, Lizzie quietly walked away to go assist the other women who had busied themselves in the kitchen, setting the food into the dishes that would be passed around during fellowship. Amanda stood there, amazed by her mother's words and pondering what message, exactly, the bishop was sending.

Chapter Twelve

In the early-morning hours, the only light in the room came from the small kerosene lantern that Alejandro had lit when he'd first woken. The flame flickered, creating a warm light that barely filled the room. The sun was not due to rise for a while, but already Amanda could hear and smell the stirrings of a new day on the farm. There was the faint scent of coffee, which meant Anna must be already up, and the distant mooing of the cows anxious for their morning milking.

In Miami, even with the endless succession of late-night concerts or recording sessions, it wasn't unusual to see Alejandro rise early. He was a night owl by necessity, up all hours of the night and well into the early dawn hours until he would finally be able to rest his head on a pillow, hoping for a few hours of uninterrupted sleep before the cycle would begin all over again. Sometimes it caught up with him, and he'd sleep for almost an entire day.

Amanda would have thought that Alejandro would have used this time away from Miami and his crazy schedule of work to sleep in. Instead, Alejandro had been one of the first ones up, eager to start each day with this new routine—one he was not accustomed to but seemed to embrace with apparent enthusiasm. Amanda was coming to the realization that country life suited him, and she even wondered if he would ever consider giving up all of his fame if offered the chance to lead the unrushed plain life of a farmer.

Alejandro stood by the side of the bed as he quickly slipped a work shirt over his white sleeveless undershirt. Amanda sat, her pillow pressed behind the small of her back against the very same wooden headboard she'd had as a child, and watched him, curious as to what he was thinking. The previous evening he had been especially jovial and had even played a few rounds of checkers with Hannah and Rachel after supper while Amanda and Anna were busy cleaning up the dishes. During her youth, Amanda had been especially fond of these quiet moments after everyone had eaten and wound down for the night. They would stand at the sink, Anna washing and Amanda hand-drying the dishes while their parents talked about the day's events. Last night, however, while they worked, Anna and Amanda had shared stories of their childhood. Sometimes one of them would laugh out loud, and Alecia or Lizzie would look up and smile. It was so nice to have everybody under one roof. Amanda could hardly remember the last time she had been with all her children and Alejandro in the same house, let alone the same room, just relaxing and enjoying each other's company.

Now, however, Alejandro appeared deep in thought.

"Why didn't you tell me, Amanda?"

The question caught her off guard. "Tell you what, Alejandro?"

"About Samuel," he said as he finished buttoning his shirt.

Ah, she thought, Anna's son. That was the reason why he seemed so serious. She wondered if he had been more insightful than she had, whether he had figured it out on his own or if Jonas had told him. After all, the fact that Samuel rarely cried, slept a lot, and kept silent for extended periods of time had not struck Amanda as odd. At least not at first. When they'd arrived, she hadn't even noticed that he wasn't sitting up on his own, at least not without support, because he was always in the arms of his mother or one of his older siblings.

"She only told me yesterday morning before church," Amanda replied, lowering her voice so that no one might overhear her from the other side of the bedroom door. "We were both so tired last night that I didn't have a chance to tell you."

Alejandro gave a slight nod of his head as he grabbed a gray knit sweater that hung on a wooden peg on the wall, near the door to their room. "It was a busy day, *sí*?"

And today would be no different, she realized.

Despite being so far along in her pregnancy, Anna certainly kept busy. The more time that Anna spent with her, the harder it became for Amanda to remember the sister of her youth. She had changed so much since Amanda last saw her.

"I noticed something about my sister," Amanda went on, lowering her voice just in case anyone was awake on the second floor of the house. "She's just so"—Amanda tried to think of the proper word—"content."

Alejandro frowned. "She was always content, no? I don't recall her ever being unhappy."

Amanda shook her head. "You didn't know her after Aaron died. She was so quiet and withdrawn. And then when she returned with Jonas, she was happy, Alejandro, but not like this. Not the way she is happy today."

He questioned her silently, with the raising of his eyebrows.

"And about Samuel," Amanda continued. "I thought it was so sad when she first told me. But her attitude about it is so . . ."

As she struggled to describe what she had observed, Alejandro finished the sentence for her. "Inspirational, *sí*?"

That was not the word Amanda would have chosen. Hearing it from Alejandro, she was taken aback. After so many years of inspiring millions of people through his own music, his comment made her realize that he, too, needed moments of motivation from others.

"I was going to say positive and so optimistic," she said slowly. But Alejandro was right. Inspiring seemed to be much more fitting. "It makes me realize how much people take for granted. If a person truly has faith, he or she knows that God will never give us a burden too heavy for us to carry."

Alejandro slipped the sweater over his head. *"¡Exactamente!"* He ran his fingers through his hair and straightened the front of his sweater. "And that, Princesa, is why I find it inspirational."

He sat down beside her on the bed. Amanda reached out to gently pluck a piece of lint from his sleeve. She was suddenly struck by how handsome her husband looked in his simple clothes. He didn't need all of those fancy designer suits or the dark sunglasses. To her, he was always attractive, but even more so here, in her childhood bedroom, under the glow of a simple kerosene lantern.

"I reckon you're right. It *is* inspiring. We have so much that we take for granted, we forget to take joy in the precious little gifts that God gives us along the way."

Leaning forward, he pressed his lips against her forehead. "Indeed, *mi amor.* It's refreshing to forget all of the stress and just . . ." He paused, thinking of the right word. "Just be. No schedules. No tours. No frantic phone calls. No interviews."

She smiled. "It suits you very well actually, you know."

"When was the last time we did this? Just escape from everything?" he asked, his forehead furrowed in thought.

She tried not to laugh. "Have we *ever* done this, Alejandro?"

He made a noise deep in his throat and stood up. "We need to do it more, then," he replied absentmindedly as he started to walk toward the door. "I'll see you at breakfast, Princesa, after the morning milking, *sí?*"

This time Amanda did laugh out loud, and Alejandro stopped.

"What is so funny, Princesa?" he asked.

"Oh, Alejandro, if all of your fans could see and hear you right now, getting ready to go milk cows in those clothes, they would laugh, too. That's for sure and certain!"

Turning around, his hand on the door handle, he gave her a big wink and quipped, "Got to go milk my cows, Princesa, because they can't wait. But you sure can, *that's for sure and certain.*" And with this, he made his exit, leaving Amanda with a smile on her face.

Anna and Amanda stood side by side in Hannah Zook's kitchen. The children were next to the kitchen table, their eyes eagerly staring at the large piles of cookies and brownies that adorned the different plates and serving trays. But first, they had to wait for the end of the silent prayer.

Most of the children were younger than Sofia and Nicolas, as the older children were still in school. The girls Isadora's age had finished their eighth-grade studies, and they stood in the background, waiting to help their younger siblings if needed.

"I haven't been to a cookie swap since . . ." Amanda paused as she tried to remember. "Why, I don't even know when the last one was, I reckon!"

Anna rubbed at the small of her back. "Probably when Aaron was still alive, *ja?*"

The casual way that Anna mentioned their deceased younger brother surprised Amanda, especially since that tragedy had triggered so much pain in their family. And it was even more surprising given that they were standing in the kitchen of Hannah Zook, the young woman who had married Anna's former suitor, Menno.

Just thirty minutes had passed since they had arrived at the Zooks' farmhouse and Amanda hadn't known exactly what to say when their hostess greeted her. After all, besides marrying Menno Zook, Hannah had also been rude to Amanda during one of her visits back to Lititz after she'd left the church and married Alejandro.

But Amanda sensed no animosity between Anna and Hannah Zook. Instead, they greeted each other as if there was no unhappy history to connect their pasts. Whatever feelings Anna may have previously harbored against Menno and his wife, Amanda could sense nothing amiss between them now.

Of course, she reminded herself, Menno broke off his engagement to Anna over ten years ago. Time had a way of healing old wounds, she reckoned.

To Amanda's relief, Lizzie interrupted them. "Your back hurting you again, Anna? Mayhaps you should see that doctor before the holiday weekend begins. You know how those Englische doctors disappear during Christmas."

"It's fine, Mamm," Anna said. "Just aches from church service yesterday. Those benches and this baby don't seem to care much for each other. You worry too much."

"That's what mothers do, Anna. Worry," Lizzie said in a point-blank manner, looking from Anna to Amanda as she spoke. Alecia nodded her head in agreement and put her arm around Lizzie's waist, which caught both Amanda and Lizzie off guard. Amanda had never thought of Alecia as particularly motherly, though being a single parent must have left her with plenty to worry about. Amanda knew that during Alejandro's youth, her mother-in-law had struggled to put food on the table and keep a roof over their heads. Like any woman with a strong maternal drive, Lizzie or Alecia would do anything for their children and grandchildren.

"*Sí*, Amanda, your mother is right. Mothers *always* worry about their children, even after they are all grown up and have lives of their own," Alecia said.

Amanda understood that the words her mother spoke were meant for her as much as for Anna. Amanda nodded and smiled at both her mother and Alecia. She was more appreciative of what her mother meant now that she herself was a mother. She thought of Sofia, Nicolas, and Isadora. Not a day went by without her praying for them. There was nothing a mother wanted more than for her children to be safe, healthy, and happy.

When they were finished swapping the cookies, Anna and Amanda gathered all the children together to leave. Everyone, even the littlest ones, carried a small tin in their hands, filled with all sorts of delicious holiday cookies to take home. There were bound to be visitors dropping in for a visit over the next few days, and the cookies would surely come in handy.

It was a short walk back to the farm, but it was cold outside, colder than it had been in the last few days. A few flakes of snow had begun to fall as they bundled themselves up and made sure all the children had the mates to their mittens. When Amanda looked behind her as she walked down the road holding the youngest ones' hands, she saw Lizzie and Alecia lagging behind, their heads closer than usual as they chatted for the rest of the way home.

Chapter Thirteen

Nicolas clung to Amanda, his arms thrown around her neck as she held him while he sobbed into her shoulder.

They sat on the sofa in Anna's kitchen, Amanda attempting to calm down her son while feeling too aware that Sylvia and Elizabeth were watching the unfolding and far-too-dramatic scene with a mixture of interest and concern. Thankfully, Anna was in the master bedroom tending to Samuel's needs and was not privy to Nicolas's meltdown.

"Please, Nicolas," Amanda pleaded as she rubbed his back. "It's only for a few hours."

But he remained inconsolable.

Sofia bounced down the stairs, the small heels of her little black boots slapping against each wooden step. Behind her trailed Isadora.

"What's wrong with him?" Sofia asked when she reached the bottom step.

Amanda gave her a warning look.

Reading her mother's thoughts, Isadora quickly walked over to Sofia and put her hand on her sister's shoulder. "Did I show you where Katie Cat used to sleep?" Her eyes shifted to where Sylvia and Elizabeth stood. "Want me to show you?"

As Isadora led her sister and two cousins outside, pausing to make certain they put on their coats, Amanda sighed in relief. Her daughter's gentleness with the younger cousins was becoming such a blessing, especially when Nicolas was so out of sorts.

For a few moments, she held her son and rubbed his back, hoping that he would calm down before Alejandro returned from helping Jonas with the horse and buggy. Without an audience, Nicolas's theatrics began to dissipate and were far less embarrassing by the time Anna emerged from her bedroom, carrying Samuel in her arms.

"Wie gehts?" Anna asked, moving to the rocking chair next to the sofa. Noticing the boy's sullen face, she settled Samuel onto her lap before reaching out to gently touch Nicolas's leg, which hung over Amanda's lap.

"Someone doesn't quite want to go with us, I reckon," Amanda said as she met her sister's inquiring eyes.

Anna clicked her tongue and shook her head in a lighthearted manner. "Such a big boy like you? Crying over something like that? Pshaw!"

With a sloppy sniffle, Nicolas moved his head so that his face was no longer burrowed into Amanda's shoulders. Just from the way he was turned, Amanda could tell that he was peering at Anna with those big blue eyes.

"Why, I heard Jonas telling your *papi* how he wanted to ask you to help them this afternoon in the barn after we return home from the quilting." She pretended to look disappointed as she shook her head. "Reckon Jonas will see you fussing and mayhaps he won't ask."

Curiosity got the better of the boy. "Helping in the barn? With what?" he asked, his voice betraying a mixture of disbelief and anticipation.

"Oh, things that only a big boy can help with!" Anna nonchalantly replied, knowing only too well that she had piqued the boy's interest. Then, leaning back in the rocking chair and repositioning Samuel so that his back was pressed against her chest, she gestured toward the child. "Why, you don't know how much your *onkel* was excited about you being here! He couldn't wait to show you how to milk the cows and feed the horses."

"He was?" Nicolas asked with a tone of incredulous but guarded excitement.

Anna nodded her head in an overly exaggerated way. "Oh *ja*! That he was, for sure and certain." She paused as if pretending to think. "Why, I even recall him mentioning letting you hold the reins of the horse and driving the buggy!"

Amanda felt Nicolas draw a deep breath.

Waving her hand in the air, as if dismissing the subject, Anna continued. "But no worries, Nicolas. Jonas can make do on his own." She sighed. "Just such a shame, seeing how much he was looking forward to it, seeing that he doesn't have a son to help." Another pause and then she added, "At least not a big one that could be as helpful as you."

Nicolas straightened up and let his eyes drop from Anna's to study Samuel. "He's gonna have to wait a long time for Samuel to help out," he remarked in a serious voice.

"That's right." Anna nodded thoughtfully.

Amanda glanced at her sister's face and was surprised to see that there was no sign of sorrow when she agreed with Nicolas. Anna's acceptance of Samuel's affliction surprised even Amanda. After all, with the new baby being a girl, there would be no future sons to help Jonas with the farm. That responsibility would be left on Jonas's shoulders and those of his daughters until they were married.

"But you're having another baby, I think?" Nicolas's eyes cast down to Anna's waist.

Anna let her free hand fall onto her enlarged stomach, barely able to contain a smile. "*Ja*, I am." She leaned forward, forcing a very serious look on her face as she motioned for Nicolas to come closer as if she wanted to tell him a secret. "But it's a girl baby. So Jonas was really looking forward to having a big boy helping him in the barn." She sat up straight and gave a little shrug. "But big boys don't sass their *mamm*, that's for sure and certain."

Nicolas remained quiet, his one hand still on Amanda's shoulder, but his grip loosened. He seemed to be contemplating Anna's words. "Well," he started slowly, "as long as I only have to go for a *few* hours . . ."

Amanda patted his back and kissed the top of his head. "That's a good decision, Nicolas. Your uncle will be so pleased."

He seemed to straighten his shoulders at her compliment. "Even though those cows sure do stink."

"Nicolas!" Amanda tightened her hold on his waist, horrified at his words.

"And no more girlie cooking things?" he asked, not heeding his mother's reprimand.

Anna laughed, her eyes crinkling. Once again, Amanda was struck by the thought that her sister looked truly joyful and at peace. Such a difference from the years immediately following Aaron's death, when Anna had fallen into a depression.

"We can color instead, *ja?*" Anna said to her nephew. "While your cousins are at school."

That activity seemed to satisfy him much better, and he nodded his head empathically.

Now that he had calmed down, Amanda suggested that he run outside to find the others and see where Katie Cat had been born in the barn. Eager to escape the confines of the house, and clearly having forgotten about having been upset earlier, he scampered down from Amanda's lap and ran as fast as he could toward the door.

"And no going near those horses by yourself, you hear, Nicolas?" Amanda called out after him.

Anna watched him, a smile still on her face. "That boy—"

"Is a handful!" Amanda finished her sentence. "It's amazing how different children can be, isn't it?"

"*Ja, vell,* he *is* a boy." Anna returned her attention to Amanda. "And he reminds me of a miniature version of Alejandro." Amanda chuckled when imagining Alejandro as a little boy and had to agree with her sister. Nicolas was, indeed, the spitting image of his father.

The door that connected the kitchen to the *grossdaadihaus* opened, and Lizzie entered, a frown on her face. Without a word, she walked over to the table and sat down in a chair. Clearly, something was bothering her.

"Mamm?" Amanda sat next to her and reached out for her mother's hand. "What's wrong? You feeling all right?"

"Hmmph."

Amanda looked over at Anna, who merely shrugged in response.

"What is it, Mamm?" Amanda insisted.

"That *woman.*"

For a split second, Amanda shut her eyes and inhaled sharply. Alecia. Of course.

"What happened, Mamm?" Amanda asked in a soft voice, her eyes glancing toward the door in case Alecia walked in.

"She is *cooking,*" Lizzie said, as if that was a criminal offense. "Preparing food for supper!"

Anna laughed. "Oh, Mamm."

"And reorganizing my pantry while she's doing it! I scarce know what to say to such a thing!" Lizzie stared at Amanda as if she expected her to do something about her mother-in-law.

"You can just reorganize it when she leaves," Amanda reassured her. "It isn't such a horrible thing, is it? A little reorganization?"

"I suppose not, but she keeps talking to herself. I can't understand her half the time," Lizzie confessed. "But mayhaps it's better that way."

"I imagine that she feels most comfortable when cooking. I think it's very hospitable of you, Mamm, to make her feel at home. I'm sure she appreciates your kindness," Amanda remarked. "Besides, the two of you seem to get along quite well."

"Hmmph, I suppose so," her mother mumbled underneath her breath. While they did appear the most unlikely of friends, clearly a bond was developing between the two women, despite Lizzie's irritation at Alecia's invasion of her kitchen, the heart of any Amish woman's home. "I just hope I recognize my kitchen when I get it back."

Both Anna and Amanda laughed.

By ten o'clock, a large van pulled into the driveway to pick them up for the quilting bee. Since Alejandro and Jonas had taken the SUV to the horse auction and there were too many of them to fit into the buggy, Lizzie had made alternative transportation arrangements with a Mennonite neighbor. It was only a short ride to the Kings' farm, where the quilting bee was being held, but Amanda enjoyed looking out the window. She had forgotten how peaceful the landscape of her childhood could be.

When they arrived at the Kings' farm, the driveway looked as full as the driveway from the church service on Sunday. Inside the stone farmhouse, the kitchen was crowded with Amish women, their dresses a rainbow of dark colors: navy blue, hunter green, deep burgundy, brown. Very few of them wore bright colors, such as pink, yellow, or purple, although several of the smaller children did.

No sooner had they walked into the house than one of the older girls from church came over and greeted Isadora as if they were old friends. Within seconds, Isadora walked off with her new friend to join the other fourteen-year-olds, who stood on the other side of the room.

"Barbie King," Anna whispered in Amanda's ear.

"Ah, of course." Amanda watched as Isadora greeted the other girls. An enthusiastic Barbie immediately introduced Isadora to two of her friends who had not been at the church service. Amanda hadn't initially made the connection between the young girl and the house that was hosting the quilting bee. After all, King was a popular name in the Lititz community.

But now, as she observed her daughter blending in with the Amish girls, Amanda couldn't pull her gaze away. The sight of Isadora laughing with the others was simply mesmerizing. When was the last time that she'd seen anyone pay such attention to her daughter? Attention on Isadora as a person, *not* as the daughter of a celebrity.

"Why, Amanda Beiler!" an older woman said in a warm, friendly voice. "I don't believe my eyes!"

Amanda smiled at the woman who approached her.

"My word, child! You are all grown up and then some!" She made a clicking noise with her tongue. With her thinning white hair and the thick glasses that covered the deep sun-weathered wrinkles under her eyes, the woman looked older than Lizzie, and although she seemed somewhat familiar, Amanda couldn't quite recognize her.

"Why, you don't remember who I am, do you?"

Embarrassed, Amanda dug deep into her memory. A spark of recognition began to grow.

"Katie Lapp," the woman said.

"Of course, of course." Amanda could feel the heat rising to her cheeks. She still wasn't certain who this woman was. After all, the name Katie Lapp was also rather common. "I'm terribly sorry I didn't recall your name," she said, still racking her memory to place the woman in her past.

Katie waved her hand at Amanda, dismissing her forgetfulness. "Nothing to fret about, child. Why, I haven't seen you in years, and mayhaps I wouldn't have recognized you, either, if I hadn't heard you were coming home for the holiday!" Clutching her hands together over her stomach, Katie rocked just a little on her heels. "And, of course, my Sylvia and her husband do remember your husband visiting with them when he first came out here." When Amanda frowned, puzzled over this remark, Katie quickly added, "Right after your accident."

Vaguely, she recalled the memory of her father, Elias, taking Alejandro to Jake Edwards's horse farm. He had returned amazed at how beautiful Jake Edwards's place was. "How are Sylvia and Jake?"

Katie smiled at a woman who was walking past them but kept her attention on Amanda. "Oh, she's just fine, Amanda. *Danke*. Six children and another one on the way. I do miss living over that way, but I've moved to my younger son's *haus* in Lititz just two years past." She paused. "After my Jonas died, you see."

Amanda was too embarrassed to admit that she had never learned of Jonas Lapp's death. It made her wonder what other things she had missed over the years: births, marriages, deaths. The cycle of life, and yet by living in the world of the Englische, the only life that she focused on was her own with Alejandro. The rest of the world seemed so removed—and no one thought to update them on anything that didn't impact their own.

"I'm so sorry, Katie."

"*Nee*, he's with God now. Much better place, don't you think?"

Amanda felt a hand on her shoulder and glanced to her left, relieved to see her mother standing there.

"Now, Katie," Lizzie said in a teasing tone, placing her hand on Amanda's arm as she guided her toward the back of the room, where the women were beginning to take seats to start quilting. "You best not monopolize my *dochder*. It's rare enough that I get to see her, too!"

While there was no malice in her mother's words, Amanda felt the sting of the unspoken complaint. She was a stranger in her family's world. And she didn't feel like she fit in. Even more telling was that the more she realized that she didn't belong, the more she realized how much she had missed it.

In the middle of the Kings' large gathering room, typically used only for hosting worship services or the rare weddings and funerals, there was a large wooden quilting frame with a mixture of kitchen and plastic folding chairs. A beautiful quilt stretched out between the eight-by-twelve-foot rails. Around the frame, most of the chairs were occupied by women, their heads tipped down as they worked on quilting the section in front of them.

Amanda sat next to her mother, still feeling more than a little out of place, even though everyone had greeted her with nothing but kindness. Anna sat on the other side of the quilt and talked with two of her friends, women who Amanda did not recognize. The older women focused on the quilt more than the company.

Reaching for the needle and thimble that her mother had brought for her, Amanda looked down at the quilt. The pattern, the Grand Dahlia, resembled a beautiful flower with seven rings of petals surrounding the center. Each ring of petals had been carefully cut and pieced together to make the top of the quilt. By the time all of the women finished making their tiny stitches to attach the quilt top to the batting and bottom fabric, over 1,600 yards of thread would be used.

But it wasn't just the work that brought everyone together. It was the camaraderie of women being together, making something with love, for a young couple in their church district or family. In this case, the quilt would be gifted to one of the Kings' younger daughters, who had just married the previous November.

Amanda took a deep breath and started to thread her needle. She missed the eye three times before someone leaned over and tossed her a pair of glasses.

Surprised, Amanda looked up in time to see Katie Lapp nod at her.

"*Danke*, Katie," Amanda said.

"No readers in that Englische world of yours, Amanda?" another woman teased, causing several women to chuckle.

Amanda remembered far too well the teasing tongue of Amish women seated around a quilt. She took no offense at being the object of a little ribbing. But she didn't feel comfortable trying to poke fun back. Instead, she put on the glasses and quickly threaded the needle.

When she finished, she borrowed her mother's small scissors to snip the thread before she gently tossed the glasses back to Katie Lapp.

"Why, Lizzie!" said Mary King. She was an older relative, who sat near the corner of the quilting frame. "You gave no mention that your granddaughter was such a good quilter!"

Amanda looked up, following her mother's gaze to where her daughter sat with Barbie King, who was showing Isadora how to quilt.

"Oh, Mary!" Lizzie shot back good-naturedly. "She's no better or worse than any other Englischer, I'm sure."

The other women laughed, and Amanda joined them.

"Now, Barbie, girl, you make certain that you teach proper now," Mary shouted across the quilt. "Her *grossmammi* says she quilts as good as any Englischer, so that means you best keep an eye on her, then!"

Barbie looked up and made a playful face. "*Ja,* Aendi. I'll keep an eye on her. What is it you do? Twelve stitches an inch?"

The women laughed again, and Mary pretended to take offense.

"Oh, you!" She shook her head and clucked her tongue. "You know perfectly well that I'm a ten-stitch quilter now. But those ten are perfectly tiny and even stitches. I'll leave twelve stitches to the young ones with steady hands and perfect vision."

The teasing continued well into the afternoon with a sprinkling of good old-fashioned gossip, making the gathering livelier than Amanda remembered from her youth. Sitting next to her mother, she felt a sense of peace and calm wash over her. When was the last time that she had enjoyed such a relaxing time with other women? Whenever she was with other women, it was always at an event, typically a fund-raiser where people would rather take photos with her than talk to her.

She thought back to the woman she had met in Michigan. It had been the closest she'd come to shedding her celebrity status and merely being a regular person engaged in a dialogue that didn't involve someone telling her how much they loved her. How could so many people love her if they didn't know her? It was a question she had asked from the very beginning of her relationship with Alejandro. The artificial affection so many felt for her weighed heavily on her conscience. Was fame so important that people forgot that she was a regular person, too?

Despite all of her good works to raise awareness of self-esteem and to raise money for the children's cancer center, Amanda had never embraced the concept of fame alone being a reason to adore a person. Such energy should be put where it belonged: with Jesus and each person's effort to follow in his spiritual path.

But unlike the Amish, Amanda was raising her children in a society influenced by fame, beauty, and power—not God.

Amanda dipped her head, concentrating on her stitches as she listened to the other women. If only she could change that, she thought. What a better world it would be for her children.

"Mami!" Sofia ran up to her, jumping up and down excitedly. "Guess what Aunt Anna said!"

Earlier, when they had arrived home from the quilting at four o'clock, Nicolas and Sofia had disappeared to help the men with the milking as Amanda prepared supper with the help of Alecia and Isadora. Anna had lain down for a short nap while Lizzie entertained the grandchildren.

Right after the supper meal, while the men went out to the barn to feed the livestock, Amanda had taken Samuel for a short walk, pushing him in a stroller down the lane. The air was cold, and they were both bundled up, Amanda in a thick coat she borrowed from Anna and Samuel under several layers of lap blankets. By the time they'd returned to the house, Samuel was sleeping, and Sofia was bursting with excitement. Amanda could hardly imagine what had made Sofia so enthusiastically happy in such a short period of time. Behind her, however, Nicolas stood with a long face, clearly not feeling as animated about what had overjoyed his sister.

"It must be something *wunderbar* to have you so happy, *mija*!"

Sofia nodded, a big grin lighting up her face. "Anna said that we could go to school with Hannah and Rachel tomorrow!"

Nicolas scowled.

Amanda laughed at the different reactions of her two children. "Now, Nicolas, that should be fun! You can sit in the same schoolhouse where I used to attend! And it will be interesting to experience an Amish school day."

He crossed his arms over his chest and pouted. "I don't know why we have to go to school on our vacation. It's our vacation! I'd rather help Jonas with the milking all day!"

Amanda smiled as his scowl turned into an enthusiastic grin. "You enjoyed that, *ja*?"

He nodded. "Oh *sí*! I did, Mami. Why, I even got to pull at their others!"

Sofia laughed. "Others? You mean *udders*!" She nudged him with her elbow. "That's why you have to go to school, goose! You aren't smart enough to know one udder from another!"

Her joke caught Amanda off guard, but when she realized what Sofia has said, she couldn't hold back her laughter. Amanda gave Sofia a quick hug. "Oh, *mi amor*, that was priceless."

Not understanding the joke, Nicolas continued to scowl.

Sofia was clearly undeterred by Nicolas's long face. "Maybe I could wear one of their dresses," she said. "And you could fix my hair like theirs?"

"I'm sure we could ask Hannah. You would look especially pretty in a blue dress."

Sofia looked up toward the sky as if contemplating the suggestion. "Can you help me ask if they would let me?"

Amanda put her arm around her daughter's shoulders and leaned over, planting a soft kiss on Sofia's head. "Of course, *mija*. Let's go upstairs, and while you are getting ready for bed, I'll ask them."

"Bed?" Nicolas practically choked on the word. "It's not bedtime yet!"

"You want to help with the cows in the morning, *ja*?" Amanda waited for him to take her hand so that she could lead him to the stairs. "Sylvia and Elizabeth must be upstairs getting read for bed. And Samuel is already sleeping in his stroller. I'm sure Hannah and Rachel are soon to follow." After dinner, Isadora had gone over to the *grossdaadihaus* to help Alecia with something, Hannah and Rachel tagging along with her. After the long day, Amanda wanted nothing more than to get the children situated so she could sink into her own comfortable bed under the heavy quilts. Her back ached and her eyes stung from quilting for so long.

Once upstairs, Amanda knocked on Hannah's bedroom door and inquired about Sofia's borrowing a dress. Hannah giggled and nodded her head.

"Here, Amanda," she said as she took down a blue dress that hung on a hanger from a peg on the wall. "This should fit her, I reckon."

Amanda took the dress and looked at it. "So pretty, Hannah. Did you make this yourself or did your *mamm*?"

"Mamm did," she admitted before quickly adding, "but I helped. I like sewing. Mayhaps I could make a dress for Sofia to keep?"

Amanda felt her heart warm at her niece's generous idea. "I'm sure that Sofia would love that, but I would only agree if she helps you."

Hannah smiled and nodded her head enthusiastically.

When she returned to the room Sofia and Nicolas shared with Isadora, Amanda held the dress up and asked, "What do you think?" She watched as Sofia studied the dress, her lips pursed and to the side. Amanda wondered what her daughter was thinking. Back at home, such a dress would have been far too plain for Sofia's taste. Now, however, when she just wanted to fit in with the others, a plain and simple dress might actually appeal to her. How ironic, Amanda thought. "Mayhaps with your white sweater?"

Sofia made a face. "Mami! The other girls don't wear white sweaters!"

"Well, I'm sure I can borrow a black one for you, then."

Satisfied, Sofia nodded. "All right, then. I think that will do."

With unbridled excitement, Sofia climbed into the bed and snuggled under the blankets. Nicolas, however, still wasn't convinced that going to school was something he had any interest in doing.

Amanda sat on the edge of Sofia's mattress. "Mammi Lizzie will be pleased to see you in this dress tomorrow."

She could only imagine that Alecia would be appalled. Unless a dress had frills and lace, Alecia felt it was too plain. And while she had been adapting well to the Amish environment, there were plenty of moments when Alecia seemed to share her disapproval with either silent criticism or unusual resolve about some things that were going on. Most of the time Amanda couldn't decide which one it was.

After tucking them into bed, Amanda gave Nicolas and Sofia a kiss and got up to leave.

"Mami?"

She paused at the door and looked over her shoulder at her son. "*Ja*, Nicolas?"

"Do you think I'll like going to the school tomorrow? It's not forever, right?"

She smiled and shook her head. "Of course not. Our home is in Miami. And so is your school."

Sofia made a scoffing noise as she started to roll over. "Miami isn't as much fun as here."

Amanda's eyes widened in surprise as she stood in the doorway. She stared at her daughter, wondering whether she should respond. She knew that Sofia was getting along well with Hannah and Rachel.

She even seemed to like playing with Sylvia and Elizabeth, although she didn't pay much attention to Samuel. But Amanda couldn't believe that she had just heard her daughter favor Lititz over Miami. A week ago, she never would have believed it was possible.

"It's just new and different," Amanda replied at last. "Everything is much more exciting when you experience it for the first time. But home will never change."

"It changed for you when you married Papi," Nicolas pointed out. "This was your home first, no?"

Amanda stared at him, amazed that such a wise observation had come out of her youngest child's mouth. Quickly, she replied, "That's different."

And yet, she wasn't so sure whether it was different.

Yes, it had been a new experience when she had left Lititz to travel with Alejandro. A life-altering experience. Quite exciting, to say the least. And while she loved Alejandro and the children with all of her heart, she was increasingly aware that she did not equally embrace their lavish Miami lifestyle. Coming home had reminded her of too many things that she missed: the scent of freshly baked bread in the oven, the sound of buggies rattling down the road, and the feeling of closeness with her family. She didn't want to think of their visit drawing to an end. Not yet, anyway.

"Now go to sleep," she said, hoping that Nicolas hadn't sensed her doubts. "You have to get up early if you're going to school with Hannah and Rachel."

As she shut the door, leaving it open just a crack so that Isadora wouldn't wake them when she went to bed for the night, Amanda sighed. Yes, she had wanted her children to experience the other side of their heritage. But what she hadn't counted on was how much they would come to enjoy it. What would Alejandro have to say about that? Oh dear, how would Alecia react if they were to stay a little bit longer?

After returning to the kitchen, Amanda joined Lizzie and Isadora on the sofa, where Lizzie was crocheting by the propane light, her granddaughter watching with quiet curiosity. After the supper meal, Alecia had promptly excused herself, escaping to the solace of her room to call her friends with the latest updates, Amanda suspected. Her mother-in-law appeared to be the only person in the family who wasn't fully embracing the country lifestyle. Amanda was sure she was counting down the days to when she would be on her way back home to Miami and her own kitchen.

"It was wonderful, Alejandro," she said, hardly able to contain her enthusiasm. "Isadora just walked right off with that girl . . ." She tried to think of her name. "Barbie King, I believe."

"Oh *sí*?"

In the flickering light of the kerosene lantern, Alejandro took off his sweater while she rubbed lotion on her hands and arms, preparing for a good night's sleep. She wore a plain white nightgown, a robe tossed over her shoulders but not fastened. The room was cold, the heat from downstairs not quite reaching it. But she didn't mind. She was too focused on the events of the day.

"It was so *wunderbar gut* to see her interacting with young girls who don't want something from her," she added.

He made a noise deep in his throat as he tossed his sweater onto the ladder-back chair.

"And, my word!" Amanda started to laugh as she remembered the quilting bee. "You should have seen Isadora stitching with those girls! Why, she took to quilting like a duck takes to water."

"A duck?" He raised an eyebrow at her and made a face. "I don't see our Izzie being a duck out of water anywhere."

"Exactly!" Amanda exclaimed. "She fit in with all of those girls. They even made plans to do something tomorrow while Sofia and Nicolas go to the school with Hannah and Rachel."

Alejandro walked over to the bed and knelt before her. "That will be good for them to see an Amish school," he said softly.

"Nicolas fusses so, but I think he's excited, too." Amanda smiled as she remembered how he had complained about going to school. "And Sofia. She wasn't as partial to the quilting, but she seems to get on quite well with her cousins. Did you know that they made sugar cookies after we returned from the quilting?"

He reached out and touched her legs, resting his weight on them. "Sugar cookies? I did not know that, no." He watched intently as he listened to her relating the events of the day. But she barely noticed as she continued.

"I shouldn't be surprised. I caught Nicolas sneaking some when he thought I wasn't looking." She laughed softly. "Oh! And then the four of them went outside and played until you and Jonas came home for milking. They were out in the field for a long time, just running through the paddock!"

For a long moment, he didn't say anything as he gently caressed her thighs through her white nightgown. She didn't pay attention as she thought back on the day. How glad she was that they had come to Lititz for Christmas! To see the transformation in her children made it all worthwhile. And despite some initial lack of enthusiasm, even Alecia had seemed to calm down and relax—something Amanda had never thought she'd see.

"It's just so amazing," Amanda gushed, still focused more on her thoughts than on his touch, "how they just adapted so fast! It's as if they've lived here all their life! Especially Izzie. I mean, none of these girls care a shake about social media and followers or even that she's Viper's daughter. It's as if here, she's free to be who she truly is. She doesn't have to live behind a façade of who people expect her to be. And to think that there's no paparazzi! What freedom they have, especially Izzie. It's like she's removing a mask that's been hiding her true feelings."

He stood up and gave a little groan as his knees creaked. Then, he reached behind her head to start removing the pins that held her bun at the nape of her neck. "You seem so happy, Amanda," he said as her hair cascaded down her back. He combed his fingers through it, his thumb gently brushing against her neck. "Do you ever wonder . . . ?"

When he stopped in midsentence, she looked up at him. "Alejandro?"

He shook his head and walked over to the small dresser, his back to her as he placed the pins on a little plate atop a hand-crocheted lace doily. *"Nada, mi amor."* After another pause, he turned around to face her. "It's good to see you so happy, *Aman-tha.*"

She knew that tone.

Aman-tha. The way that her name rolled off his tongue made her bite her lower lip. He stared at her, his gaze smoldering. Even after all of these years, Amanda never tired of her husband's attention. She stood up and crossed the room to where he stood by the dresser. For a moment, she remained silent. Raising one hand, she brushed her fingers up his arm and let them rest on his shoulder. She could feel his muscles twitch, and she suppressed a knowing smile.

"I like being happy," she said softly, moving her hand to gently brush aside a loose lock of hair that hung over his forehead. "But, Alejandro, I'm always happy, as long as I'm with you." Gently, she ran her hands along his chest and hooked her fingers over his belt, giving it a slight tug. "You," she said, "make me happy."

"Umm." He took a step, gently moving her backward and toward the bed.

She felt the side of the mattress hit the back of her knees and without thinking, she sat down.

"You like me happy?" he mumbled as he began to slowly unbutton his shirt, his eyes still holding her gaze. "I like you happy." The way he enunciated each word made her look up. He raised an eyebrow as he began to slide his shirt off his shoulders. "We are the perfect couple, no?"

"*Ja*, we are," she whispered.

"And it doesn't matter where we are, does it?" he said, looking at her as he tossed his shirt on top of his sweater. He lowered himself over her, slowly crawling onto the bed and forcing her to lean backward. She placed her hand on his shoulder, bracing herself as he hovered above her. "I do, however, like that we are here." He leaned forward and kissed her shoulder. "In this room." Another kiss on her neck. "By ourselves." Her ear. "Until morning."

She smiled at his words and shut her eyes. "That's a good place to be, *ja*?" she asked in a soft voice.

"*Sí*," he purred into her ear. "I've thought about you for a long time today."

"A long time?" she teased.

"*Sí*. All day."

"All day?"

He stroked her cheek with his thumb and nodded.

"That is a long time, then."

"You have no idea, Princesa," he murmured in mock despair.

"Well, I'm here now."

"And I intend to take full advantage of the long night ahead of us."

"I love you, Alejandro," she whispered as she raised her arms and wrapped them around his neck. "Thank you for bringing us all home for Christmas."

He paused for just a moment, his lips barely touching hers. But then, he whispered back, "And I love you, Amanda."

Just as his lips found hers at last, she realized that she had called Lititz her home, and she wondered if that was why he had hesitated. But as he held her in his arms, his gentle kisses distracted her, and she forgot about her blunder. After all, her home would always be exactly wherever Alejandro was.

Chapter Fourteen

The following afternoon, as she was tidying the upstairs bedrooms, Amanda heard a soft knock on the door.

"Amanda?"

She turned around and smiled at Rachel, who stood in the doorway on one foot, her other tucked up and hooked around her knee as she balanced on one leg.

"Home already from school?" she asked as she finished fluffing a pillow and placing it at the top of the bed.

"Mamm says you need to come downstairs," she announced in Pennsylvania Dutch.

Oh help! Amanda thought as she quickly hurried out of the room and down the stairs. Anna must be having contractions again.

But when she made it to the landing, she was surprised to see Anna standing by the sink, peering out the window. Even more startling was the fact that she was not alone. Lizzie and Alecia were both there, their shoulders touching as they struggled to look outside.

"What on earth?" Amanda asked.

At the sound of her voice, all three women turned around in unison and stared at her. Lizzie and Anna wore astonished expressions on their faces, while all of the color had drained from Alecia's.

"You have to see this, Amanda," Anna said, waving her arm frantically for her sister to join them. "You won't believe he's done such a thing."

"Who's done what?" Amanda asked as she joined them at the window.

Alecia stepped aside to make room for her. "That son of mine," she said, her voice clearly expressing her displeasure. "I don't understand why he would do such a crazy thing. My son is too generous for his own good." Then, under her breath, she added, "It's not even his farm." When Amanda met her eyes, Alecia shook her head and walked away.

Outside, a large truck and trailer were parked in the driveway. Alejandro stood with Jonas as they talked with the driver while another man emerged from the back of the trailer, leading a horse. Carefully, the man turned as he tugged on the lead rope, and the horse, hesitantly at first, jumped down and took a few steps along the driveway before stopping in front of the other three men. The younger children were running around the yard, their lunch pails tossed on the ground near the front walk.

Amanda gasped. "A Dutch harness horse!" She had always liked that particular breed of horse, with its majestic gait when it pulled the buggy. A well-bred one had a coat so black that it almost looked dark blue in certain lights. And this one had a full white blaze running from between its eyes to the tip of its nose.

Amanda watched the horse as the man walked it in a small circle while Jonas pointed at its legs and said something.

"He's beautiful!" She turned and looked at her sister. "Why, Anna! I didn't know Jonas needed a new horse. Did he buy it yesterday, then?"

No one responded.

She looked over her shoulder and frowned. "Anna?"

Anna pressed her lips together, suppressing a secretive smile, and shrugged. "*Nee*, Jonas did not buy a horse yesterday."

From the other side of the room, Alecia made a noise of displeasure.

Returning her attention to the men and the horse, Amanda saw Alejandro step forward and run his hands along one of the animal's shoulders and then down its leg. "I don't understand," she said. "If Jonas didn't buy it . . ." And then it dawned on her. For the second time since she had walked into the room, she caught her breath. "Alejandro bought it?" She looked at her mother, who averted her eyes, and then at her sister, who looked far too amused to suit Amanda. "Whatever was he thinking, Anna?"

"I'm sure I can't answer that. But *he* certainly can."

Amanda scowled at her sister's teasing tone and headed toward the door without another word. It made sense now why Alecia was so unhappy.

It was cold outside, even though the sun was shining. In the distance, a few clouds were forming, and the wind sent a chill through her. She hadn't stopped for a coat so she rubbed her arms with her hands as she walked over toward her husband.

"Princesa!" he said with a broad smile. "You like?"

She stopped in her tracks, her mouth opening as if to say something, and then she shut it again. He looked so happy, totally elated, as he stroked the luxurious coat of the horse.

"Now this," he said teasingly, "*this* is real horse power." He winked at her. "Better than my Porsche, *sí*?"

"Alejandro?" she managed to say, trying her best to remain calm. "What is this all about?"

But he did not respond to her question. Instead, he walked around the horse, examining it from the other side. "Gorgeous. Just gorgeous," he muttered more to himself than to Amanda, completely absorbed in the moment.

While she couldn't argue with that statement—for the horse was, indeed, magnificent—she still wanted an answer to her question. "You bought a horse, Alejandro? For what purpose?"

He raised his head, his concentration broken by Amanda's voice, and looked at her over the horse's withers. From the expression he wore, Amanda realized her question genuinely surprised him. "For driving, Princesa," he responded as if it was the most sensible answer in the world.

"Driving *what*?"

"Our new buggy."

"What?" she exclaimed, incredulous about how casual he was behaving over an acquisition that she thought utterly crazy.

After patting the horse's shoulder, he walked over to Amanda, placing his hands on her arms. He knelt just enough so that he could look directly into her eyes. "Amanda . . ."

None of this made sense. For a moment, she wondered if he had gone insane. "What do you intend to do? Ship the horse and buggy to Miami so you can drive it to the studio?" She knew the answer to that question without him responding. She gestured toward Jonas. "Are you expecting him to tend to it when you aren't here, Alejandro? Which, might I remind you, is *always*."

He shrugged and added sheepishly, "*Mayhaps* we need to visit more often."

She leaned forward and whispered, "You don't need a horse and buggy for 'more often.' It's a burden on them to have to tend to it. And you know that, Alejandro."

"*Sí, sí,*" he said dismissively, returning his attention to the horse. "We can talk about this later."

"I wish you had talked to me about this before, to be perfectly honest."

Alejandro reached up and took her chin in his hand, still looking directly into her eyes. There was a tender expression on his face, and he hovered so close to her that, for a moment, Amanda thought he might kiss her. "Surprises, Princesa. It keeps everything fresh."

"Fresh, perhaps, but these types of decisions need to be planned, Alejandro. Who will care for this horse when we are no longer here?"

He leaned down and gently brushed his lips against her cheek. "A minor detail, *mi amor.* Now, let me settle with the driver, and then Jonas and I will take the horse for a drive. But afterward, I want to take you out." Once again, he leaned over, and this time, he brushed his lips against hers as he whispered, "Alone."

Dumbfounded, Amanda stood there, staring after Alejandro as he returned to the other men. He kept looking at the horse, his eyes shining with delight at his new acquisition. What was going on? It was as if Alejandro was transforming into another person right before her very eyes.

Back in the house, Amanda avoided Lizzie and Anna. Instead, she joined Alecia in the sitting area. "What is going on with Alejandro, Alecia?"

Her mother-in-law shook her head, her lips pressed together in a tight line. "I have asked myself that question many times over the years. As if I would know the answer. I only know that when my son gets an idea in his head, there is no changing his mind."

"But a horse! He bought a horse!" she exclaimed in disbelief.

Cheerfully, Anna added from the kitchen, "And a buggy."

Amanda looked at her, astonished that her sister seemed so pleased at having apparently kept the secret. "You knew?"

With a sheepish smile, Anna quickly turned and began wiping the counter, confirming the answer through her silence.

"This just doesn't make sense," Amanda mumbled to herself. Over the last few days, she had noticed how happy Alejandro had increasingly become. But she had never known him to do something so rash. He hadn't become the superstar that he was without precise planning and perfect execution. When it came to his finances, Alejandro was meticulous and very careful. And although she knew Alejandro would pay for the horse's upkeep, it would be an added burden for an already overworked Jonas. Alejandro wouldn't do such a thing to Jonas or her family. He'd always taken care of his family and friends, and that included Anna and her husband. No, there was definitely something else going on, but neither Alejandro nor her sister appeared ready to share it with her.

Amanda resolved not to say anything else to Alejandro about it. She knew it would only be a matter of time before he told her the reason he had made such an impulsive purchase. After all, they were partners in the marriage, and Alejandro never made a major decision, whether personal or professional, without first consulting with her unless he had good reason to do so. She might not understand why he did certain things, but she knew that he would explain his rationale eventually.

Alecia, however, had a different reaction. Rather than remain quiet, she continued to question her son's acquisition. Amanda refused to comment, knowing better than to disrespect her husband by feeding into Alecia's fretting. Yet, Amanda's silence did nothing to deter her. While Alejandro and Jonas went driving with the new horse, Alecia continued to pace the floor and shake her head, mumbling to herself in Spanish and occasionally complaining out loud about why her son would make such an impulsive purchase in a place that he hardly visited. Within an hour, she had worked herself into such a frenzy that she asked for some Tylenol and excused herself to take a nap.

"That's a fine idea," Anna said as she stood up, rubbing the small of her back. "I think I'll follow Alecia's example, if you don't mind." She walked over to where Samuel was playing with his toys, lying on his stomach on an old quilt covering the floor. "And I reckon you, little one, could use an hour or so before the rest of the *kinner* lose interest in the new horse and want their supper!" She bent down to pick up her son, wincing as she straightened up.

***

Amanda sat at the kitchen table and chopped vegetables to toss into the boiling water. She wanted to make a nice soup to go with the fresh bread that cooled on the wire rack by the stove. From time to time, she would look up, glancing at Isadora, who was sitting on the sofa watching Lizzie crochet a small lace doily as she rocked back and forth in the rocking chair. The thin thread seemed to slide through Lizzie's fingers as she crocheted. Amanda had also liked to watch her mother when she worked with such fine thread. She would try to follow her mother's fingers as they worked, but they moved far too fast for her to ever understand how she made such delicate and pretty doilies.

"Mammi Lizzie," Isadora asked, her big eyes still staring at Lizzie, "when did you learn how to do that?"

"*Ach*, child!" Lizzie set her work upon her lap and shook her head as she tried to formulate an answer. "Oh my. I'd have to think about that. Seems my own *grossmammi* taught me how to do this when I was just a tad older than Sofia."

Isadora sat on the edge of the sofa, her eyes bright and shining. "Really?"

Lizzie glanced up to the ceiling as she thought back in time. "Let's see," she said slowly. "*Ja*, I was no more than eight years old when I started to crochet. Started with small washcloths. By the time I was ten years old, I was working on baby blankets. I remember that my parents gave me some yarn and a new crochet needle for my birthday that year." She smiled at the memory. "But I didn't start crocheting with fine thread like this until later."

Amanda watched the interaction between her mother and Isadora. She couldn't help but feel a pang of remorse. Why hadn't she taught Isadora how to crochet? In fact, when was the last time she had crocheted at all? She used to love crocheting blankets, but somewhere along the way, she had stopped. Amanda couldn't exactly remember when or why. Perhaps when she became too engrossed with her role dealing with the public. When she had first married Alejandro, she took her yarn and needle with her on some of their trips. But when her role as a public figure began to develop, Alejandro's publicity team had placed increasing demands upon her until finally he'd arranged for her to have her own team of people to overbook her schedule. Amanda found less and less time to sit and relax. Now, although she didn't travel as often with Alejandro, she still had to balance being a mother of three with her weekly commitments. Free time to crochet was a luxury she had lost a long time ago.

And that meant that teaching her children how to crochet simply never had entered the picture.

"Would you teach me, Mammi Lizzie?" Isadora asked.

Lizzie's mouth opened in surprise. It was clear that Isadora's question had dumbfounded her. "Why, of course, child!" She reached down to dig through her bag of yarn that was tucked behind her chair. After fishing around, she withdrew an extra crochet hook and handed it to Isadora. "Pick out a color yarn from that box over there, and I'd be happy to show you."

Watching her mother and daughter sit together, Isadora listening intently while watching Lizzie's fingers as grandmother taught granddaughter a skill that had been passed through the family for generations, brought tears to Amanda's eyes. She looked away, ashamed that she had not taught her own daughter something so very basic to her heritage. But then again, it was Amanda's heritage, not Isadora's.

"Mami?"

Amanda's concentration was broken by someone tugging at her skirt. Sofia stood behind her, a worried look on her face. Amanda knelt down before her daughter. She hadn't heard Sofia come inside and wondered why she wasn't playing with the other children. *"Ja, mi amor?"*

"Do you think I might learn, too?" she whispered, nervously glancing toward her sister and grandmother.

Amanda forced a smile that hid her tears. She felt joy at the fact that her daughters wanted to learn something so basic to her childhood, but at the same time shame at her neglect in denying them such a simple skill that would've created so many bonding moments between them.

Lost bonding moments and only herself to blame for it, she realized. And yet there was still time to change all of that. Right now, right here.

"Come, Sofia," Amanda said as she reached out for Sofia's hand, a look of resolution on her face. "Let me show you the way my *mamm* taught me." Sofia placed her hand inside her mother's, the warmth of the small child's touch lingering in Amanda's heart long after, together, hand-in-hand, they walked over to the sofa and joined Isadora and Lizzie.

Chapter Fifteen

"Back in my country, when I was a little girl," Alecia was saying to Nicolas as they sat on the sofa, talking while Anna and Amanda made breakfast, "I used to tend to the household chores at your age, too, Nicolas. We didn't have a cow, though. Goats. Lots of goats. But the milking process was the same." Alecia smiled nostalgically as Nicolas stared at her with an expression of childlike wonder.

"You lived on a farm?"

She nodded, clearly pleased that she had captured his attention. "*¡Sí, claro!* Not as big as this farm, though."

"Did it smell as bad, Abuela?" he asked as Amanda gave him a look of warning.

Alecia waved off Amanda's concern with Nicolas's comment. "*Ay, mija*, he's just a boy. Besides," she said in a lowered voice as she leaned toward Nicolas as if telling him a big secret, "goats smell just as bad as the cows, but you get used to it. A person can adapt to almost anything over time. But once you live on a farm, a piece of you always misses it."

Amanda's mouth opened, just a little, when she heard Alecia say that. For the first time that week, Amanda took a good hard look at Alecia and suddenly recognized that there had been a subtle transformation in her. Could it be that being here had brought back forgotten memories for her mother-in-law as well? Amanda never had imagined such a thing could happen and yet, why not?

Alejandro had told her stories about Alecia's difficult childhood in Cuba. She had grown up in a rural area of the island that, with a little stretch of the imagination, sounded similar to Lititz. Of course, the weather in Cuba was nothing like Pennsylvania, but she had lived with her family on a farm.

Yes, from the stories Alejandro shared and from what Alecia was telling Nicolas now, Amanda knew that her mother-in-law had been born into a very simple life. Later, as a young single mother, she had emigrated to America, settling in Miami as she struggled to make ends meet and raise her young son. Her life had made a complete 180-degree turn.

And yet, as Alecia reminisced, there was a distant but happy look in her eyes. Was this experience bringing those memories back to Alecia?

Amanda looked over again at her mother-in-law and realized that she might have misjudged her. After all, the changes that came with her son's whirlwind fame couldn't have been easy for Alecia, either. In her life, she'd gone through a lot of adjustments, making many sacrifices for the happiness of her only child. Amanda, of all people, understood that.

She reached over and patted Alecia on the shoulder, giving her a small smile of understanding. Alecia's eyes widened, and she returned the smile. After all, they both loved Alejandro with all of their hearts. Amanda suspected that tonight Alecia would not be retiring early to her bedroom to call anyone. In fact, Amanda was certain that the Amish lifestyle was beginning to grow on her mother-in-law.

After listening to Alecia and Nicolas interact, Amanda made her way to the kitchen and put on an apron. She intended to take over the cooking so that Anna could sit and relax. Her back had been hurting her for the past two days, and Amanda found herself wondering if her sister was experiencing contractions or perhaps false labor. Either way, with Alecia and Isadora helping, Amanda could surely handle preparing the breakfast meal and school lunches.

Hannah and Rachel walked out of their parents' bedroom door just off the staircase with Samuel in Hannah's arms. His head was tucked beneath her shoulder, hiding his face from the others.

"Oh, will you look at that!" Anna couldn't hide her joy. "He's playing shy now!"

Rachel spread a crocheted blanket on the floor and sat down so that Hannah could set Samuel down beside her. Sofia ran over to join her cousin, helping her to steady the child on the blanket. They sat on either side of him and tried to balance his little body as he wobbled and teetered, his two chubby legs splayed out in different directions.

Nicolas leaned against Amanda while she stood over the stove. "Is Papi taking us to the schoolhouse again today?"

Amanda flipped the pancakes in the skillet. "I'm sure he could," she said. "Unless you want to walk in the snow."

He caught his breath. Clearly, the prospect of walking in the snow was much more appealing than being driven. "I wanna walk to school!"

"My word!" she said, laughing.

At the table, Lizzie finished brushing Sylvia's hair and, after setting down the brush, began to twist and roll her long hair into a proper bun.

"Don't you go to school in Miami?" Sylvia asked.

Nicolas nodded. "But I don't get to *walk* to school!" he said, as if he were being denied a great privilege.

"Oh?"

He shook his head. "Or take a bus. Mami has one of the drivers take us in a car."

Lizzie's laughter subsided, and she raised an eyebrow as she looked at Amanda. "I see."

"It's too far away for them to walk," Amanda said as she slid the spatula under the pancakes and moved them to the waiting plate.

"A little more exposure to fresh air might do them well," Lizzie said as she finished with Sylvia's bun and reached out for Elizabeth, who was waiting to have her hair done as well. "And it sure seems that your little one enjoys playing outside well enough."

Amanda couldn't argue with her mother on that point. Ever since the cookie swap, Nicolas had spent almost all of his free time in the barn. Sometimes he played by himself; other times he managed to persuade his sister and cousins to join him. It wasn't a hard sell for Sofia, as she loved to wander the farm and play with the animals, especially the kittens in the barn.

"It's not something they can do in Miami," Amanda admitted, realizing how horrible that must sound. "I mean, at least not without security and then, of course, if people recognize them . . ."

Lizzie clicked her tongue and shook her head. "Not to be able to play outside! Well! I never heard such nonsense." Then, setting the hairbrush on her lap, she leaned forward as if she were telling a secret to Nicolas. "When I was your age, we always walked to school, Nicolas. Even when it was raining outside."

"And snowing?" he asked.

"Oh *ja*! Especially in the snow. Sometimes my older *bruder* would pull me down the road to school on a sled!" She laughed at the memory, her eyes crinkling at the corners. Picking up the brush from her lap, she began to pull it gently through Elizabeth's hair. "Why, those are some of my best childhood memories!"

Nicolas lit up at the mention of a sled. "Do you have a sled here, Mammi Lizzie?"

Hannah answered for Lizzie. "*Ja*, in the barn."

"Can we take it to school?"

Out of the corner of her eye, Amanda saw Anna's back stiffen. While Nicolas was organizing the logistics of which cousin would pull him on the sled to school, Amanda walked over and placed her hand on Anna's shoulder. "Everything alright?" she asked quietly.

Anna nodded but that was her only response. Clearly, she wasn't going to admit that something was wrong in the presence of the children. Amanda would have to wait for them to leave before she could confront Anna and find out why her sister was so quiet this morning.

By the time the children were dressed, lunches were packed, and coats were all zipped up, Amanda found herself breathing a sigh of relief. Through the open doorway, she watched Sofia and Nicolas as they ran with Hannah and Rachel toward the barn, intent on fetching the sled that Jonas had volunteered to find for them.

A few minutes later, Hannah and Rachel pulled the old wooden sled down the driveway and toward the road. Nicolas was happily sitting on it with a big grin on his face, while Sofia brought up the rear, swinging the red-and-white lunch cooler in her hand.

"My word!" Amanda said as she closed the front door when they finally disappeared around the corner of the dairy barn. "I have to admit it's nice to have a quiet break."

She moved to the kitchen table and sat down across from her sister. "Honestly, Anna, I don't know how you do it every day!"

"Oh, they are such big helpers around the farm," Anna said cheerfully. "That Hannah is like a little mother to Samuel, too. When I'm milking the cows in the morning, she often gets up to tend to him. And makes breakfast, as well." There was more than a hint of pride in her voice.

Amanda remembered how, when their baby brother Aaron had been born, they'd both taken on much more responsibility. While Amanda managed to help with more of the outdoor chores, such as the gardening and the milking, it had been Anna who took over a lot of their mother's morning routine. But Anna hadn't needed to tend to three younger sisters and a developmentally disabled brother.

"Oh my," Anna whispered, placing her hand on the side of her stomach.

"Kicking?"

Anna shook her head. "*Nee*, my back is stiff, and it hurts a bit."

"Maybe Alejandro should take you to the doctor," Amanda suggested.

Anna shook her head. "I'm fine," she replied with a forced smile. "Besides, we have so much baking to do. I promised to bring cookies and granola bars to the school pageant tomorrow."

At this remark, Amanda made a sound of disbelief. Hadn't Samuel been born over two months early? The complications of the birth had not only denied the baby oxygen he needed but had also endangered Anna's life. Even if Anna was further along than she had been with Samuel, Amanda couldn't understand why her sister would chance the health of her unborn daughter, especially with the doctors monitoring her so closely.

"Mamm? Don't you think Anna should go?"

Lizzie looked up from the devotional that she was reading. She took a moment before responding and studied Anna as she sat at the table. Her expression changed from one of relaxation to one of growing concern. "Well, now . . ." She set aside her booklet and stood up. "You do look a bit worn, Anna."

"I just need to lie down a spell," she argued.

But neither Amanda nor Lizzie looked convinced.

Crossing the room, Lizzie glanced at the clock. "Mayhaps we might call the doctor," she said, placing her hand on Anna's forehead. "Just to be safe. It's after nine. They should be open yet."

Abruptly, Anna pulled away from her mother's hand. "I don't have a fever," she said with a little laugh. "Just some backache, I reckon.

Carrying Samuel all the time along with all this extra weight," she added, pointing to her stomach, "is bound to hurt my back. That's all."

Lizzie glanced at Amanda and raised an eyebrow. Amanda knew that her mother was not comfortable with Anna's nonchalant attitude about the pain she was experiencing.

Anna started to stand up. "I'm fine," she said as cheerfully as she could. "See? Besides, I need to get to that laundry so that it can dry in the basement. Then we need to start the baking for the—" She stopped talking midsentence and bent over, her hand immediately pressing against her stomach.

"I'll go get Jonas," Amanda whispered to her mother as she hurried out of the kitchen. Not even pausing to grab her coat, she hurried out the door to the barn to summon her brother-in-law.

The freshly fallen snow crunched under her shoes, and she slid, just once, from a fine layer of ice hidden beneath it. She chastised herself for not having realized that Anna had been experiencing contractions the previous day. Her sister had grown unusually quiet early in the evening and had retired shortly after she'd put Sylvia and Elizabeth to bed.

Oh, how she prayed that everything was all right with this new baby. If labor came early and the baby was born with problems similar to Samuel's, that would present even more burdens for Anna.

As it was now, Amanda had no idea how her sister would manage the cleaning, the laundry, the cooking, the sewing, and all of her other chores with three children not yet attending school *and* a new baby. Not to mention that Anna usually helped Jonas with the morning milking. It was too much for one person to handle, and Lizzie could only do so much to help her.

Amanda found Jonas in the back of the barn, busy washing the milking equipment. Although she didn't see him, she could hear Alejandro talking to Isadora near the cows. Not wanting to alarm anyone, Amanda tried to keep her voice low and calm as she addressed her brother-in-law.

"Mayhaps you may want to come inside, Jonas," she said softly. "Anna's feeling some pains."

Immediately, he shut off the faucet and wiped his hands on his jacket. "Some pains, you say?"

"She says it's nothing, Jonas, but I know that her back was hurting yesterday. Even the day before, I think."

He nodded his head, raising his hand to remove his hat and wipe his forehead with his sleeve. "She didn't sleep much through the night, either. I was wondering . . ."

Amanda could see the worry creep into his eyes. Childbirth was stressful for any couple, presenting many concerns: Would the baby be healthy? Would the mother be all right? Would the delivery, which for the Amish was normally without anesthesia, be difficult? But Amanda knew that this labor presented extra stress for both Jonas and Anna. And if anything happened to her, Jonas would have even more added to his already heavy load.

"Perhaps Alejandro could take her to the doctor," Amanda offered. "Just to have her checked out, especially with the holiday so near."

When they entered the kitchen, Lizzie was seated next to Anna, holding her hand as she silently prayed.

Jonas set his hat on the counter and walked over to his wife. "What's this I hear?" he asked as he pulled out the chair beside her. "Having some back pains, Anna?"

"It's nothing, I'm sure."

"Hmm." He studied her as he rubbed his chin, scratching at his beard. "Mayhaps we best let the doctor decide that, Anna."

Anna started to argue with him. But another pain overtook her, and as she caught her breath and held her stomach, Jonas quickly looked up at Amanda and nodded his head.

"I'll go fetch Alejandro," Amanda said before Anna could put up a fuss.

Once again, she headed toward the barn. This time, however, Alejandro and Isadora were already walking back, their heads bent together as they talked. They didn't notice Amanda as she approached them. When she called out Alejandro's name, they both looked up, startled.

"What's wrong, Princesa?" he asked with concern.

She glanced at Isadora, not wanting to upset her daughter, but decided that she was old enough to know what was happening. "Anna needs to go to the doctor. She has some pregnancy pains."

Isadora's eyes widened. "She's going to have the baby? While we're here? Now?"

"Looks that way," Amanda said. "She needs to go to the doctor, Alejandro."

Without asking any additional questions, Alejandro placed his hand on her shoulder. "I'd be happy to take her, Amanda. Let me fetch my keys and warm up the car."

Before Amanda could say another word, he had disappeared in the direction of the house. Moments later, she saw him walking behind Jonas and Anna toward the SUV. Both men helped Anna get into the vehicle before joining her. Alejandro gave Amanda a quick wave, a serious expression on his face as he drove away from the house.

With Isadora's help, Amanda tackled the remaining tasks that usually would be Anna's or Jonas's. She was thankful for the work, which kept her busy during the day; otherwise, she knew that she'd be consumed by worry. Several hours after he had left, Alejandro called to inform her that, as they'd suspected, Anna was indeed in labor. Amanda felt a mixture of excitement and fear. Welcoming a new life into the world was always a time for celebration, but Amanda worried that something might go wrong again with the birth.

When the children arrived home from school, Amanda reassured them that everything was fine and that soon they'd meet their baby sister. Thankfully, Lizzie and Alecia helped care for the children, and the evening passed quickly. Still, Amanda couldn't stop herself from being anxious. Later that evening, when she finally put the children to bed, Amanda found herself alone in the kitchen. Her body ached from exhaustion. For almost a half hour, she sat in the chair by herself, praying to God that he would take care of her sister. When the clock chimed nine times, Amanda sighed and slowly got up. She blew out the lantern and headed for the stairs, hoping that she would easily drift off to sleep. She wanted to wake in the morning to hear the news about her sister and the baby instead of worrying about it all night.

"Princesa, wake up." Alejandro nudged her softly.

Amanda's eyes flitted open, and it took her a few seconds to adjust her eyes to the dark room. Alejandro was standing by the bed, and from what she could see, it appeared that he was already dressed for a day of work in the barn, except when Amanda looked around the room, she realized the morning had not come yet.

What was going on?

"Is everything alright?" she asked groggily. Panic started to set in. Was something wrong with her sister or the children?

Alejandro must have sensed Amanda's worry because he quickly shook his head and patted her lightly on the arm.

"Nothing is wrong. It's actually very good news, *mi amor*. Your sister had her baby just two hours ago."

"What?" Amanda replied, still trying to get her bearings. Her mind was in a fog.

"*Sí*, it's true. Your little niece has made her grand entrance into the world."

"She did?" Amanda asked in wonder.

"*Sí*. She did," Alejandro whispered back to his wife.

"And she is . . . ?"

He smiled down at her as he set the flashlight he had been holding on the nightstand. "Perfect in every way, Amanda. And Anna is just fine. She's insisting that she come home tomorrow, but the doctor convinced Jonas to have her stay an extra day." He chuckled to himself as he bent down to remove his boots. "Her determination reminds me a little of someone else I know."

Amanda sank back into the pillow, ignoring his comment and focusing on the joyous news. "How wonderful! What perfect timing that she had her baby while we are here!" She watched as Alejandro started to get undressed. "To think, if she hadn't, we might not have met our new niece for a long, long time."

In the limited light from the flashlight, she saw him pause, obviously reflecting on her statement.

"And how amazing for the children!" she added. "They've never been able to share in the excitement of a cousin being born!"

As he unbuttoned his shirt, he appeared deep in thought. She was about to ask him what was wrong when he turned to her. "I had forgotten how small newborns are," he said. "And if I didn't know any better, I'd believe this little girl is a born performer."

Amanda laughed. "A . . . performer?"

"¡Sí! I heard her crying all the way in the waiting room! Such strong lungs!"

"Not to mention a captivated audience waiting with bated breath to meet her," she added as she pulled back the covers so that Alejandro could join her underneath. "I don't know who is more excited . . . Sofia, Nicolas, Isadora—or you."

Alejandro wrapped his arm around Amanda, pulling her against his body as he kissed the back of her neck. He gave a soft sigh, one that sounded surprisingly similar to the one that Amanda had given as she watched the children walk to school earlier that morning.

"It's late and you can barely keep your eyes open, Princesa."

"You must be exhausted, too," Amanda remarked.

"I'm used to it, but you're right. We should both go to sleep. Tomorrow will be a big day."

"Good night, *mi amor*," he whispered into her ear.

She lay in his arms, listening as his breathing slowed, sleep finding him quickly after such a long and exciting day. How beautiful and plentiful are God's gifts to us all, she thought as she shut her eyes, hoping she would be able to fall asleep as quickly as Alejandro had.

Within minutes, she, too, drifted off, her head nestled in the crook of Alejandro's arm as he held her, his chest pressed against her back in a loving embrace.

Chapter Sixteen

In the morning, Amanda heard Alejandro get up, and without his asking, she slid out from beneath the covers.

"Stay sleeping, Princesa," he whispered in the darkness. "I can handle the chores. It's too early and cold."

But she refused. Jonas had stayed at the hospital with Anna and the new baby, and she knew that milking all of those cows was practically impossible for just one person, especially with that new milking system.

So when Alejandro bundled up in a heavy winter coat, she put on Anna's work coat, buttoning it up to her throat so that she didn't catch a chill. She shivered as they walked outside, her cheeks feeling the blast of cold before the rest of her body did.

Alejandro opened the door to the dairy barn and stood aside, waiting for her to step through first. Alejandro hadn't put the cows to pasture the previous evening because the temperatures were supposed to dip well below zero, which meant that, in addition to feeding and milking the cows, they would have to clean the manure from the cement floors.

Amanda walked through the barn, careful not to slip on the slick floors, and gave each cow some grain while Alejandro disappeared to the back of the barn where the milking pen was. She knew that he needed to wash the equipment, making sure that it was sterile, even though he had done the same after milking the cows the previous afternoon.

When she joined him in the new milking pen, the sun had still not begun its ascent and the only light came from the propane lantern that hung overhead.

"All fed?" he asked when he saw her.

She nodded, her eyes taking in the room. She tried to figure out how, exactly, this new milking system worked. The pit in the center of the room appeared to be where Alejandro would stand while the cows were herded to stand beside the railing. Strange contraptions that looked like octopuses hung from a pipe that ran horizontally below the ceiling and toward the back of the room. Certainly, that was what sucked the milk from the cows' udders and transported it to the holding tank at the far end of the barn.

"Let's start bringing them in, *sí*?" Alejandro said. Without waiting for her to respond, he walked through the open doorway into the pen where the first cows would be herded to await their turn for milking.

In the quiet moments of dawn, they worked side by side. It didn't take Amanda long to understand how the new automatic milking machine operated. It helped that Alejandro took charge and jumped down into the milking pit. Without being told, Amanda began to herd the cows, two at a time, into the cordoned-off holding area so that Alejandro could sterilize their teats before attaching the milking cups to each one.

It was an unspoken division of labor, exactly like their marriage had always been. Over nine years of working together, in perfect unison. Whether they were in Miami performing at a concert or working inside a barn in Lititz, they balanced each other by providing unwavering support. Even when their travel schedules were grueling, they operated in sync with one another. The harmony in their marriage was something that any other woman would have found difficult to achieve. For Amanda, however, it came naturally.

While Amanda waited for Alejandro to finish, she stood back and watched him perform his tasks, not once complaining about the stench of cow manure or the physical work. She couldn't help but smile as she wondered what his fans would say if a photo of him looking like this suddenly appeared on social media.

"Princesa?"

She looked up, her thoughts broken off at the sound of his voice. "Hmm?"

"You look like your thoughts are a hundred miles away."

She leaned against the metal door that kept the cows in the milking corridor. "If your fans could see you now," she said with a small smile.

He chuckled and tossed a brown paper towel into a bucket. "I think they would be surprised to see Viper knee-deep in cow dung instead of lying on a lounge chair by a pool somewhere. Geoffrey would certainly have a heart attack. Not exactly exuding sex appeal, am I?"

"I don't agree at all," Amanda protested in a soft voice. "I find you rather appealing just like this."

Alejandro's eyebrow arched and, in an alluring voice, he added, "You do, do you?"

She tried to hide her smile.

As he stood in the concrete milking pit, he leaned against the lowest rung of the railing that surrounded it. He crossed his arms over his chest. There was something soft in his gaze as he stared at her.

"You always have sex appeal," she whispered at last. "To me."

He took a deep breath and glanced at the cows that were gathering behind the fenced area of the pit. "Well, I think you'd better stop right there unless you want to give the cows a show, no?"

Amanda blushed and returned her attention to the work at hand. After a few moments of silence, she said in a soft voice, "It's been nice. Being here."

He started to lean more heavily against the railing but thought better of it, as the concrete wall of the pit was dirty. Pushing away from it, he took a step toward her. Neither one cared how dirty they were after doing the morning chores. He touched her arm and pulled her toward him, embracing her loosely against his chest.

"I reckon that I just forgot what it was like, spending time together as a family without the crush of the media and the constant obligations. It's given us time to . . ."

She hesitated. How could she describe what she felt? She had grown so accustomed to schedules and people and smiling for cameras that she had forgotten the simple values of her childhood. Even more important, she now realized how much her children needed exposure to these values. Their lives were far too chaotic, yet, at the same time, they were insulated and sheltered, too. The same children who traveled abroad on a regular basis, eagerly navigating the world of pop culture, couldn't even walk to school. "Time to just *be*. To live life the way it was meant to be," she finally added, giving a little shrug of her shoulders. "Don't you ever feel that way, Alejandro? At least just a little?"

She couldn't help wondering what he was thinking, given the way he continued to look down and study her face.

He took his time before he responded, never once looking away from her. *"Claro, mi amor,"* he said at last in a gentle, nostalgic voice. "Spending time with the family without the demands of managers and music labels, fans, and paparazzi *has* been nice."

She sensed that he had more to say. "But?" she coaxed.

"But nothing. It's been very nice."

His lack of further commentary surprised her, and she blinked. "That's it? Just . . . nice?"

He laughed. "Did you want me to disagree with you, Princesa?"

"I'm . . . I'm not sure," she admitted cautiously.

The truth was that she wasn't certain *what* she wanted, but she hadn't expected him to agree with her. Where was his lecture about how wonderful their lives were—the house, the yacht, the trips, and the money? She had thought that he would have brought up the private schools and advantages for their children; they would, after all, never starve and had golden opportunities available to them without putting forth any effort.

But he hadn't. Instead, he had agreed with her. And she certainly didn't know what to make of that. In the past, everything had been about work for Alejandro. The only time she'd ever seen Alejandro relax in such a way had been when he first came to the farm after the accident in New York City. Even on their extensive vacations abroad, he always had people around him and was always aware of the cameras. It had been only on this trip that no one had paid any attention to the international sensation known as Viper. Even the paparazzi had neglected to show up to sneak photos or follow them on their outings.

"It's been so different this time," she said, breaking the silence. "I didn't think you'd enjoy yourself so much."

"Does it please you?" he asked.

"It pleases me, yes," she confessed. "But I worry that you are anxious to return to your life."

In response to her admission, Alejandro playfully groaned. "I will never understand women. I haven't said anything about *our* life because I am happy here with you and the children. We are living *our* life, no? That is all that I need to be happy."

"Is it?"

He took a deep breath and studied her expression. "Why would you question that, Princesa?"

She shrugged and averted her eyes. "You agreed too readily with me. It doesn't feel sincere."

"*¡Ay, mi madre!*" He released her from his hold and ran his fingers through his hair. "I would think you'd be happy that I agree with you, no? Isn't that what all wives want from their husbands?"

"Not me. I only want to please you, Alejandro," she answered honestly. "To support you in your life, both professionally and personally."

"I feel the same, *mi amor*," he replied in a more serious tone. "I live to make *you* happy. And you seem to have found that here. Same with the children."

"But it's not real, Alejandro. We are just pretending, aren't we?"

For a long moment, he stood there, a puzzled look on his face. She wondered what he was thinking, if she had crossed a line. But she spoke the truth. In a few days, Christmas would be over, and they would leave Pennsylvania. The relaxation would end the moment they arrived at the airport and the cell phones began to blow up with messages and e-mails. Social media would again become Isadora's primary focus, and the younger two children would be reunited with their nanny once again, freeing Amanda to continue with her obligations while Alejandro returned to travel and appointments and, eventually, more concerts. Their brief hiatus in Pennsylvania was nothing more than a staged break, a momentary what-if that would be forgotten within days, if not hours.

When he didn't respond, Amanda started to say something, wanting to explain all of that to Alejandro, but they were interrupted by a loud hissing noise. One of the teat cups had popped off the udder of the cow closest to her. The suddenness startled her and she jumped, shaking off the solemnness of their discussion. Instead of reprimanding her for casting a somber cloud over what had been a shared morning of togetherness, Alejandro chuckled as he glanced over his shoulder at the cow.

"Seems like this is a conversation we can continue later, Princesa." He winked at her and returned his attention to the milking.

***

"Mamm's not going to be home for the pageant," Rachel stated in a matter-of-fact voice.

"No, sweetheart, she's not." Amanda gave her niece a gentle hug. "But we'll be there and so will Isadora and Mammi Lizzie . . ."

"And Abuela?"

Amanda smiled at the sweetness behind the question. "*Ja,* Abuela will be there, too."

"But Mamm will be home for Christmas, *ja?*"

Amanda nodded as she buttoned up the back of Rachel's dress for school. She had managed to find time to call the hospital and check on Anna. Jonas had answered the phone and reassured her that both mother and baby were doing fine. There had been no complications, and Anna preferred that her sister attend to the children rather than come to the hospital to visit.

"That's what I was told," Amanda assured Rachel. "Your *daed* said that they would be home tomorrow. And with your baby sister, too."

Hannah walked into the room, her hair loose and ready for Amanda to fix before they went downstairs for breakfast. "Who's going to help Mamm with Samuel when she comes home with the new baby?"

It was a question that Amanda had been asking herself since Anna had left for the hospital the previous day. Lizzie helped as much as she could with the children, and Alecia had even colored with Sylvia and Elizabeth before supper. To Amanda's surprise, Alecia had been such a help to her and her mother while Anna was at the hospital. She couldn't have managed without her. Yet Amanda had shouldered the bulk of the responsibility for tending to her nieces and nephew. And she had immediately realized that, even though Samuel had an almost continuously pleasant demeanor about him, he required close to 100 percent of Anna's attention when he was awake.

How on earth would Anna help Jonas, tend to Samuel's unique needs, and care for a newborn?

"Oh, well," Amanda said after a brief delay to collect her thoughts. "I'm sure both of you will certainly help out."

She noticed the way that the two girls furtively exchanged a look between them. It was a look that only two sisters could share. And Amanda knew exactly what it meant.

Amanda sat on the bench in the second row of the schoolhouse. Samuel sat on her lap, propped up against her chest. He played with a small toy, a wooden cow that was his current favorite, occasionally lifting it to his mouth to chew. The battery-operated lights that the schoolteacher had placed at the center of each windowsill created a warm and cozy glow in the room. With all the people crowded into the one-room schoolhouse, it was warm enough that Amanda didn't need her shawl.

She was flanked by Lizzie and Alecia. Sylvia and Elizabeth sat next to Lizzie while Alecia sat upright and leaned forward as she watched the children at the front of the large room. Alecia was dressed in her finest as usual, and there was a distinct air of pride about her. Amanda smiled to herself as she thought how much Alecia had started to embrace her role within her family. She was definitely not the same woman who had set foot in Amanda's mother's house the day they'd arrived. She watched with her complete attention as the grandchildren stood fidgeting before Amanda.

Thankfully, the teacher had let Sofia and Nicolas stand right behind Hannah and Rachel. That way, it was easier for the three women to watch all of them.

The teacher stepped in front of the children and faced the audience. She was a young woman with big brown eyes and a cheerful smile. Quite different from the stoic and emotionless educators that her children had, Amanda thought. No wonder Sofia and Nicolas liked it so much.

"We want to thank all of you for attending our holiday pageant," the teacher said, her voice carrying surprisingly well through the crowded room. "The children have been excited about this day, working hard for many weeks." She glanced over her shoulder at her students, a benevolent smile on her face. "Christmas is such a special time of year, a time when we share our joy and faith with family and friends. At Christmas, we celebrate the wondrous gift that God has given to us, the greatest gift of all: Jesus, the Son of God, born to all mankind for the forgiveness of all sin."

She paused, waiting to allow the audience to quietly reflect on her words.

"Today, we hope that you enjoy our Christmas pageant as we share the love of the Lord with each and every one of you."

When she stepped aside, a silence fell over the room. From the back, someone coughed, and a few of the children shuffled their feet while waiting for their cue to start.

The older students standing in the back of the room began to sing the first line of the song to the tune of "Jesus Loves Me," and when they came to the chorus, they stopped so that the younger students with their cherubic voices could sing in turn:

In a land and time far away,
Upon a manger filled with hay,
Christ the wondrous baby lay.

Shepherds on a hill that dark night,
Watched their sheep under starlight,
Until beckoned by one so extra-large and bright.

Plain Christmas

They followed the star to where it hung
Over the inn in Bethlehem.
Angels sang from the heavens above,
About God's gift: the son he loved.

Jesus the Savior slept in the manger
Prayed over by his parents and strangers.
While the angels continued to sing,
Proclaiming the birth of the newborn king.

As she watched her daughter and son singing along with the other students, Amanda felt a lump forming in her throat. Both Sofia and Nicolas sang without any fear of standing in front of people that they didn't know. When Nicolas stumbled over a word, Sofia gently nudged him with her shoulder, as if encouraging him to continue anyway. Without even looking, she could sense Alecia's joy as the children sang.

It dawned on Amanda that this was the first, and perhaps last, time that her children would perform in a Christmas pageant with their peers. Success had robbed her children of so many of the simple pleasures taken for granted by so many children—and adults! Fame and wealth might buy fancy houses, yachts, and stylish clothes, but those were just things that, once acquired, usually lost their value in the eyes of the beholder anyway. What mattered most were the things that money could not buy, such as children singing in a school pageant, baking cookies with their cousins, and learning to crochet with one's mother and grandmother.

She turned around and sought out Alejandro where he stood in the back of the room. There was a look of pride on his face as he watched his children performing in unison with the other students. Usually, he was the one on the stage with every pair of eyes staring at him. He smiled to himself, his head moving just a little as he listened to the song.

And then his eyes glanced in Amanda's direction. When he saw that she was watching him, he held her gaze with such a thoughtful intensity that she wondered if he had been thinking the very same thing she had. But just as soon as the thought crossed her mind, he winked at her and returned his attention to the front of the classroom, where the children had moved to the side of the room, a few of them slipping behind the hanging curtain to prepare for the highlight of the show: the reenactment of the Nativity scene.

Amanda knew what came next. When she was growing up, it had been the same every year: the younger children acted out the Nativity scene while the older students took turns reciting the second chapter of Luke to the audience. And each year it was always the highlight of the pageant, especially when the children were particularly creative with their props.

A tall girl, probably no older than thirteen, stepped toward the corner of the "stage" area and gently cleared her throat. She looked nervous as she began to recite the first verses:

*And it came to pass in those days, that there went out a decree from
Caesar Augustus that all the world should be taxed.
And all went to be taxed, every one into his own city.*

Finished with her section, the girl gave a quick smile in the direction of her parents before she stepped aside for another student, a boy this time, to continue the recitation. Only this time, before he began to recite his verses, two of the younger children emerged from behind the curtain.

White sheets covered their regular clothes, and each had a black cord tied around the waist so they looked as if they wore biblical-style garments. It was clear that they were playing the roles of Mary and Joseph.

Slowly, the two actors began to trudge across the front of the room, Joseph clearly having practiced how to look like he was trudging through a hot desert. Every few steps, he stopped, pretending to wipe the sweat from his brow and shaking his head at the tedious journey ahead of him. A few of the parents in the audience chuckled, which only seemed to encourage him to continue his theatrical display with even more intensity.

While Mary and Joseph made their way across the room toward the other side, the other young boy began speaking his lines:

And Joseph also went up from Galilee, out of the city of Nazareth, into Judaea, unto the city of David, which is called Bethlehem, because he was of the house and lineage of David;

To be taxed with Mary his espoused wife, being great with child.

As he finished speaking, Mary and Joseph had completed their journey and now faced a dark curtain that hung from the ceiling. A little boy poked his head out from behind the curtain and, pretending to scowl at Mary and Joseph, he shook his head emphatically as if to say no. Joseph tossed up his hands. Then he turned to Mary and shrugged his shoulders while holding out his hands, palms up.

Clearly, there was no room at that "inn."

Amanda couldn't help but give a soft laugh at his performance. She wasn't alone. Several people in the audience joined her, including, to Amanda's surprise, Alecia.

"Such a character, that boy," Alecia whispered into her ear. "Reminds me of Nicolas, *sí*?"

A third student stepped forward and continued reciting the Scripture.

And so it was, that, while they were there, the days were accomplished that she should be delivered.

And she brought forth her firstborn son, and wrapped him in swaddling clothes, and laid him in a manger; because there was no room for them in the inn.

The girl acting as Mary knelt down by a makeshift manger, which looked suspiciously like the box Amanda had been looking for after Nicolas had "borrowed" it the day before. Amanda saw him standing with the other children and caught his eye. When he grinned at her, she knew that her suspicion was correct.

There were two more younger boys, dressed in sackcloth and walking with shepherds' crooks, or, in their case, small cast-iron stakes that they probably brought in from their mothers' gardens. A third student stepped forward to recite the next section of Luke.

And there were in the same country shepherds abiding in the field, keeping watch over their flock by night.

And, lo, the angel of the Lord came upon them, and the glory of the Lord shone round about them: and they were sore afraid.

To Amanda's surprise, Hannah appeared from behind the curtained-off area dressed as the angel. Behind her were four other little girls, one of whom was Sofia. Amanda caught her breath and, without thinking about it, reached out to hold her mother's hand. Her feelings of emotion went beyond a lump in her throat now, and tears filled her eyes. She had to blink rapidly and make a conscious effort at containing them.

And the angel said unto them, Fear not: for, behold, I bring you good tidings of great joy, which shall be to all people.

For unto you is born this day in the city of David a Savior, which is Christ the Lord.

And this shall be a sign unto you; Ye shall find the babe wrapped in swaddling clothes, lying in a manger.

The angel made a wide gesture with her arms and turned to walk toward the manger, then stood behind it as if hovering protectively over the baby that "slept" inside the box.

And suddenly there was with the angel a multitude of the heavenly host praising God, and saying,

Glory to God in the highest, and on earth peace, good will toward men.

When the four young girls representing the multitude of the heavenly host finished pretending to say the words as the student recited their lines, they twirled twice and slipped back behind the curtain. Amanda placed a hand on her chest, trying to catch her breath from having watched two of her children perform in the Nativity scene for the very first time.

And it came to pass, as the angels were gone away from them into heaven, the shepherds said one to another, Let us now go even unto Bethlehem, and see this thing which is come to pass, which the Lord hath made known unto us.

*And they came with haste, and found Mary, and Joseph, and the
babe lying in a manger.*

The two shepherds walked over to where Mary and Joseph knelt by
the manger-box. They stood nearby, pretending to gaze into the box.
The one shepherd leaned over too far, and before he or the audience
knew what was happening, he fell forward. In trying to steady himself,
he leaned against Mary, who almost fell into the manger as well. The
shocked look on her face coupled with the embarrassed expression on
the boy's face caused a ripple of laughter in the audience. But the children managed to recover quickly and acted as if nothing unusual had
happened.

*And when they had seen it, they made known abroad the saying
which was told them concerning this child.*

*And all they that heard it wondered at those things which were told
them by the shepherds.*

The children who had not performed in the Nativity scene stepped
forward and began to sing "Hark! the Herald Angels Sing." After they
finished the first stanza, the actors stood up and gathered together with
the other children, joining in with the singing.

Amanda couldn't help but notice how their faces shone. She
remembered her own school years and how she had felt when she performed for her parents and her grandparents. It had been a wonderful experience knowing that she, along with her classmates, could give
something so very special and meaningful back to the community,
especially during the holidays.

How wonderful that Sofia and Nicolas had been given the opportunity to feel the very same thing.

At the end of the performance, the children stood in front of the parents, holding hands as they awkwardly took a humble bow. Then, with the teacher announcing that the pageant was over, they scattered to join their proud families. Several women began to unwrap trays of freshly baked sugar cookies and other sweets, setting them on the edge of the teacher's desk at the front of the room, where the children had just performed.

"Did you see? Did you see?" Nicolas asked repeatedly as he jumped up and down, hanging on Lizzie's arm.

Sofia grinned at her mother.

"You were all wonderful," Lizzie said, recognizing all four of her grandchildren who had performed.

Alecia smiled at Sofia and Nicolas. "Such talented children!" she said, her face glowing with pride. And then, remembering that Hannah and Rachel had performed, too, she added, "All four of you."

"Can we go get cookies now, Mami?" Nicolas asked eagerly.

"It's 'may we,' and yes, you *may*, but please take Sylvia and Elizabeth with you."

"I'll go with the little ones," Lizzie said. "I see Jenny Fisher over there anyway."

Alecia stood beside Amanda, both of them watching as Nicolas and Sofia followed behind Hannah and Rachel to raid the table of sweets.

"Such a wonderful experience for them," Amanda said with a sigh. She noticed Alejandro at the back of the school, talking with several other men. With the exception of his clothing and lack of a beard covering his jawline, he certainly fit in with the others.

"And for us, too," Alecia pointed out. "What a treat it has been to see my grandchildren in an environment that allows them to just be children!"

Amanda reached over and took Alecia's hand in hers. And together they stood there, taking in the scene of happy children laughing as they talked about the pageant and parents and grandparents complimenting each other on their children's performance. Isadora stood near the doorway with her newfound friend, Barbie King. They were giggling and whispering to each other with an occasional glance in the direction of three teenaged boys on the other side of the room.

It was a moment that filled Amanda's heart with so many emotions. She felt happy and sad at the same time, grateful for having been blessed with this moment but disheartened as she knew that, all too soon, it would come to an end.

She pressed her hand against her chest and said a small prayer to God, thanking him for seeing fit to give her this special moment to share with her entire family.

Chapter Seventeen

The morning before Christmas felt very much like every morning since they had arrived. Regardless of the special day, Jonas and Alejandro had awoken before sunrise to milk the cows while Amanda shivered in the chilly kitchen, waiting for the propane heater to warm up the room while she began to prepare the morning meal.

In the quiet of the pre-dawn, she found herself humming one of her favorite hymns from when she was a child.

"What song is that, Mami?"

She turned around, startled to see her daughter descending the staircase. "What are you doing up? It's so early and still cold down here, Izzie." She met Isadora halfway and greeted her with a warm hug. "Why don't you go back to bed for a spell?"

But Isadora shook her head.

"It's Christmas Eve," she said. "I wanted to help you in the kitchen."

Amanda's mouth opened in surprise. With the exception of baking cookies or cakes, it was usually just Amanda working beside Señora Perez. Cooking was not something her children did. "My word, Izzie! I don't even know what to say!"

Isadora gave a little shrug as if Amanda's praise embarrassed her. "Yeah, well . . . don't get used to it," she said in a serious voice, even though Amanda knew that she was teasing. "What can I do to help?"

For the next half hour, Amanda and Isadora worked side by side, mother and daughter making dough for fresh bread and biscuits. While they waited for the dough to rise, they sat down at the table, Amanda drinking coffee while Isadora enjoyed a hot chocolate.

"Mami, do you ever wonder . . . ?" Her voice trailed off and she bit her lower lip.

"Wonder what, sweetheart?"

She seemed nervous and avoided her mother's eyes. "Well, you know . . ." She started to play with the edge of a paper napkin, her fingers tearing off little pieces and rolling them into gravel-sized balls. "Like, what would have happened if you'd stayed here?"

Amanda pursed her lips and studied her daughter.

Isadora glanced at her and then looked away. "I mean . . . do you ever think about that?"

Did she ever think about that? More often than she would ever admit. Not to her daughter. Not to Alejandro. And, on some occasions, not even to herself. But she would never say that to her daughter. "Oh, sweetheart, that was such a long time ago," Amanda answered thoughtfully. "And I love you children and your father so much that I wouldn't change any decisions that I made."

There, she thought, secretly pleased with herself. She had answered Isadora's question without telling a lie. While she'd been taught to live by the Ten Commandments, she'd always felt she could compress all of them into two basic groups: stealing and lying. People who dishonored God, their parents, or spouses stole respect, while murderers stole someone's life. With her strict upbringing, she could never imagine anyone breaking *those* commandments. But it was the ninth commandment, *Thou shalt not bear false witness*—such a clear and simple commandment—that Amanda had to carefully navigate at times, especially when the children asked her questions that she simply did not feel were appropriate for her to answer.

But Isadora had seen through her reply. "That's not really an answer, Mami."

Amanda sighed. Especially after her conversation with Alejandro the previous morning, she didn't know how to answer her daughter. From the determined expression on Isadora's face, however, Amanda knew she wasn't going to get off easy.

"Izzie, sometimes it doesn't make sense to dwell upon what simply can't be," she finally said slowly, carefully selecting her words. "God has plans for us, and sometimes things happen for reasons that we just can't understand. One of my favorite passages in the Bible states, *'For I know the plans I have for you,' declares the Lord, 'plans to prosper you and not to harm you, plans to give you hope and a future.'* When I met your father, God had something in mind that I never could have conceived. Look at how many children the Princesa Cancer Center helps."

Isadora narrowed her eyes as she contemplated what her mother was saying. "And all of the young girls you used to help with their self-esteem when you traveled on tour with Papi?"

Amanda was impressed by Isadora's example. She often wondered if her children truly understood the things she did to help others. "Exactly. God's plans might often confuse us and seem as if he expects the impossible—"

Isadora interrupted her. "You mean like a simple Amish girl marrying a famous Cuban music star?"

She laughed. "I guess that did seem impossible, didn't it, now? But that just proves that with God, all things *are* possible. And I could never look back and ponder over all the what-ifs. In a way, that would be questioning God's plans."

Isadora nodded her head as if understanding what her mother meant, but there was still something lingering in her mind.

Amanda reached out and covered her daughter's hand with hers. "Hey, now, Izzie, what's this about?"

Taking a deep breath, Isadora exhaled and the tension left her face. "I don't know, really," she said apologetically. "I've just been thinking, Mami. Thinking and remembering when I was here with Aunt Anna and Mammi Lizzie. I might not remember exact details, but I remember how I felt. And . . . well . . . this week I've felt the same way."

"And how is that?"

She shrugged her shoulders and averted her eyes. "I've thought about this and didn't want to say anything, especially with it being Christmas and all . . ."

Amanda braced herself as she gently coaxed her daughter to unload her burden. "You didn't want to say anything about what, sweetheart?"

Isadora raised her eyes and stared at her mother. "I . . . I feel happier here."

Amanda tried not to react, hoping to hide how astonished she felt about Isadora's confession.

But Isadora didn't seem to notice as she continued talking. "It just seems so much calmer here, like life is about"—she paused, struggling to voice whatever had been bothering her—"about living. Papi seems so much more relaxed. You seem happier. And Sofia and Nicolas . . . me, too, I guess . . . we have so much more freedom than in Miami."

Freedom? Amanda tilted her head as she digested her daughter's words.

Isadora needed no encouragement to continue. "They can run around outside without being bothered by fans or photographers. And I've made friends—*real* friends—who don't want to just use me to meet someone in Banff or other singers. I mean that's cool and all, but it's really nice to realize that people can like me just for me, not for who they think I am."

"What are you saying, Izzie?" Amanda whispered, although she thought she already knew the answer to that question.

But Isadora didn't have time to respond. The door in the mud-room opened, and Alejandro hurried through it, along with a cold burst of air. After shutting the door, he stomped his feet on the floor and slapped his arms against his sides as he walked into the kitchen.

"Brr! It's freezing out there!" He began to take off his coat when he noticed Isadora sitting at the kitchen table with Amanda. "*Ay!* What is this? A girl party or is there room for me?" He hung up his coat and joined them at the table. He sat down on the bench next to Isadora and wrapped his arm around her shoulders, giving her a sweet, fatherly hug.

She smiled and leaned her head against him.

"Looks like more snow," Alejandro said. "Makes for a white Christmas. The children will enjoy that, no?"

"That will be a first for us," Isadora said. "It's kinda cool, the snow and all."

Alejandro glanced at his daughter. "Oh *sí*? That's a far cry from what you thought about coming here." He gave her a teasing nudge with his shoulder. "What happened to you missing all of your friends in Miami?"

Amanda quietly got up and moved over to the stove to pour Alejandro a cup of coffee. She tried to make herself busy so that Isadora could talk with her father about what was on her mind. As she waited for Isadora to respond, Amanda shut her eyes and said a quick prayer.

When she had first began traveling with Alejandro, he had warned her many times to be careful of whom she confided in and befriended. Over the years, Amanda had kept most people at arm's length; she knew from watching Alejandro how often people tried to get close to him because they wanted something from him. He had warned her that it would be the same for her. At first, she hadn't believed him, but she had quickly learned that he spoke the truth.

It was the one thing that Amanda had wanted to shield her children from, and clearly, she had failed.

"I made a friend here," Isadora said at last, her voice low as she spoke. "And she doesn't know what Banff is."

Alejandro made a soft noise in his throat, but he didn't respond. Like Amanda, he waited for their daughter to share what was on her mind.

"In fact, Papi, she doesn't know who *you* are . . . or Mami or me," she continued. "She doesn't want anything from me. At least nothing more than friendship."

"It's good to have friends," Alejandro managed to say when she remained silent. "True friends, *sí?*" Amanda saw recognition in Alejandro's eyes, no doubt thinking about Geoffrey, his manager for the past eight years and one of the only people both of them truly trusted.

"I wouldn't know, Papi," Isadora said with no hint of malice or sass. "She is the first one I've had. Everyone else just wants to use me to get to you!"

"Ay, Isadora!" he cried out.

Amanda cringed and, as she bit her lower lip, looked up in time to see Alejandro lean his head back. His eyes closed and his shoulders sagged under the weight of his daughter's words. He took a deep breath. After opening his eyes, he ran his fingers through his hair. He shook his head, just a little, as if disagreeing with something in his own mind.

"That hits below the belt," he said in a defeated voice.

Isadora tilted her head to the side, lifting her shoulders as she made an apologetic face.

He turned toward Amanda. "Did you talk to her? Is this about your . . . your 'just be' speech?"

Amanda handed him his coffee mug and stepped backward. She held up her hands in front of her. "Don't look at me," she said. "These are her words, not mine."

Alejandro arched an eyebrow at her, considering her denial without absolute confidence.

"Alejandro!" Amanda's mouth opened. "You know I would no sooner lie than . . ."

He seemed to recognize the fact that Isadora had spoken to him from the heart and not for any other reason than that was how she felt. He drummed his fingers against the table, the noise sounding loud in the quiet of the morning. "Well, *mis princesas*, I suspect that there is not much that I can say to make you feel better, but I can assure you that there are many sacrifices that we all must make in life. What little you gain in one area, you always lose in another. The trick is to find a balance between what you can expect to lose before you accept the gain."

He reached over and gently patted Isadora's shoulder.

"I know, Papi," she said softly.

"Now, moving on, there is something you can help me do after breakfast, Isadora," he said, giving her a playful wink. "We can talk more then, no?"

Immediately, Isadora brightened and nodded her head. Amanda realized that the times when father and daughter shared private moments alone were far and few between. Indeed, throughout Isadora's life, most of her time was spent with Amanda or with Amanda and Alejandro. And when neither of them was around, she had been left with Alecia or a nanny, except for the brief period when Amanda had left her in Anna's care while she was on tour with Alejandro.

The quiet solitude of the early-morning hours, so conducive to serious discussion, was suddenly interrupted. Simultaneously, Hannah and Sofia ran down the stairs while Lizzie entered the room, carrying a baking pan covered with tinfoil.

"I made a little breakfast casserole," Lizzie announced as she set the pan on the stovetop. "If you put it in the oven at 350 degrees, it will be ready when the rest of the *kinner* awake. Thought it would save you some time this morning."

There were no words for Amanda to express her appreciation for her mother's thoughtful gesture. With Anna returning home later that day, Amanda had a long day ahead of her. She needed to delegate cleaning chores to all of the children as she tried to focus on the preparations for the Christmas Day meal. It was going to be an all-hands-on-deck type of day, that was for sure and certain.

"She's home! She's home!" Rachel ran down the stairs and headed to the door, where she joined the others and anxiously waited, her nose pressed against the glass as she stared outside.

"Oh now," Lizzie called out from the rocking chair. "You'll catch a cold if you don't step away from that door. There's a draft over there."

The children, however, either chose not to listen or simply could not hear Lizzie's voice over the sounds of their own excitement. Amanda quickly herded the children away from the door. Bringing a newborn into a house filled with other people was nerve-racking enough, and Amanda did not want the children crowding their mother the moment she walked through the door.

Eagerly, both Alecia and Lizzie joined Amanda to watch Anna's arrival from the kitchen window. Alejandro had parked the SUV in the driveway, and Jonas walked around the side of the car to open the door for Anna. There was a moment's pause as she fussed with removing her newborn baby from the car seat.

"Did everyone wash their hands, now?" Amanda asked suddenly, gesturing the two smaller girls to the sink. Isadora was holding Samuel, and with a look of compassion, Amanda relieved her of that duty. "Let me take him," she said as she put him on her hip. "And remember, girls, no crowding around your *mamm*."

It took a few minutes for Anna to move from the car to the house. She walked slowly, holding the baby in her arms. Jonas followed behind, the diaper bag slung over his shoulder.

By the time Anna made it into the house, Amanda had the children lined up in a row, patiently waiting to meet the newest member of the family.

"Oh my!" Anna said as she let Jonas take the baby so that she could shrug off her coat and set it over the back of a kitchen chair. "Look at all of you!" She gazed around the room, her eyes wide open and a smile on her lips. "And you've all been so busy! Look how everything is just spic-and-span clean!" Despite appearing tired, she radiated joy. "What a *wunderbar* welcome home from my family!"

"Hey, I helped, too!" Nicolas said. Sofia jabbed her elbow into his side, and he cried out.

Anna laughed. "I'm sure you did, Nicolas. And you *are* family, silly. Now, let me sit down in the recliner by the window and introduce you to your new sister." She looked directly at Nicolas as she added, "And *your* new cousin."

For the next hour, the family crowded around the recliner, taking turns sitting on the sofa so that they, too, could hold the baby. Amanda stood next to Alejandro and watched. As her entire family gathered around, staring in awe at the new baby, a new life that had been created and gifted to them, the miracle of God's love had never seemed more apparent to Amanda.

Chapter Eighteen

"*¡Feliz Navidad!*" Alecia sang out as she walked into the kitchen, greeting everyone with her arms spread wide, a warm smile on her face.

Sofia and Nicolas jumped up from the table where they were eating breakfast to run to their grandma, almost tipping her over in the process.

"Abuela!" Nicolas reached her first and wrapped his arms around her hips.

Sofia tried to muscle her way past Nicolas, but he wouldn't release his hold on Alecia.

"Nicolas, be careful!" Amanda called out from the table. She was sitting next to Elizabeth and Sylvia, helping them as they ate the pancakes that she'd made for breakfast.

"*Ay*, Amanda," Alecia said with a laugh. "He's just excited. That's boys for you."

When she finally had untangled herself from Nicolas and managed to give Sofia a warm embrace, Alecia made her way over to the table, pausing to give each of Anna's daughters a quick hug.

"There's coffee on the stove if you'd like," Amanda said.

"*Gracias, hija*, but I've already had two cups with Lizzie." She sat down at the table, eyeing the pile of plates on the counter that needed to be washed. "How did your sister do last night?"

When Amanda had come downstairs to start preparing for the day, Anna had joined her for a while until the baby had begun crying. She already looked tired, with dark circles under her eyes, but she remained upbeat and cheerful, even if she was drained physically.

"As well as can be expected with a newborn," Amanda said as she leaned over to wipe Elizabeth's mouth. "Getting up to nurse every three hours is exhausting, but looking into that sweet cherubic face is such a priceless reward."

Alecia looked around the kitchen, her eyes scanning the thread with the Christmas cards hanging over it. There was a wistful look in her eyes, and Amanda wondered what she was thinking. Probably homesick for Miami and the festivities that were undoubtedly taking place at her sisters' and brothers' houses. With so much extended family, every holiday seemed bursting at the seams with people and children, food, and desserts. And while most Amish families were large families, often with nine or ten children who were grown and had their own little ones, the Beiler family was not large. And that meant fewer people to gather around the holiday table.

"It'll be quieter here today," Amanda said, feeling as if she should apologize to her mother-in-law.

Alecia glanced around at the children still seated at the table. "Quieter can be a nice change, *sí*?" She straightened her shoulders and managed to give Amanda a small smile. But there was still a wistful expression on her face.

The sound of a horse and buggy pulling up to the house interrupted the morning greetings.

"I wonder who that is," Amanda said and started to stand up when Isadora ran through the door.

She was out of breath, and her cheeks were pink from the cold. But her eyes shone bright, even as she leaned over and took several deep breaths. "Mami, Papi said you need to go outside. He wants to take you on a buggy ride."

Amanda glanced at Alecia, who scowled at the mention of the buggy. It was still a sensitive topic, especially with his mother, this horse and buggy that Alejandro had purchased.

But the thought of a nice buggy ride on Christmas morning was not unpleasant to Amanda. Her stomach suddenly filled with butter-flies. Leave it to Alejandro, she thought, to do something special that made her feel like a teenage girl being courted.

"I want to go, too!" Nicolas whined.

Isadora shot a look in his direction. "Let Papi and Mami spend some time together," she scolded. And then, softening her tone, she said, "And we can make some of those cookies that you liked so much at the school pageant."

After putting on her coat, Amanda hurried outside to get into the awaiting buggy. She laughed when she saw that Alejandro had hung bells from the side mirrors as well as a small sprig of mistletoe from the roof.

He waited until she settled onto the seat next to him before he leaned over and snuck a quick kiss. "Merry Christmas, Princesa," he said as he pulled back and smiled at her. "The children's present to us . . . time alone!" He stepped off the brake and urged the horse to begin walking down the driveway toward the road.

"Oh, I'm not so sure that Nicolas was too thrilled about that gift."

Alejandro laughed. "That's for sure and certain."

His use of that phrase, so common among the Amish, made her glance at him with a quizzical look on her face. But he was concentrat-ing on driving the horse and didn't notice her reaction.

At the end of the driveway, he leaned forward and looked both ways before he gently tugged on the right rein, the horse quickly turning in that direction onto the street outside the farm. As the horse began to trot, it tossed its head, and its thick black mane flowed against its neck. The rhythmic song of its hooves pounding against the pavement lulled Amanda into a sense of relaxation that was luxurious in its simplicity.

"What a *wunderbar gut* idea!" she said, exaggerating a heavy Pennsylvania Dutch accent.

"I reckon I come up with a few good ones from time to time, *ja?*" he teased back.

"You reckon?" she repeated, laughing at his word choice.

He leaned to the side and nudged her with his shoulder. "I do, Princesa."

They rode in silence for several minutes, Amanda staring at the farms that they passed and Alejandro focusing on driving. Several buggies were parked in the driveway of a neighbor's house, and as they continued down the road, she noticed there were few cars on the road. That only made for a more pleasant drive.

She sighed and tilted her head just enough to rest it against his shoulder. She felt as if she could just ride in the buggy all day, watching as Alejandro's hands held the reins as he occasionally slapped them gently against the horse's back so that it continued trotting at the same pace. The wheels rumbled against the road, and she knew that if she shut her eyes, she could fall into a light sleep. But she didn't want to miss one minute of this special time with her husband. After all, time spent with Alejandro was always the greatest gift of all.

The ham cooked in the oven and the potatoes boiled on the stove, giving the kitchen a pleasant aroma and with it the hint of the savory supper they would all soon share as a family. Amanda had a chance to step back and relax for a few minutes. The house was still quiet. While Anna was resting in her room with the baby, Jonas had announced that he was going to walk over to a neighbor's farm with Samuel so that they could wish them a Merry Christmas. Amanda suspected that he wanted to get some fresh air more than anything else. Lizzie had baked two pecan pies that she sent along in a basket. And Alejandro had accompanied the children outside to play in the snow before supper.

Quiet.

As she sat in the rocking chair, Amanda listened to the sound that "quiet" made. The ticking of the clock that hung from the wall seemed louder. Outside the windows, she could hear the whirl of wind blowing, just enough to make her appreciative of the fact that she was sitting inside by the propane heater.

Earlier that morning, Jonas and Alejandro had placed a folding table next to the regular table. With both covered with a white hand-sewn linen tablecloth, they made one table long enough to accommodate the entire family, as well as the bishop and his wife. And before they had gone outside to play, Isadora, Hannah, and Rachel had set the table, carefully placing Lizzie's old china at each spot while Sofia had followed with the utensils.

Amanda rested her head against the back of the rocking chair and shut her eyes for a moment. How different this was from what her children always experienced in Miami! Of course, without the decorations and Christmas tree, it didn't feel like the Christmas they had become accustomed to and came to expect, year after year. But it sure felt more like *Christ*-mas to Amanda. And she felt happy that her children were able to experience it.

"*Ay*, Amanda! You look so peaceful!"

At the sound of Alejandro's voice, she opened her eyes and greeted him with a relaxed smile. "You're back so soon?"

He shook the snow from his shoulders before he slid his arms from his coat. "*Sí*, it's too cold," he said as he hung the coat on a hook near the door. "But those little ones . . ." He chuckled as he shook his head. "They don't feel the cold, no? Isadora's watching them as they sled down that hill in the back."

"Oh help! The little ones will fall asleep for sure before it's time to have our meal!"

Alejandro nodded and leaned against the doorframe. "*Sí*, I think you're right." He glanced toward the stove, his eyes falling on the coffeepot on the back burner. "Any coffee left?"

"Let me get it for you." She got up and walked to the stove. "Go sit by the heater to warm up, Alejandro. Take the chill off."

But he didn't move from where he stood. His arms were crossed over his chest, and his gaze followed her as she reached for a coffee cup from the cabinet.

"I haven't seen your mother since Mamm brought over those pies for Jonas to take to the neighbors. Is she resting?" Amanda asked as she waited by the coffeepot.

He gave her a little shrug. "Or calling her friends in Miami."

"Ah, of course." She reached out and touched the coffeepot, testing to see how warm it was. "I wonder what she's saying to them." It wasn't a question, just a general musing.

"Probably telling them how wonderful everything is."

She laughed and looked at him, expecting him to raise an eyebrow or make a face in jest at his comment. But, to her surprise, his expression remained serious.

"I wasn't teasing you, Princesa."

Amanda raised her eyebrows. "Seriously?"

"Seriously."

While Alecia had calmed down over the past few days, Amanda would not have gone so far as to say her mother-in-law thought Lititz was *wonderful*. Just that morning, when Alecia had swept into the kitchen with her Christmas greetings for everyone, Amanda had sensed a hint of disappointment lurking beneath the surface of her smile. Had she misread Alecia's reaction? Was it possible that Alecia, too, was enjoying herself more than Amanda thought?

After Anna had gone to the hospital, Amanda had noticed that Alecia had become more subdued and pensive, as if deep in thought. What could be on her mind?

"Well," Amanda said at last.

"Well, indeed." His lips twitched, the hint of the smile he was suppressing giving her reason to pause. She knew that look all too well. He was up to something. And with it being Christmas, she knew he was capable of anything.

She put her hand on her hip and pursed her lips. "Alejandro, what are you up to?"

"Nada, mi amor," he said, his expression suddenly turning serious once again. But he still could not hide the sparkle in his eyes.

"Uh-huh!"

This time he laughed out loud as he walked over to her and wrapped her in his arms. Gently, he rocked her back and forth as he held her pressed to his chest. *"Ay,* Princesa, always so suspicious!"

By the time the bishop and his wife arrived, the children had finished their hot chocolate, and Hannah and Sofia had washed and put away the cups. Rachel was sitting on the floor with Samuel. Nicolas lay in front of them, playing with the wooden barnyard animals while making funny noises. Samuel laughed and leaned forward, trying to grab the animals from him. Every so often, Nicolas would let him have one, then gently take it back, ensuring that the toddler would not get upset. It was a game they had made up between the two of them.

"Merry Christmas," the bishop said cheerfully as he entered the room, removing his hat and setting it on the edge of the counter. His wife walked in behind him, a basket slung over her arm.

Catching Isadora's eye, Amanda gestured toward their guests, and she hurried over to take the basket.

"*Danke*, Isadora," the bishop's wife said. "Just some pies that I thought we could enjoy after our meal."

"Come in and get warm," Amanda said, feeling a little awkward since it wasn't her place to welcome guests, but Anna still had not emerged from the bedroom after her nap. And Lizzie had returned to the *grossdaadihaus* to check on her baked sweet potatoes and green bean casserole.

"Smells like a *wunderbar* feast in here," the bishop said as he crossed the room to sit down on the sofa. "We had our *kinner* over last night, so this is a real treat to be here this afternoon. Sharing fellowship with friends on this special day."

Amanda tried to avoid glancing at Alejandro. In all of the years that she had interacted with the bishop, she had never seen him so jovial. Most of her memories involved him scolding her about the paparazzi that flooded the streets when she had returned to the farm with Alejandro.

"And I saw that someone decorated the white fence with fresh greens," the bishop's wife said, her voice light and cheerful.

This was news to Amanda. She frowned. "I wonder who did that!"

Alejandro coughed into his hand and looked away, the guilty expression on his face exposing him. "It was Isadora's idea," he confessed.

"It looks beautiful!" the bishop said and turned toward his wife. "Next year we must consider doing the same."

Amanda's mouth opened in surprise. She couldn't believe that the bishop would approve of holiday decorations. How much he had changed!

The door to the bedroom opened, and Anna emerged carrying the baby in her arms.

"Oh now, look at this!" She gave a little gasp as she looked around the room. "Why, not only does it smell like Christmas, it feels like it, too!" She moved over to the sitting area and carefully sank down into the rocking chair, repositioning the baby in her arms. "And look at this! Oh, my, my, my! Nicolas! I think you have made a new friend in Samuel!"

Nicolas looked up from where he lay on the floor. "He's my cousin, Aunt Anna, not a *friend*."

"Well, that is true," she admitted, nodding her head as she spoke. "But he sure doesn't have any other cousins like *you* here to play with him. That makes it extra special."

Sofia piped up and added, "And cousins can be friends, too, right, Mami?"

Amanda wiped her hands on a dish towel before walking over to join the bishop, his wife, and Anna. Earlier, upon his return from visiting the neighbors, Jonas had set out folding chairs so that everyone had a place to sit while they visited. "Of course they can be friends," she said. "Just like sisters can be friends."

Anna made a noise of appreciation. "That's right."

Nicolas made a face. "Do I *have* to be friends with Sofia?"

"Nicolas!" Amanda gave him a warning look, even though the other adults chuckled at his comment.

"Aw, now, don't be too hard on the boy," the bishop said, another remark that surprised Amanda. "Siblings don't always get along now, do they?"

"Mamm says they're supposed to," Rachel said, happy that she could contribute to the conversation.

"What about loving thy neighbor?" Jonas quipped lightly.

"Ah!" The bishop held up his finger. "Good question, Jonas. The Bible does say that, doesn't it?"

"I'm not *her* neighbor . . ."

Amanda stared at Nicolas, willing him to stop misbehaving.

The bishop pulled at the knees of his pants as he leaned forward toward Nicolas. "Mayhaps not the way you define it, but she is certainly a neighbor as God defines it."

Sofia moved over toward where Amanda sat and leaned against her shoulder. "What does that mean, Bishop?"

"*Ja, vell,* it's simple, really." The bishop leaned back and stroked his gray beard as he spoke. "God is our father and that makes us all God's children."

Out of the corner of her eye, Amanda saw Nicolas and Sofia exchange a look. She cringed when she realized what they were thinking. Please don't say it, she willed. Please.

"But," Nicolas began, looking at Amanda and then Alejandro.

Amanda shut her eyes and waited for the inevitable.

"Papi is our father."

She felt as if her son's words had knocked the wind out of her lungs. How much more apparent could it be that Amanda and Alejandro were not raising their children within a church?

But the bishop did not react with a scowl or harsh words. Instead, he nodded his head. "*Ja,* that's true, for sure and certain. Papi is your earthly father, but God is your heavenly father. And if we are all children of God, that means that even our neighbors are our brothers and sisters. And Jesus tells us,

Let us love one another, for love is from God and everyone that loves is born of God and knows God. The one who does not love does not know God for God is love."

For a moment, Amanda almost asked him why he was not quoting the King James version of the Bible. But she refrained, realizing that her observation was not as important as the message spoken.

Her thoughts were interrupted when Lizzie came through the door with Alecia right behind her. They both carried a piping-hot dish of food. As they walked to the table to set them down on crocheted potholders, they simultaneously greeted the two newcomers with a cheerful "Merry Christmas!" Everyone smiled.

Amanda took the opportunity to hurry over and start preparing the other platters and dishes. Without being asked, Isadora came over to help her. Thankfully, Amanda heard Lizzie starting a conversation with the bishop and his wife, asking them about their Christmas Eve with their family. As the bishop's wife began telling stories about her children, grandchildren, and even several great-grandchildren, Amanda sighed in relief. She was safe from any more blunders from Nicolas. For now, anyway.

By the time all of the dishes were on the table, everyone had taken a turn holding Anna's baby, cooing over how small her little hands were and what a blessing God had bestowed upon them, just in time for Christmas. With the baby sleeping, Anna let Jonas put her down in the crib in their bedroom.

"Well now, I guess it's that time," Lizzie announced, her signal for everyone to gather around the table and take their seats.

The younger children sat at the folding table, Sofia making certain she sat between Hannah and Rachel on one side, with Nicolas, Sylvia, and Elizabeth on the other. Isadora glanced at her mother and waited for direction as to where to sit: with the children or with the adults.

"You sit next to Mammi Lizzie and Abuela, Izzie," Amanda offered, as she sat down as close to Elizabeth as she could. She knew she'd need to help her nieces with serving the different plates and didn't want to put that burden on Anna.

With everyone seated at the table, the bishop bent his head, a signal for everyone else to do the same. Amanda gave Nicolas a stern look and prayed that he wouldn't say or do something inappropriate during the silent prayer. Obediently, he bowed his head like everyone else. They remained like that for a long moment, each person saying a silent prayer of thanks until the bishop lifted his head and reached for the nearby plate of ham. Immediately, the noise of Christmas supper began. People reached for different dishes and then, after filling their plates, passed the dishes to the person beside them. At one point,

Amanda couldn't keep up with the dishes going by, having to tend to the two little girls next to her.

"Having some trouble down there, eh, Princesa?" Alejandro said.

She gave him a helpless look, and laughed at his gentle ribbing.

For most of the meal, the conversation centered on updates about the different families in the church district. During her years living at the farm, Amanda had never realized how much work was required of the bishop and his wife. Just that day, they had visited with six families, a fact that amazed Amanda, considering how much food still filled both of their plates.

"Ah *ja! Gut* food, Lizzie." He looked at Amanda. "And Amanda! You've become a fine cook in that Englische world of yours."

"No better than anyone else, I reckon," she said modestly and with a hint of a blush crossing her cheeks. If Amanda could draft a list of the Amish people she knew who avoided expressing praise for fear that the recipient would become prideful, the bishop was certainly at the top of it.

Alejandro leaned back as he pushed his plate away. "I don't know, Bishop," he said in an offhand manner. "Her cooking seems to have improved quite a bit since we've been here!"

Amanda stared at him, her mouth agape at his comment.

"In fact," he went on with a satisfied grin as he put his hands behind his head and leaned back just a little, so that the chair tipped slightly away from the table, "a man could get used to this fine cooking!" He looked across the table at Isadora and winked. "Right?"

Isadora sighed, but it sounded artificial when she said, "Oh, I sure will miss all of this home cooking when we leave on Tuesday."

Amanda shifted her gaze from Alejandro to her daughter, a dumbfounded look on her face.

"And playing with my cousins!" Sofia added, putting her arms around Hannah and Rachel.

Never one to miss out on an argumentative exchange in support of his sisters, Nicolas cried out from his end of the table, "And cookie swaps and sledding."

Alejandro gave Nicolas a sideways glance.

"I mean . . . uh . . ." Nicolas frowned and leaned over the table toward Sofia, whispering in her ear. "What was I supposed to say?"

"School!"

"Oh yeah." He turned toward his mother. "And school!"

Amanda said incredulously, "Now I know something is going on! You fuss over school all the time, Nicolas."

He held up his hands and looked at his father with an I-told-you-so look on his face. "I knew she wouldn't believe *that* one."

"What on earth is going on here?" Amanda demanded as she looked at everyone staring at her. "Alejandro? Can you please explain?"

He placed his hands on the table and, with an overly dramatic exhalation, stood up. "Perhaps it's time to bring in the present, *sí*?" He directed the question toward the children, who eagerly jumped up and left the kitchen with their father.

Amanda glanced at her sister and then her mother, wondering if they knew what Alejandro was up to. Anna focused on Samuel, as if intentionally avoiding Amanda's inquisitive look while Lizzie stared straight ahead, both of them obviously intent on avoiding her eyes. Even Alecia seemed preoccupied, her finger tracing an imaginary line on the tablecloth. Clearly, they know something I don't, Amanda realized.

From the mudroom, she heard the sound of Alejandro moving something and the hushed whispers from the children. Whatever it was seemed to be heavy. When they finally walked into the room, the four of them carried a box, the children holding a corner while Alejandro carried the bulk of it. As he set it down in the center of the floor, she could see that whatever was inside wasn't truly that heavy, but he had wanted the children to participate.

Amanda felt uncomfortable as she realized that, now, everyone was directing their attention at her.

"I . . . I thought we discussed the no-gifts policy this year," she said, directing her statement to Alejandro.

"Perhaps it's not just for you, Princesa," he said playfully. "But I do think we all agree that you are the one who should open it."

A chorus of different voices, a mixture of enthusiastic "yes" and "ja," responded to his statement.

"Well, this is a little more than unexpected," she said reluctantly as she slowly got up from the table. "And more than a little awkward."

Isadora stood back and pulled Sofia and Nicolas to stand on either side of her. She held their hands as they watched their mother move toward the box. Amanda paused in front of them and wagged her finger at them. "You know I don't like surprises," she whispered, which only caused her children to giggle.

"Now, before you open this," Alejandro said, using what Amanda called his professional interview voice. "This is a gift for everyone in the family." His glanced in the direction of the bishop and his wife. "Well, almost everyone," he said in a joking manner that caused the bishop to chuckle.

Amanda was confused. "Well, then I don't understand why I didn't know about this."

He leaned over and whispered loud enough for everyone to hear, "Because we all know you *don't* like surprises, which is the very reason *why* we wanted to surprise you, Princesa."

This time, Hannah and Rachel joined her children when they began to giggle again, and Amanda thought she even saw Jonas snicker.

"So, without further ado . . ." Alejandro looked at the children. "Drumroll, please?"

Nicolas did the honors and made a noise with his tongue as he pretended to be tapping the top of an imaginary drum.

Oh help, Amanda thought as she felt the heat rise to her cheeks. She didn't like this at all. It was one thing when she was the center of attention among strangers because it helped Alejandro. Being the center of attention within her family was quite another. But she knew that refusing to play along with Alejandro would be fruitless. Not only would that cause an unpleasant (and unwanted) scene, it would also disappoint not just her children but, from the looks of it, her nieces and the others smiling and watching her, too.

"Oh, very well then," she said with an exasperated sigh of defeat.

She stood by the side of the box, which was almost three feet tall and wide. The top was taped, and she looked around for a knife to slice through it. Alejandro cleared his throat and handed her a pocketknife that he had had tucked in his pocket.

"So prepared," she teased.

"Like a Boy Scout."

Slicing the length of the tape, Amanda felt her heart beating rapidly. Whatever the gift was, she knew that Alejandro had put a lot of planning into it. He had never made such a public display of a gift to her. Well, she thought as she carefully handed the knife back to him and caught the mischievous smirk on his face, at least not since he had given her an engagement ring at that awards dinner in Los Angeles nine years ago.

She pushed aside the two flaps of the box and saw the edges of white packing foam.

"Oh help!"

She tried to pull at it but couldn't. Whatever was inside was too cumbersome for her to lift.

Jonas got up and joined them, helping Alejandro lift the foam packaging from the box. That, too, was taped, and Alejandro again held out the knife.

"Such mystery," she said, trying to sound good-natured.

As she started to slice the last pieces of tape, she heard Anna stand up and join Jonas so that she could see. When Amanda glanced up at her, she saw that her mother, Alecia, the bishop, and his wife were doing the same.

Once again, she handed the pocketknife to Alejandro, and he promptly shut it before sliding it into his front pocket.

With all eyes watching her, Amanda lifted the packaging to see what this over-the-top display had been all about.

Gasping, Amanda dropped the piece of foam onto the floor near her feet. For a moment, she could only stare at what was tucked so carefully inside. Raising her hand to cover her mouth, she felt it trembling as she tried to make sense of what she saw.

A mailbox.

A dark-hunter-green mailbox with a red flag and white lettering that spelled three names: Beiler, Wheeler, Diaz.

Stunned, not just by the present itself—for surely it had required much planning and thought—but because she was suddenly hopeful about what the gift meant. At the same time, she was frightened in case she was mistaken. Amanda pressed her lips together and blinked her eyes. She felt that all-too-telling sensation of tears welling up and threatening to trail down her cheeks. When Alejandro placed his hands on her shoulders and bent down to peer into her face, she stared at him and whispered in a voice that was both hopeful and incredulous, "What does this mean?"

He reached up and brushed aside a stray tear that had escaped. "It means, Princesa, that you are home." He paused, glancing around the room at everyone who stood around them. "We *all* are home."

"I . . . I don't understand. What are you saying, Alejandro?"

"It means that I heard what you were saying, Amanda. I listened to Isadora, too. And I saw what you saw when we were at the school pageant. There is more in life than just a constant push for more success, more money, more things. And our children need to have the chance to experience the balance." He gave her a tender smile. "To be with their family." He glanced at Alecia, who stood behind Isadora. "*All* of their family."

"But . . ." Her mind struggled to grasp what he was saying. "But . . . but you can't just move away from everything!"

He raised an eyebrow, giving her a sideways glance. "No? Says who?"

Her mind whirled with conflicting thoughts and emotions. "Well, for one, you have contracts, Alejandro." For a moment, Amanda forgot that the rest of the family stood there, listening to their conversation. "And your production company. All of that is in Miami." She began to think of all his commitments, which made what he was suggesting seem even more impossible. "And concerts. Why, on New Year's Eve, you have to perform in Atlanta *and* Miami!"

"*Escúchame, mi amor,*" he said in a soft but pointed tone. "There are some things that are more important than success, no? Being with my family is one of those things. From the very beginning, you have taught me that." He hesitated before he continued speaking, taking a moment to study her reaction. "It won't be easy to juggle everything, I know that. But there is no reason why Lititz, Pennsylvania, cannot be our home, too." He glanced around the room, his eyes pausing on his children first and then on the rest of Amanda's family. "This is where our family is."

Amanda's gaze darted in Alecia's direction. "But . . ."

"Princesa," Alejandro said, redirecting her attention back to him. "I said that all of us made this decision. And that includes Mami."

None of what he said made any sense to Amanda. "Where . . . where will we live?"

This time, it was Lizzie who answered her. "That patch of land at the end of the lane? Your *daed* never cleared it of trees. Seems like it's high time to put it to good use, Amanda."

"And Papi's going to build us a brand-new house," Sofia chimed in.

"With a room for Abuela to come visit whenever she wants," Isadora said.

"But I have to keep going to school," Nicolas added in a disappointed voice.

"We all have to go to school, you goose," Sofia added lightly. "Even Izzie!"

Amanda looked at each one of them, realizing that this was not an idea that had just occurred overnight. It was something, perhaps just a small seed, that had been growing in Alejandro's mind. For how long, she couldn't speculate. She did, however, wonder if that had been part of the reason why he'd agreed so readily to coming to Lititz for the holidays.

"Alejandro," she said in a soft voice, "you've worked so hard and for so long to build your career."

"Now it's time for me to enjoy the fruits of my labor," he pointed out. "And with the people I love the most: my family."

"But . . ." Amanda looked down as the words faded from her mouth.

"You are happier here with your family, no? The children are freer here, too. And I can breathe easier without the press and public hounding me all of the time. And just because this is our home base doesn't mean we won't spend time in Florida. So what is your 'but'?"

Amanda looked up into his eyes and resolved to tell him the truth.

"What if you regret this decision? Aren't you worried that your fans will forget you if you aren't as active and visible?" she asked with concern.

"Are you worried I will be like Banff, so six months ago?" he teased, winking at Isadora, who laughed at his words.

Amanda shook her head, dismissing his attempts at humor. This was, after all, a decision that would have long-lasting consequences in their lives. As much as she wanted this—the opportunity to provide her children with the chance to grow up in a world that did not include paparazzi and fame, constant change, and travel—it was a huge decision.

"I'm being serious, Alejandro," she said sternly.

Alejandro pulled her into his arms and gently brushed away a strand of hair from her face. He spoke his next words very carefully. "The only regret I could ever have is not spending more time with you or my family. And as for my career, I've done all that I set out to do. I've lived a life most people could only dream of. But that gets tiring. I realized how much I was missing from my children's lives. I want to be part of watching them grow up. No, Princesa, you are wrong. It's time to begin putting that chapter of my life behind me. Slowing down a bit and enjoying life with you, with the children, and with the rest of our family."

Just as Amanda began to protest once again, she felt Alejandro's lips softly pressed against her own, silencing her words with a quick kiss. When he pulled back, she stared into his eyes, looking for any hint of uncertainty, any doubt, but she found none. Instead, she saw genuine happiness on his face.

"Welcome home, Princesa. You are where you belong." He glanced around the room, his eyes looking at each of the people who watched them: her mother, her sister and her husband, her nieces and nephew, her children, his mother, and even her former bishop and his wife. When he returned his gaze to meet hers, he gave her a smile and gestured toward them. "We all are."

Epilogue

The metal wheels made a rumbling sound against the pavement as the large black gelding maneuvered the gray-topped buggy past the new mailbox and down the long driveway. The woman driving the buggy wore a simple blue dress with a small floral pattern, and her hair was pulled back into a neat, tight bun at the nape of her slender neck. She held the worn leather reins loosely in her hands, occasionally tugging at them just a little to remind the horse that she was in control. In truth, the horse was casually guiding itself. Strange and *gut*, she mused, how horses, so independent and curious by nature, enjoy doing certain things over and over again: the same meals at the same hours, the same routes on which to travel, the same time to be turned out in their paddocks, the same routine, day in and day out.

As she neared the old farmhouse, a man suddenly opened the screen door, distracting her from her thoughts. Alejandro stepped outside onto the weather-worn porch, with the door slightly ajar, held open only with his foot, while he leaned against the doorjamb. With his arms crossed over his chest, he watched her. There was the slightest hint of a smile on his lips. Her heartbeat quickened at the sight of him.

She lifted her hand and waved through the open side window of the buggy.

Stopping the horse near the barn, she jumped down, careful to hold the bottom of her long dress so that she wouldn't stumble or trip on it. Once her feet were firmly set on the ground, she ran her hand down the front of her skirt, brushing away some of the horsehair that had floated through the open buggy window while she had been driving.

Grabbing the reins so that the horse wouldn't move, she began to unhitch the gelding from the buggy. When she glanced over the sweaty neck of the horse, she saw that Alejandro had joined her. Without being asked, he unsnapped the tug line from the shaft on the other side so that they could gently roll the buggy backward.

Once the buggy was a safe distance away and the horse could back up without hitting the shafts, they worked together and finished unharnessing the horse, removing the driving saddle and the breast-plate before unbuckling the reins. He pulled the right rein through the small metal rings of the harness before he reached for hers. When she handed it to him, he folded them both in a way that they could easily be hung from the hook inside the barn's small tack room.

Amanda removed the horse's bridle and led the animal through the open barn door, guiding the gelding into its stall for the night. As she went to get some hay, she noticed Isadora's orange cat sleeping on top of several bales. Amanda paused and rubbed the cat's head, smiling as she thought of the irony. Almost ten years ago, Katie Cat had slept in the very same place when just a kitten. Now, after a decade, she, too, had returned to the farm and, like the rest of Amanda's family, seemed much more content.

"Excuse me, Katie Cat," Amanda said as she tore two flakes of hay from the bale, resulting in a scornful look from the cat, who clearly did not appreciate the disruption to her sleep. Amanda carried the hay to the horse stall and tossed it into the stable before checking to make certain that the horse had enough water until morning.

"*¿Todo bien?*"

She peered over her shoulder again and smiled at his short-sleeved white shirt; with the two top buttons undone, she caught a glimpse of his tanned skin just slightly marred by the blue line of a tattoo. When he stood before her, she reached her hand out toward him and traced the outline of the ink on his bare chest, her finger lightly tickling his skin.

He reached for her hand, holding it tightly for a long moment before raising it to his lips and kissing her fingertips.

"Don't," she whispered in a soft voice while trying to hide her grin.

"*Ay, Princesa,*" he murmured warmly as he put his arms around her waist and pulled her closer against him. "You were gone too long. *¡Mucho tiempo!*"

She gave a little laugh. "Not even two hours. If that."

"As I said, too long."

"You survived, I see," she said with a teasing smile on her face.

"*Sí, mi amor*, I survived."

From behind him, the noise of a child's laughter caused them both to glance toward the house at the same time.

"But barely," he went on.

Leaning forward, she placed a soft peck on his cheek. "It's good to have you back, Alejandro," she whispered. "I missed you while you were in Miami last week."

"You survived," he quipped, teasingly tossing back her own words.

"But barely." She smiled.

He laughed and leaned over to brush his lips against hers.

When he pulled back, she reached up and pushed his hair back from his forehead so that she could see his blue eyes. "It's been good this spring, hasn't it?"

"I think so, *sí.*"

"You like helping Jonas."

It wasn't a question, but he answered her anyway. "I do, Princesa." He turned his head toward the back paddock, where the frame of their future home stood. "It will be nice when the house is finished, no?"

She nodded her head. "Yes, but I will miss all of us being together in the evenings. It's nice to be surrounded by family."

He returned his attention to her, staring down into her face. He raised his hand and brushed a stray piece of hair from her cheek. "It's nice to just be with you, Amanda. While I like being here as much as I can, I must confess that I'm looking forward to you returning to Miami with me next month. Time with you, alone."

Truth be told, she was looking forward to that, too. Over the past few months, she felt as if she spent more time away from him than with him. While he got everything situated, flying back and forth to Miami and Los Angeles, Amanda had stayed with the children at the farm. Next week, however, she would leave them for the first time since they had made the move to Lititz. She would travel with Alejandro to their home in Florida. Both of them had meetings, but she had managed to schedule hers to fall during a two-week period of time. And for one week, Alejandro had insisted she spend some time with him alone on their yacht before they returned to Pennsylvania for the rest of the summer.

Amanda glanced over her shoulder at the buggy, which was filled with the many boxes of groceries that needed to be put away. The children would return from school soon, Sofia and Nicolas happily walking home with Hannah and Rachel while Isadora took the bus from the local high school. "Let's carry in the groceries, then," she said. "You can keep me company while I cook, *ja*?"

"I'd rather stay right here, Princesa," he breathed into her ear. "Alone and with only you."

"I have a lot to get done." She sighed halfheartedly.

But Alejandro made no move away from her. Instead, he pulled her closer still, whispering into her ear, "You know I'm not a patient man, Princesa, and even less when you are this close to me."

She looked up into his piercing blue eyes and gave him a soft smile as she teasingly replied, "Patience *is* a virtue."

He sighed. "A virtue I have yet to master, *sí?* Maybe you can teach me?" His eyebrows arched up in a suggestive manner.

"All right, then." She nodded thoughtfully before adding, "First lesson? Help me bring all of this food into the kitchen."

He laughed when he realized that she had, once again, maneuvered the outcome of one of their conversations to her benefit. "That's not exactly the lesson I had in mind, Princesa."

She laughed, too, as he tightened his grip around her waist. "All in due time," she teased. "Right now, I have to cook . . ."

"And then . . . ," he murmured softly.

"You will have to wait and see."

"I know, I know. All in good time, *sí?*" He leaned toward her, his lips almost brushing against hers. "After all, you are a very good teacher."

"*Danke,*" she whispered, her hands placed squarely on his shoulders and her eyes staring up at him. "Now, I'm afraid that if you won't let me go, there won't be any dinner. What kind of a wife would that make me?"

Reluctantly, he gave her a soft kiss and a last squeeze before releasing her from his arms. He took her hand in his, and together they walked toward the back of the buggy. He turned the black handle and lifted the rear hatch of the buggy. Effortlessly, Alejandro picked up a box of groceries. Amanda watched him as he did this, her heart filled with pride for her husband. She was never more in love with him than she was now, as he worked silently beside her in the quiet of the country life.

They walked side by side back toward the house. When they neared the front door, he paused for a moment and breathed in the many wonderful smells of the farm and its surroundings before placing the two boxes on the wooden porch and opening the door for her to enter. She made her way toward the kitchen as he followed behind with the groceries.

They were home.

Acknowledgments

No book is ever written by *just* the author. That cliché phrase *"It takes a village"* is true for every writing endeavor, regardless of who is typing the words. As many of you know, this series grew from my love of the Amish culture and religion and from my celebrity crush on Pitbull. As far as I was concerned, the third book of the series, *Plain Again*, was the finale. However, that was not meant to be the end.

One very special person, Amy Hosford, convinced me that Amanda and Alejandro's journey was not quite finished. She encouraged me to continue exploring their relationship. As a result, three more books followed: *Plain Return* (Book Four), *Plain Choice* (Book Five), and this book, *Plain Christmas*, which isn't necessarily part of the series as it is written to stand on its own.

Without Amy's personal encouragement and never-ending support, Alejandro and Amanda would have faded away from Times Square on New Year's Eve at the end of *Plain Again*. We never would have seen that *happily ever after* isn't always a smooth ride, but that with faith, love, and perseverance, the destination is definitely worth the journey.

I also want to acknowledge other key components of my little village: Marc Schumacher (my "hub"), Michelle Dawn, Lisa Bull, Marisol Abuin, and Gina McBride. Besides brainstorming, proofing, editing, and critiquing, each of them has helped talk me "off the ledge" on many an occasion. And trust me, *that* is not a task for the faint of heart!

About the Author

The Preiss family emigrated from Europe in 1705, settling in Pennsylvania as part of the area's first wave of Mennonite families. Sarah Price has always respected and honored her ancestors through exploration and research about her family's Anabaptist history and their religion. For over twenty-five years, she has been actively involved in an Amish community in Pennsylvania. The author of over thirty novels, Sarah is finally doing what she always wanted to do: write about the religion and culture that she loves so dearly. For more information, visit her blog at www.sarahpriceauthor.com.